JINXED

Wayward Mage Book One. Also includes the prequel, Hands of Fate

ANN GIMPEL

Hands of Fate

A WAYWARD MAGE SERIES, PREQUEL

Urban Fantasy

By
Ann Gimpel

**Tumble off reality's edge into a dangerous world fueled
by lore and magic**

Contents

HANDS OF FATE, A WAYWARD
MAGE PREQUEL

Copyright Page

The Myth

What better place than the misty, magical Scottish Highlands to spawn myths rife with dark edges? The ruins of Rait Castle are near Nairn and Inverness. As castle ruins go, this one has a rich history complete with feuding clans and a Romeo and Juliet spin.

The two battling clans were the Cummings and MacIntoshes. Major movers and shakers in thirteenth-century Scotland, the Cummings rose to power through a series of advantageous marriages. At one point they boasted four earls, thirty belted knights, and the Lordship of Badenoch. Riding high, they took control of lands previously belonging to the MacIntoshes and other clans as well.

The Cummings fought for King Edward I of England against Robert the Bruce when the Scottish wars for independence broke out in the twelve and thirteen hundreds. The MacIntoshes were staunch Bruce supporters. After

Bruce won, the MacIntoshes petitioned to get their lands back—including Rait Castle.

The petition was unsuccessful; bad blood ran deep.

Meanwhile, one of the Cummings daughters fell in love with a MacIntosh (ergo, the Romeo-and-Juliet motif). When her father hatched a cunning plan to invite the MacIntoshes to dinner under the guise of improving inter-clan relations, he had a far more wicked agenda. After an evening of merriment and entertainment, when a special phrase was spoken, he and his fellow clansmen planned to mob the MacIntoshes and slaughter them.

All well and good, except the daughter had a trysting spot with her lover. Next to a large standing stone, she told him of the plan, so the MacIntoshes came prepared to fight back. And they knew the magic phrase that would spawn destruction.

After the ensuing bloodbath, the laird of the Cummings clan was one of the few left alive. Suspecting his daughter of betrayal, he chased her through the castle. She clambered out a window, hanging onto the sill. Her father raised his sword against his own blood and chopped off her hands.

The maid fell to her death, and, to this day, a handless woman haunts the ruins of Rait Castle.

One more aside, and we'll dive into the story part of things. *The Handless Maiden* is a German fairy-tale from the 1800s. Many similar stories bloomed from its roots. Like all fairy-tales, they deal with journeys and transformation by going into a forest where the heroine's deepest fears and most powerful dreams are realized.

In all the variations of this particular tale, the transformation is from wounded child to whole, healed woman, from miller's daughter to queen. In the process, her hands are restored, but it's the least important part. She finds her personal power and comes into her own as a woman. Too bad the Cummings maid wasn't handed the proper script. She might have kicked her father in the balls and told him what a jerk he was for trying to trick the MacIntoshes.

But wait! There's far more to this tale than meets the eye. Twists and turns galore, and a red-hot romance to boot. Catch you on the other side, dear readers.

Book Description: Hands of Fate

Fitting in has never been in the cards. Not part of the hand Fate dealt me. My superpower is animals, magical and otherwise. They adore me. Birds and insects too. Back when the Celts still roamed the Highlands, I begged them to shed light on how I came to be since my power is unique.

You can guess how well that went. They're a taciturn, entitled lot. I didn't shed a single tear when they packed up and left Earth.

Other mages don't care for me. They don't trust my one-of-a-kind magic. On my more generous days I don't blame them. For now, I run a tiny detective agency in the Scottish Highlands. Mortals are quick to hire me because I always solve their problems. Using magic is cheating, but they'll never find out.

One fine afternoon, a Sidhe sought me out. His power surpassed mine by a factor of ten, so I was suspicious as hell, but he was too profanely gorgeous to turn away...

As usual, no one to blame but myself when my life skids off the rails.

Chapter One

Scottish Highlands, Early Twenty-First Century

Mud flew up from churning hoofs, staining the backs of my legs. This is why I seldom ride in shorts, but the sun was out. Impossible to resist a rare sunny day in Scotland's hinterlands. That's the thing, though. If I'd tarried long enough to change clothes, the sun could have taken a powder.

Not could have, most likely would have.

My cell phone vibrated against my leg. I reached for it but changed my mind. I was having way too good a time to look at any screen. Whoever was calling could jolly well leave me a message. For once, I was mostly caught up. Jumping into my battered old black Range Rover hoping for a riding partner had been a whim. I often have them, but rarely indulge myself. It's why I wore denim shorts, an old black T-shirt, and ratty running shoes with holes in them instead of more standard riding attire.

A horn honked from a nearby road. Raising a hand, I waved. If I'd been truly neighborly, I'd have cantered over, but I guarded my painfully few moments of solitude with all the vigor of a gang member protecting his turf.

I worked way too hard. Between my private detective business and my other, much quieter pursuits, I rarely had even a quarter hour to call my own. Animals adore me. All of them, enchanted and otherwise. It's my biggest gift on the magical end of things, and why the cream-colored unicorn didn't hesitate when I raised my mind voice hinting at the prospect of a ride. The bunch of her strong muscles under my bottom said she'd happily maintain our breakneck pace forever.

She could. We'd been there, done that.

She's a pro at hiding her horn, and she fools mortals, but the other horses know all too well she's nothing like them and give her a very wide berth. Marked with boulders and sodden ground, verdant countryside flashed past. I breathed deep. Spring was in the air, such as it was here. At least the days of ground fog and dense frost were gone for a few months.

The horn honked again. Fuck. Shading my eyes with a hand, I twisted to get a look at the car and whistled. Shiny. Black. Sleek. A Mercedes convertible I'd never seen before was driving about the same pace Becca and I were moving. After waving once more, I turned my attention forward.

"Who's he?" the unicorn asked.

"No idea."

"He seems to know you," she pressed, and then added, *"He's a mage."*

Double fuck. I hadn't bothered to check. Magic isn't common in the modern world. In truth, it's so uncommon, I never expect to run into anyone who wields power. Not by happenstance. The few of us in the region all know one another. Not that we get together or anything.

Eh, they might, but I'm not included.

They don't like me. I'm an oddball in the magical realm. So much of an outlier, there's not even a name for me beyond animal wizard. Or the woman who charms animals. I can even turn creatures against their bonded mages, not that I would or anything. Unless I was truly pissed off.

We were still charging forward. The man driving the Benz had upped the ante on honking. Clearly, he wasn't going to go away. It meant he probably knew what I was. Even the weakest mage can sense power in others.

Phooey. On the slim chance I was mistaken about his intentions, I made a show of dragging on the reins. Both they and the bridle were only for show; I drew the line at additional tack and always rode bareback. As Becca slowed, I turned us toward the macadam lane where the Benz was and stopped when we were still a respectable distance away.

Within shouting distance, but not so close he could snare me in a spell. Not easily, anyway. My power isn't terribly strong on the face of things, but all I have to do is put out the call. Every bird, animal, and insect in a five-kilometer radius will come on the run to defend me, their mage, their queen.

"Hello," I called. "I don't believe we've met." It was politer than what I wanted to say, which was along the lines of what the fuck do you want.

The driver killed the engine and opened the door. Tension in my thighs and tense fingers on the reins told Becca to be ready to bolt if he even looked as if he were about to raise power against us. Soothing waves of unicorn enchantment circled me as she signaled assent.

Unfolding long legs, the car's occupant got out and nodded a greeting.

I stifled a gasp and hoped to hell I hadn't been as obvious as I feared. The dude was Hollywood gorgeous. Slightly over six feet, sleek, and graceful with the same broad-shouldered, slim-hipped build of all his race. He was dressed in an expensively cut tweed jacket, linen shirt, and black pants with shiny loafers peeking out. Inky-black hair had been layered and reached collar level. I bet he'd spent more on that haircut than I earned in a month. With a high forehead, sculpted cheeks, a square chin, and dark eyes with eyelashes any woman would gladly kill him for, he was quite the package.

And then I looked closer. "For fuck's sake," I muttered, "it's a glamour."

Sure enough, a male Daoine Sidhe lay beneath all that glory. Not that he was any slouch. They're royalty in the Sidhe world. Legends suggest any mortal who lays eyes on one in their true form would be lost forever. They'd fall hopelessly in love, never satisfied with any lesser being.

The dark hair and eyes were the same. The chin more pointed, and of course, the ears. A pair of black wings set with jewel tones were folded across his back. How in the hell did he manage in the car without crushing them?

He glided closer, a predatory look on the human version of his face. "Very good, my dear," he purred in a pure American accent. "You know what I am, and I know what you are. You're a hard woman to find, Abria MacLeone."

"Bullcrap," I shot back. "No one else has ever

complained." Setting my mouth in a tight line, I went on, "Why are you looking for me?"

"To hire. Why else?" He sounded genuinely mystified.

But then, so was I. His power outshone mine by a magnitude of perhaps a hundred. What in the hell could I do that he couldn't manage on his own?

"What's your name?" I started with the simple shit and draped an obvious truth net between us—in case he was tempted to lie. Names hold power. The one he called me was my current alias. My real name is buried so deep no one knew it.

Except me, and I aimed to keep it that way.

"Blake Townsend, Earl of Galloway." He offered a slight bow.

His words pinged true off my spell, so I reeled it in. "That's a hell of a long way from the Highlands," I commented, not bothering to ask why any Sidhe carried a title reserved for mortals. Perhaps he was bored.

He shrugged. "I have a task in this part of Scotland. You'd be absolutely perfect for it, my dear." The predatory expression was back in full bloom.

Oh-oh. I've never trusted smooth talkers, and Blake-baby was the original.

"How'd you find out about me?" I was stalling for time to figure out how to say no and head for the hills. I could tell Becca we were done. Fleet-footed darling that she was, she'd run like the wind. But Blake had hunted me down once. It meant he'd do it again. I had to stand my ground and put this problem to bed here and now.

"We keep tabs on...everyone," he replied in response to my question.

He might be profanely gorgeous, but the fine hairs on the back of my neck prickled. I didn't care for the idea of anyone "keeping tabs on me."

"I'm really not interested in working for you," I said flatly and picked up the reins. "Find someone else."

"But we need you." Compulsion flowed thick as honey, lacing his words into a convincing mix.

I reached for my mind voice to tell Becca we were through. Ha. No such luck. The Sidhe had placed a barrier between me and my power. And he'd managed it so sneakily, I'd never noticed. Fury vied with annoyance. I could have kneed Becca and accomplished the same goal. Instead, I jumped off the unicorn and stomped to face Blake.

Good. We were about the same height. Establishing credibility is simpler when I can stare into someone's eyes.

"Now. You. Look. Here," I gritted through clenched teeth.

This time, a calming spell rose from him, wafting around me with the scents of mint and rosemary with hints of vanilla. "I mean you no harm," he murmured.

Wishing my truth spell were still in play, I glared balefully at him. "Then you will unwind whatever you stuck between me and my power."

"Fair enough. On one condition."

"What?" I snarled. He might be gorgeous, but I wanted to rip his eyes out and feed them to a flock of crows. Better yet, I'd have the crows grab his eyes, while I—

He smirked, probably plucking all the colorful murderous intentions from my mind. "The condition is you'll stick around long enough to hear me out."

I shook my head. "Nope."

"Then we might be standing here for a long while. Unless you don't care about leaving with your power intact."

I crossed my arms under my breasts. "Is this the way the Daoine Sidhe usually operate? With threats? I never partner with anyone I don't trust, and I sure as hell don't trust someone who leverages magic to bully me."

"But you'd have left," he protested. "I saw it in your mind."

"And that's just plain rude."

"What?" He sounded baffled.

"Helping yourself to people's thoughts to further your own ends."

He narrowed his eyes and fanned his wings. "You do it."

"Not to manipulate someone into doing what I want them to." I flapped a hand in his direction. "What did you want to hire me to do that's so all-fired important it brought you from the southern end of Scotland?" I could at least pretend to listen and play nice. Once I got my magic back, we'd see what happened next.

Becca chose that moment to trot forward and poke the business end of her horn into his neatly pressed shirt. "Unhand her magic," the unicorn whinnied. "Do it now."

Interesting development. I hadn't asked Becca for assistance, but maybe she was sick of the Sidhe's patronizing attitude too. Hoofbeats thundered across the moor. I smiled. Blake had missed the obvious. He may have shackled my power, but he'd assumed Becca would stand by and do nothing.

Big mistake for someone who should have known better. The unicorn could end him if she chose. Not without penalty.

She'd draw down the wrath of every other Sidhe, Daoine and otherwise.

A herd of unicorns masquerading as horses surrounded us. Nine more, some black, some silver white. Their clean horsey smells were a welcome change from the capitulation casting Blake was doing his damnedest to ram down my throat. With an audible clank, the shielding around my power fell away. Guess he knew when he was outgunned. He could kill one unicorn, or even two or three, but the others would gut him.

Besides, unicorns are sacrosanct in the magical world. Kind of like dragons, they're revered, treasured.

Blake held his hands up, palms out. "Apologies. We got off on the wrong foot."

"You think?" I inquired caustically.

"I do. Will you allow me to outline the task I sought you out for?"

"What if I say no?" I dropped my arms to my sides, waiting. What I needed to hear was he'd figure something else out and not continue to hound me.

He grinned engagingly. "I'm hoping you don't, but if you do, I'll manage on my own."

Fuck me. His grin was captivating. It was hard not to smile back, but I held a stern expression. "Right answer. You have five minutes."

"Do you still require our presence?" A black unicorn laid his horn on my shoulder.

I wrapped my fingers around it, soaking in love and magic. "I'm good. The Sidhe has seen the error of his ways."

Blake winced. I bet he wasn't chastised often. For anything. The black unicorn said, "Call us if you need us." With the exception of Becca, the herd wheeled and galloped away kicking their hoofs skyward and whinnying up a storm. I wasn't the only one thrilled about the sunshine.

"Just the three of us," I said. "Your five minutes begins now."

Whirring from overhead disabused my "just the three of us" observation. A flock of hawks and crows scribed patterns in the air above our heads. All it would take would be the slightest indication from me, and they'd descend on Blake and his fancy set of wheels. You'd be surprised how much damage beaks can do to aluminum, steel, and paint.

Blake cast a glance skyward. "You have quite the following."

"Down to four minutes," I replied and snapped my fingers.

He nodded and faced me squarely. "The rumor was you command animals. I can see for myself it's true, and—"

I held up a hand. "I do not command anyone. They do my bidding because they adore me. I was born with links to all living creatures, including insects. It's been helpful when I've been in warmer climes. Scorpions are a better deterrent than any type of magic."

He laughed. It was unexpected, and surprisingly warm. "There's never been another mage quite like you."

I narrowed my eyes and worked to identify the inflection beneath his words. Finally, I gave up. "What's that supposed to mean?"

"You're one of a kind and ideally suited for the problem I've run up against." He drew his dark brows together. "I suppose I'm down to three minutes now, so I'd better get cracking. Long ago, over five centuries, I was lord over the Highlands."

"News to me," I muttered. I'd been here during that time, and I'd never so much as caught a glimpse of him.

"From a magical perspective," he clarified.

I shook my head. "Still not buying it. The Celts were in ascendency, not the Sidhe."

"We ran things from the, ah, sidelines." An exasperated breath puffed from between his lips. "I'm certain you remember what prima donnas the Celtic gods were. They required kid-glove treatment, and—"

"Hush!" I hissed. "Haven't seen them for a long while, but they may have set sentinels in the stones. Speaking ill of them was never tolerated."

Blake nodded. "I rest my case. Prima donnas. Delicate. Required a whole lot of praise, often when it wasn't merited. Frankly, we all breathed a sigh of relief when they left.

"But I'm off on a sidetrack, and you requested the quick and dirty version. During the middle of the 1400s, a clan war grew ugly. About what you'd expect from that era. Feuding families, an ill-advised love affair, and treachery at its finest."

I creased my forehead in thought; his words took me back to vague memories, but clans at odds with each other were scarcely an anomaly back then. More of an exception would have been long periods of relative peace. He watched me, waiting for me to say something.

"Go on," I urged.

He nodded. "The scene of this particular disaster was Rait Castle, and—"

"I remember that," I broke in. "Laird Cummings was a total rotter. More's the pity he wasn't counted among the dead that day."

"A little-known fact," Blake continued smoothly, "was his

daughter was a changeling. One of us. It was why she was attracted to the MacIntosh lad."

My eyebrows shot up. "He was one as well?"

"Um-hum, and under my protection." Blake twisted his mouth into a sour expression. "You can see how well I fulfilled my obligation." He hesitated for a beat, perhaps arranging his thoughts. He needn't have. My five-minute limit had flown straight out the window.

"I rescued my changeling after her father cut off her hands. I'd have restored them—and her—but she forbade me. I assumed she'd come to her senses sooner or later, except it never happened. She preferred weeping and mourning her lost love. Years passed, and my band of Sidhe prepared to relocate. I came to her, offered to bring her with us, but she blamed us for her misfortunes. Said if we hadn't stolen her parents' human child—for our own nefarious purposes—she'd never have ended up stuck between the human and magical worlds."

I cocked my head to one side. "True enough. What happened to the fellow from the other clan? I assumed he was killed, but if he was a changeling as well…"

"His power was considerably stronger than hers. When I found his body, his spirit and his magic were long gone. He'd discarded one form and latched onto another."

"You never found him?"

"Nay, and I deployed scouts."

I digested what he'd said so far. Above us, the birds had settled into slow, steady circles as they kept a close eye on me. Becca stood quietly by my side, clearly intrigued by Blake's tale.

"It's all quite interesting," I told him, "but I'm not seeing where I fit in."

"Because I haven't gotten to that part yet," he said and rocked from foot to foot. "I have tea in the car. May I offer you some?"

I arched a brow. "Nope."

His chiseled lips twitched with amusement. "Not in my best interest to poison you."

"Maybe not, but you do want something. Eventually, you'll get around to spitting it out." I stopped shy of mentioning both food and drink could be laced with compliance spells.

"I will, indeed. I had business in this region. Complaints of a Cait Sith reached me. They don't belong on Earth. Members of my court offered to come in my stead, but I hadn't left the southlands in quite some time and was in the mood for a journey."

"Why Galloway?" I inserted a sidebar.

"Because it's near a portal to Underhill."

At least he was answering my questions. "Mmph. Cait Sith is another name for Cait Sidhe, right?"

He nodded reluctantly, as if loathe to claim any relationship with the renegade cat. "The Cait wasn't hard to locate, but he is impervious to my power."

I rode herd on the "aw gee" and "poor baby" that danced in the back of my throat. As a mage with relatively modest power, I'd be damned if I'd feel sorry for the Daoine Sidhe, whose magic was limitless by comparison.

Spinning a hand, I said, "Keep going. We're closing on why you chased me down."

"Aye, we are. When I dug deeper, the reason the Cait could resist me was he'd glommed onto Roya's magic.

Between the two of them, he's set himself up as laird over the other Cait Sidhe. They're not pleased."

A light crackled to life over my head. "They're who called you. The other Cait."

"Aye."

"Roya must be Laird Cumming's daughter. The one who lost her hands."

A curt nod validated my comment.

"Are you certain she was a reluctant recruit?" I asked.

"Nay, I'm not."

I rolled my shoulders straighter. "You want me to deal with the Cait."

Blake bobbed his head up and down. "Exactly. Tell him he must release Roya, and—"

"What if it was a mutual pact?" I asked and hurried on. "Even if it weren't, my gifts don't work like that. Creatures follow me because they're drawn to my type of magic. I don't do anything special. It just happens. If the Cait resisted you, what makes you think he'll want anything to do with me?"

"We will work together. I will conceal myself, and—"

"Oh hell no. I've never deceived an animal. Not certain I'm capable of it. If I did, word would spread, and no one would trust me anymore."

He frowned. "Hadn't considered that angle."

I gave him points for admitting he wasn't perfect. How would he do with me taking the lead on this problem? No time like the present to find out. "Tell you what," I said and watched him closely. "Meet me at midnight at the ruins of Rait Castle. We'll see what unfolds."

Whatever I'd expected it wasn't him grabbing my hand

and kissing the back of it. "Thank you, Abria. I shall be forever in your debt."

Tingles began where his lips touched my hand. As they passed up my arm, they turned to a long blast of desire that stole my breath. I snatched my hand back and did my damnedest to cloak my obvious reaction to him.

"Be careful of promises," I warned. "We may not meet with success, and you might end up furious with me, if events don't proceed as you expect."

"My word is my vow and not dependent on outcomes. See you in a few hours." He bowed low, turned, and retreated to his car.

Becca and I stood and watched him drive away. The birds had departed at some point, and I vaulted onto the unicorn's back. For the next hour, we rode along in silence, enjoying the still-sunny day, a soft breeze, and relative solitude.

"What do you make of that?" Becca asked.

I didn't have to ask for clarification. "Not sure. Have you heard about a group of Cait Sidhe around the Rait Castle ruins?"

"No, but I'll ask the others."

It was a sound plan. I'd ask as well. She left me next to my Range Rover with promises to be at the assigned meeting spot at midnight with a few other unicorns. Her support warmed me. No better warrior than a unicorn since they can end the immortal. Dragons can too, but I hadn't seen one of them in the Highlands in over 300 years.

As I drove back to my closet of an office on the outskirts of Inverness, Blake's dark hair and penetrating wicked eyes kept intruding. No matter how hard I tried to push him to a back burner, he bounced back. When I started imagining how he'd look sans clothing, how his hands would feel trailing across my flesh, I put a lid on it.

Tried to.

My trysts have been limited to mortals for the best of reasons. Other mages don't like me, but it's generally mutual. And my interest in a forever relationship with another immortal falls into the less-than-zero range.

So what was I doing giving Blake access to a huge chunk of mental real estate? Good question. No answers jumped to the fore.

To divert myself, I dredged out my phone, breaking the law about cell phones and driving, and checked messages and texts with one eye, keeping the other on the road.

It's just tonight, I told myself. *He'll be gone after that. Surely, I can keep it professional for a few hours.*

Famous last words. Why was I so certain they'd come round to bite me in the butt?

Chapter Two

As I slogged through my afternoon, talking with clients and researching fixes to problems, parts of Blake's story bothered me. If Roya had truly been a changeling, why hadn't she levied power against her father—before he chopped off her hands.

The only explanation I could gin up was she'd always resented her magical side and had never learned to use it. Power is like any other talent. Even if the substrate exists, it still requires practice to whip it into useable shape. As I turned things over and over, looking for patterns, I decided her association with the Cait had likely been forced on her.

If she'd rejected Blake and the Daoine Sidhe, she wouldn't have willingly linked her fortunes with another variant of Sidhe. Caits were notoriously difficult to get along with. Aloof like their cat side, they were kind of a my-way-or-the-highway bunch. Roya had been alone for over half a millennium. What possible inducement could the Cait have offered to entice her?

None that I could envision.

At least I wasn't thinking about Blake. Not directly, anyway.

Another question was why place two changelings in the same spot? What was it about Rait Castle that had drawn the Sidhe's attention? I've never been part of a Sidhe inner circle, but my primitive understanding of changelings was the Sidhe always had ulterior motives when swapping out one of their own for human babies. Motives that extended beyond whatever they did with the infants, which wasn't pretty.

Let's just say none of those little ones ever grew up.

Even though no one was riding herd on me or breathing down my neck, I made a good-faith effort to keep normal business hours. Nine to seventeen hundred, four days a week. When Blake had groused I was tough to find, I'd known he was lying. All he would have had to do was stop by my office and read my posted hours.

And wait.

Yeah. That last part was a showstopper. He probably wasn't in the habit of waiting for anyone. Running on autopilot, I closed out my day. Receipts were flowing well this month, not that it mattered. I didn't need money, but I did appreciate my job. It ate up time, which I had a whole lot of. Absent my detective business, I didn't know quite what I'd do with myself.

I've been a lot of things over the years. Until recently, those endeavors fell within the magical realm. Science put the kibosh on that, so I've become creative. Working alone was critical since I frequently utilized my gifts—or animal spies and associates—to solve cases.

Anyway, things were perfect for now. I'd figure something else out when this well ran dry. My one-bedroom apartment was right above my office. Kept things convenient. I opened a couple of cans for dinner, showered, and dressed in dark trousers, a black stretchy top, and a faded jacket that had once been black but was now more gray than anything. Stout brown boots completed my Nancy Drew-for-hire outfit.

All the while I congratulated myself on not lusting after Blake constantly. The quick flares of heat didn't count. I tried to come up with more about our task that might prove useful, but I'd thought it into the ground. I felt a tiny bit sorry for Roya. She'd never had much of a say in her life, and now she had no life at all—unless you counted her ghostly haunting of Rait Castle.

It's always a good idea to show up early, so I was behind the wheel ninety minutes before our agreed-upon meeting time. My plan was to drive closer and teleport the rest of the way. I could have managed a travel spell from my house, but it would have depleted my magical stores for a couple of hours.

I found a secluded parking spot about ten kilometers from Rait's ruins and left the Range Rover. Taking more care than usual, I levied power for the rest of the journey, leaving myself about half a kilometer to walk. I opened my senses and my power while I was on the move, testing the area. Voices, small and otherwise, crowded into my mind.

All the animals who lived nearby inquired if I needed them. Their devotion made me smile.

"Maybe," I sent back, followed by, *"Caution. Danger could be near."*

Variations of my flock vowing to protect me with their furry and feathered lives flowed through me until I called for quiet before the Cait came to investigate. I felt them too, strutting this way and that across the moor as if they'd claimed it as their own.

Was that the true problem? Blake and the Daoine viewed all of the Old Country as their personal fiefdom. Since the Cait had never pledged allegiance to the rest of the Sidhe, their independence must grate. Another unanswered question was why Blake gave a crap about Roya. He'd intimated it was because of her Sidhe blood, but mages leave the fold all the time. No one goes after them—or hires someone else to— unless they play a critical role.

It circled me back to the mystery of two changelings dropped near one another at the same point in time.

As I walked, I gathered the bits of my seeking magic and reshaped it into a ward. What was left of the walls of Rait Castle came into view. Along with it, Cait Sidhe romped and danced on the castle green. An odd iteration of mage, they're the size of an average mortal but in feline bodies. Preferring to walk upright, balanced on their hind legs, they appeared harmless.

I knew better. I'd tangled with them a time or two. Their saliva is poison and their nails deadly sharp. One of their preferred tricks is opening flesh to bone level and spitting into the wound. No wonder they'd broken ranks with the other Sidhe, who viewed such tactics as unspeakably primitive.

"We are here," Becca announced in very private mind speech.

Hopefully, we meant her and the other unicorns. Not

wanting to call attention to myself or give away my position, I didn't answer. Instead, I assessed the various Cait Sidhe. Didn't take long to determine which one had shanghaied the handless maiden.

Eh, probably shouldn't call her a maid. My bet was she'd opened her legs for the MacIntosh lad. Nothing like stardust-laden lust to addle the brain. I swallowed a snort. The lust part was good advice for me where Blake was concerned. I'd searched for him when I was getting the lay of the land, but he wasn't here yet.

Or perhaps he was. With his magic, he could be squatting behind a ward and I'd never know the difference. Becca would, though. *"Is Blake here?"* I asked her.

"Aye."

"Where?"

A set of images flooded past. Interesting. He'd taken up a post inside the ruined tower. I'd never have thought to look there. For one thing, it's a terrible position to fight from. The Cait could surround him, and he'd have hell's own time kicking his way free.

Except he wasn't fighting. I was the front line. He'd said he'd stand with me, or some such thing, without fleshing out any of the details. We'd agreed he wouldn't remain hidden. He'd welched. Part of me strongly considered teleporting back to my car and driving home. If it hadn't been for Roya's plight, I would have.

Damn men, anyway. Magical or human, they're all the same. You cannot count on them to honor their commitments—or be forthcoming with relevant details. He had something up his sleeve, but he'd neglected to include me in the loop.

I fumed, but deep-sixed my anger. It was counterproductive, and one of my worst flaws. A few deep breaths centered me, so I added several more until my head was clear. I've always thought well on the fly—when I wasn't immersed in fury—and a plan was shaping up. Like I'd told Blake, I'm not a shady adversary.

Unlike him, I meet my problems head on.

Sometimes it works, and sometimes I'm sorry I didn't take a cagier approach. Usually, though, I'm dealing with mortals and their world. That wasn't always true. Before magic was forced underground, plenty of my clients came from the mage realm. They might not like me and view my brand of enchantment as inferior, but it's tough to argue with results.

Enough mental meandering. Time to whip this baby into something other than lurking on the sidelines.

Being taller than your adversary is an advantage, so I whistled quietly. None of the Cait so much as twitched a whisker. They probably thought I was a bird. Becca melted from shadows, and I vaulted to her back, shucking my ward as I did so.

We trotted forward, angling for the Cait who'd subsumed Roya. I raised a hand in greeting. Pleasant words died on my lips when the Cait twirled to face me fangs bared.

"Get lost," he snarled in garbled Gaelic.

Sheesh. Did they have their own dialect?

Aiming for a surprised expression, I replied, "Why? Becca and I just arrived. We heard the sounds of revelry, and—" Too late, the clank of a truth spell I hadn't sensed in time revealed the sketchy nature of my reply. I hadn't been lying. Not exactly, but neither was I completely forthcoming.

Becca pranced from side to side, spreading unicorn enchantment. Many of the Cait drew closer, fascinated by her. "Why do you wish us to leave?" I asked.

"You weren't invited." The Cait narrowed almond-shaped green eyes. His black fur quivered with outrage, and a line of hackles lifted along his back. I'd have missed them if he wasn't tossing his body this way and that.

"Still not seeing the problem." I jabbed him with magic so obvious he flinched, and then I feigned surprise. "Why are you carting a ghost around?"

"Freeeee meeee," pushed past his mouth as a muffled wail.

Mmph. As I'd suspected, Roya wasn't a willing participant. "Why not let her go?" I murmured, softly infusing my own brand of compliance.

"This is none of your affair." The Cait started toward me, but Becca lowered her head, horn pointing dead center at his chest. He stopped. No one with half a brain charged a unicorn. He might be furious with me, but not so angry he was willing to risk Becca's wrath.

The night, which had been dark as pitch, took on a glow as a half-moon scudded from beneath thick cloud cover. I took it as a solid omen and established links with a rich variety of animal life to augment my power. I'd pave the way for Roya to disentangle herself. Once she was free, we'd see what happened next.

Damn Blake nine ways to Faery. He was still hiding in the blasted tower.

Because Roya had relinquished much of her physical body, distinguishing the margins where she stopped and the Cait began was relatively straightforward. Even a hedge witch can tell protoplasm and spirit apart.

The Cait glowered at me, certain I was up to something, but unsure quite what. When I was nearly done, I gave it another shot. "You may as well let her go," I purred. "What you've done is a violation of the Covenant among our kind."

"You are not one of us." He inserted significant pauses between his words.

I shrugged. "So? The Covenant applies to all with magic. Last I checked, you're not exactly welcomed in polite Sidhe company."

A long, disconsolate howl rose from the Cait. No longer dancing, they'd formed a circle around Becca and me, one that was drawing closer. Had they come to a decision?

Something like damn the unicorn, full speed ahead.

Blake intimated the other Cait had summoned him. More bullshit. This group felt solid to me, aligned behind their leader, the one who'd taken Roya. Why had he lied? What secrets was he struggling to protect? I'd bet my last farthing it had something to do with why the changelings had been positioned here.

Should I mention the other unicorns? Or my almost completed separation spell? What in the hell were they so protective about? Between Blake's secretiveness and this bunch, I had to be missing something elemental. I tightened a leg against Becca's side, urging her to turn in a circle so we could assess what we faced, but she remained immobile, horn at the ready.

The howl from earlier was nothing compared with ungodly shrieks rising from fifty Cait throats as they lunged toward me.

Fuck this.

I ripped Roya out of the Cait, not worrying what I

damaged. He hurled curses at me while spitting blood. The specter of a wasted young woman dressed in rotten rags guttered past. Her long red hair was tangled and matted; most of her flesh had putrefied, and of course, her hands were missing.

How? Magical creatures live forever. If not on Earth, then in the *Dreaming*.

A Cait flew through the air and landed behind me. Tired of dicking around, Becca drove her horn through the Cait who'd kidnapped Roya. She bucked to dislodge the one behind me.

Claws raked down my back. Peachy. Just peachy. Next he'd spit in them, and then all my magic for the next month would be allocated to healing. I dragged a dirk from a thigh sheath and thrust behind me, jabbing it into any part I could reach. At least the bastard stopped clawing me long enough to grapple for the blade.

"In a pig's eye," I shouted and flashed around. My movement knocked him off Becca.

Roya was free. My task was done. The smart move would be to teleport back to my car, go home, and soak my abraded flesh, but I was beyond furious. Bastard Cait. They'd had no right to attack me. I opened my mind voice and summoned my allies. All of them.

Go home, an inner voice shouted.

Not done here, I told it.

Wolves and deer and rodents and hawks raced to comply. Within seconds the Cait were set upon by every manner of beast in the region. I should have been an assassin instead of a detective. Bloodlust raced through every channel in my body, pushing the pain from my wounds aside. I love a good scrap.

Becca cantered this way and that. Between her horn and my brand of destruction, we mowed a broad path. My back and shoulders burned, though. Rather than settling out, they were getting worse.

"Blake," I shouted. "Now would be a good time to show yourself."

A glistening spot in the air next to me turned into a gateway. He strode through. "You're doing a fine job without me." He looked pleased.

I jumped down, shocked when my knees almost didn't hold me upright. Crap. I needed to get out of here while I still could. What had been the castle green was littered with Cait corpses. Wolves ripped into them. Stags gored them. Hawks drove their beaks into eyes and ears, shrieking victory.

Roya's spirit was nowhere in sight. I didn't get it. She'd haunted the castle since losing her hands. Why leave now?

My vision swam; I shivered, first burning hot then freezing cold.

"Abria?" Blake's tone shifted from a victory chant to grave concern.

I opened my mouth to ask him to get me out of here, but my lips and tongue refused to cooperate. The ground rose up to meet me. Becca's frantic whinnies collided with Blake's deep voice shouting questions. Consciousness flirted like an unwilling lover before spinning on her heel and walking out the nearest door.

Chapter Three

I fell forever, plummeting past one pit and into another. Fell creatures started for me, realized what I was, and backed off. Unwilling to aid me, they couldn't harm me, either. Interesting. Monsters have given me a broad berth in the past, but I'd assumed they retreated because of my battle companions.

That hadn't been it at all. Great. If I lived through this, I'd file that tidbit away.

Abominations with dual and triple heads and more teeth than anyone had a right to drifted in and out. I smelled the poison from my wounds, harsh and acrid. When I reached a hand behind me, I connected with bone. Aw crap. That wasn't promising. My body wasn't healing itself.

It wasn't even slowing the spread of the black river of sludge coursing through my blood. How had the Cait become so lethal? Other Sidhe used magic, not chemicals.

Another swan dive. Another pit. I had to do something.

Damn Blake. He hadn't lifted a finger to bail me out. If it weren't for him, I'd never have been on that green. Never have known about Roya's plight. It was her own damned fault she'd been kidnapped.

I opened and closed my eyes. Didn't make a whit of difference. Endless blackness spread around me. I conjured a mage light, shocked when it shimmered next to me casting pallid blue illumination.

If I could kindle light, it meant I still had magic. So far, so good. I sent some to my shoulders and upper back. Not a whole lot. Nothing I did would effect a cure, but maybe I could slow the progression. Buy myself time to teleport somewhere.

"Think," I croaked. Yeah, that did a whole lot of good. Crappity, crap. My thoughts were all over the place.

Where was I?

"Doesn't matter," I croaked. Teleport spells required an endpoint. The beginning was irrelevant. Crap on a cracker. I must be in worse shape than I thought if I had to remind myself of such an elementary fact.

I've been in shitty spots before, but this one took the prize. Taking care to not make any mistakes, I crafted a spell. Keeping it simple, I visualized my car. Whether I was capable of driving remained to be seen, but my phone was in the car. I could always summon assistance and lie my head off.

Maybe tell them an animal had attacked me.

I dropped my head into my hands, holding my temples and yelling at myself to start over. My car wasn't where I needed to be. Neither was my home. I needed a healer, a magical one. Too bad I didn't know any. Western medicine wouldn't know what to make of my problem. Whatever they dosed me with would make it worse.

Minutes rolled past with me holding my head. I had to do something, but a crippling inertia held me in its maw. Could the Cait poison possibly be the culprit? I didn't see how, but then I didn't understand a lot of things about any of the Sidhe.

"Blerg," I muttered, shocked by how shaky my voice was. "Should have kept that in mind when Blake rolled up." I'd told him I didn't trust him. Why in the goddess's name hadn't I followed my instincts, told him no, and stuck with it?

The flare of anger was welcome. Like I've said, it's my go-to place, and right now it added energy to my depleted state.

"Blake! Blake! Blake," I shouted—if the squeak arising from my throat could be characterized as a shout. "You fucking bastard."

"Abria!" His deep voice resonated all around me. "Thank all the gods you called my name three times. I know where you are now. You have every right to be furious, but save it for later. Do not fight me."

My head twisted from side to side, but only darkness reflected in the glow from my mage light. Was it really him, or was my overtaxed brain adding hallucinations to the mix?

"Build me a portal," I demanded, all too aware I was scarcely in a position to stipulate anything.

"Aye, lass, but first I had to find you. Steady."

My hands clenched into fists. Was my tired mind playing tricks on me? Maybe none of this was real. The Cait magic pulsing in the background could be weaving its nefarious effects until the clock ran out and escape was no longer possible.

Did any of it even matter?

I was fresh out of ideas. Letting go of the power I'd rustled up to attempt to teleport out of my prison, I fell another hundred feet. Or maybe a thousand. I'd lost my ability to judge. I tasted blood and realized I'd bitten through my lower lip.

My heartbeat was slowing. I moved magic from my back and circled the center of my body, urging everything to function as it should. It might stave off the inevitable, but not forever.

The immortal don't fritter through much time imaging how they might die. I was no exception. I'd never given it a second thought. Until now.

I might have railed against my existence, but I'd be damned if it ended here.

Something floated off to the left. Narrowing my eyes, I focused on a spectral form swimming toward me. "Roya?"

She moved faster, propelling herself through the air with arms and legs. When she got close, she wrapped bony arms around me and held on. The compassion I'd felt for her spilled through me in a rush, displacing my earlier anger. Scents of the Sidhe surrounded me, the clean smells of the natural world. Rain-wet forests and damp stone.

She had scant magic, but she poured what little she had into me. Because even weak Sidhe magic is way more than I possess, I noticed the difference. My head cleared; my heartbeat stopped jumping all over the place.

"Blake is coming," she said into my mind. *"You were far. Traveling is simpler for me than him."*

"Thank you."

"Nay. Thank you. You saved me. The Cait unearthed the secret.

He was dredging it from me bit by bit, but you got there before he knew everything."

"He's dead. What he knows or doesn't is irrelevant."

I wanted to ask her what secret, but didn't. Some knowledge isn't mine to hold. Sidhe enchantment swathed Roya and me. No portal, but I'd take help from any quarter. The casting solidified, and the place where I'd fallen and floated dropped away. A well-lit cavern took its place, but I was too trashed to take in any details other than it had to be a Sidhe dwelling from the scent and impeccable furnishings.

They'd always had a taste for the finest. Roya still clung to me. Blake wrapped his arms around us both. "You can let go," he told her. "Your task is over. You did well."

She untangled her arms from around me. Tears flowed down her ruined face as she shook her head. "Nay. He almost, almost pulled everything from me. I couldn't stop him. My role as guardian was compromised."

Without Roya's magic to sustain me, I sank to a thick rug covering much of the cavern floor.

"Hold," Blake told Roya and dropped to his knees next to me. Placing hands on my back, he began a low chant. The chill that had invaded my bones took a long while to retreat. I faded in and out, but gradually, when I opened eyes I didn't realize I'd closed, I felt more or less like myself.

When I looked for Roya, she wasn't there. "Where are we?" I asked.

"Underhill. I needed its power to augment mine while I called you back."

As an experiment, I got my feet under me and walked to a nearby chair, sinking into it. Blake sat across from me.

"I owe you an explanation," he said.

"You do," I agreed after discarding a far more caustic *ya think* as counterproductive.

"Rait Castle sits atop a portal system leading to many worlds. We never worried about it until the MacIntoshes built that castle. The pull of the otherworld is strong. A few mortals were sucked through, which could have been disastrous. Their presence pollutes all portals and could render the entire system unusable."

"Hence the changelings," I murmured.

Blake nodded.

"Why not tell me the whole story up front?" I asked, not understanding the need for subterfuge.

"They are our secret," he replied. "As such, not mine to reveal."

"You are now," I pointed out.

"After what you went through, you deserved to know. How are you feeling?"

"Better. Whatever you did counteracted the Cait poison."

"It wasn't only that. The portals are deadly to anyone without Sidhe blood, and one of the Cait tossed you squarely into them."

I licked dry lips. A goblet materialized on a table next to me. For once, I didn't question it, but drank a mildly carbonated alcoholic mixture that tasted of honey and flowers.

"The Cait planned to commandeer the portals," Blake went on. "Once they controlled them, they could have made our lives miserable."

"Your very own version of a clan war."

He smiled softly. "Good analogy."

My goblet was apparently set to auto refill, the level replenishing itself no matter how much I drank.

"Ready to go home?" he asked.

I nodded. "Back to my car at least. Where's Roya?"

He shut his eyes for a long moment. "She finally accepted my invitation to the *Dreaming*. She will bide there for eternity, having served her people well."

I was glad for her. She'd been handed a shit deal all the way around. Her consternation at failing to keep the portals secret had been genuine.

"Feel like company?" Blake asked.

"Huh? When?" I hadn't understood his question.

"May I accompany you to your car? Or would you rather I sent you alone?"

The question was simple enough. Why was I having such a tough time answering it? After a pause so long it was growing awkward, I blurted, "Company would be welcome."

His smile broadened. "I was hoping you'd say that. You fascinate me, Abria, and very little does."

He got to his feet and held out his hands. I grasped them, never expecting he'd throw his mind open to me.

Chapter Four

I saw myself reflected in his thoughts, a generous version of me with tangled red hair skirting my ass, and my green eyes brimming with curiosity. In his vision, animals surrounded me, vying to get as close as they could. The stark lines of my face had softened, and I might have had a few more curves than the real me does.

That last made me smile.

Curious what else he'd share, I walked the paths of his memories. He was old beyond reckoning, one of the original Sidhe to make the journey from their ancestral lands. He didn't rush me or kick me out.

When I finally withdrew, dawn was breaking, and we stood next to my battered Range Rover. The air was damp and fresh, sweet with the promise of a new day. "Why'd you do that?" I asked, suddenly not in a rush to get into my car and drive away.

He tilted my chin with an index finger and gazed into my

eyes. His were inky black, but I'd missed the scattering of silvery flecks like a bunch of tiny stars. "I wanted you to know who I am," he replied.

"Aye, but why?" I reverted to Gaelic.

Before he could answer, Becca galloped into the clearing followed by the other unicorns. Wolves, deer, foxes, raccoons, and all manner of smaller rodents converged on us. Birds dropped out of the sky, landing on our shoulders, my car, and the ground. Surrounded by the swell of their concern and their love, I stroked and patted and leaned into one after another.

The insects were slower, but they too crawled or flew to me.

"Guess the word went out," I murmured.

"How could it not?" a gray wolf woofed. "We fought the Cait for you, and then you vanished."

"You are our heart, our life." A stag lowered his head so I could touch his towering antlers.

"You ensure our continuance," the wolf went on and rubbed his muzzle on my leg.

Blake bowed to first one and then another, deferring to their claim on me. The sun was well on its way to midheaven before my charges departed. "That was one of the most beautiful things I've ever seen," he murmured.

I'd known they loved me but misjudged the extent of their devotion. "They are truly amazing," I agreed.

"As are you." He'd moved off to one side but came near enough to drape an arm around my shoulders. "You asked why I shared my journey with you. I don't have a pat answer because it's not something I've ever done before."

Blake drew me against him. Where the length of his side

connected with mine, something hot and primitive flared to life.

He no longer felt haughty or patronizing. He may have welched on our plans for the previous night, but he'd also saved my life. What I did next ran far deeper than simple gratitude, and it surprised me.

"Would you like to come home?" I asked. Because I was looking at him, it was impossible to miss the joy that lit his eyes, making the silver flecks dance like an arcane light show.

"Very much. If you're certain it's what you want."

I nodded and turned in his arms until we stood face to face. "For now, yes, but nothing is ever promised."

"Understood." He dropped his hands onto my shoulders. "I have been alone for a very long time, as have you."

I started to ask how he knew, but figured he'd snatched it out of my mind. "No commitments," I went on. "But we can take this day to day."

"Good enough for me." He kissed my forehead lightly. What was it about his mouth? Everywhere it landed, shivery waves of delight cascaded through me.

I grabbed his upper arms and closed my mouth over his, desperate for the feel of his lips on mine, for the press of his chest against my breasts. A low, feral moan burst from him. I felt his need in the pit of my stomach, and it thrilled me. Hard and demanding, his kiss didn't miss a beat. He tasted sweet like the beverage I'd drunk in Underhill.

Slow and lazy, he teased my lips with his tongue until I opened to him. Equally slowly, he swept his tongue back and forth until the interior of my mouth caught fire. At least it matched the inferno roaring through me. My nipples formed hard peaks. All the moisture in my body headed south, slicking my thighs with need.

My legs shook. The only solid certainty in the world was the man in my arms running fingertips down my back and cupping my ass to draw me even closer to the hot, hard length pressing into my belly. Cars whizzed past. The occasional horn honked. A few wolf whistles told me we needed a more private spot.

Breath rasped in my throat, and my heart beat as if it wanted out of my chest when I pulled away and pointed at the car. The same savage growl, reminding me of a lion on the prowl, rushed from him. Somehow, we put enough distance between ourselves to get into the Range Rover.

He reached across the console and settled a hand over my upper thigh. Once I tapped the ignition and rolled onto the narrow country lane, he settled his palm over my sex. Hussy that I am, I spread my legs to improve his access.

"You want us to crash, right?" I laughed.

He joined me. I adored his laugh. Deep, rich, musical. "Not the end of the world," he said through his mirth.

"Maybe not, but how do we explain our miraculous survival when the poor sods in the other car didn't make it?"

He waved a dismissive hand. "We wipe a few minds, alter a few memories. Easy as pie." His other hand was buried between my legs, rubbing and teasing.

His touch was incredible, but I wrapped a hand around his wrist. "We both wait," I said firmly.

"Whatever milady wishes," he murmured and snapped his fingers. A silver flute dropped out of nowhere, and he plied me with old folk tunes for the rest of the drive.

The music flowed through me and around me. "Related to

the Pied Piper of Hamelin?" I teased.

He lifted his lips from the mouthpiece long enough to say, "I'll never tell."

I parked in my usual spot behind my building. These were normal working hours for me, so I opted for the most expedient route to my apartment. My closed sign still hung in the window. No need to alter it. I hadn't checked my phone, and didn't plan to.

"I live upstairs," I explained.

"Say no more." He pocketed the flute. The click of door locks buffeted me just before he moved us from the car to my home with a flick of his wrist.

I whistled. What would it be like to command power like that? My humble abode rose around us. I considered apologizing it wasn't grander but didn't. I could live more elegantly, but this pleased me, and I'd be damned if I'd change anything no matter how much I lusted after someone.

Blake wrapped his arms around me. "This is way more than lust," he said.

I snorted. "What? You live inside my head?"

He shrugged and drew me closer. "Get used to it."

Words vanished, replaced by a flurry of clothing hitting the floor. His shiny shoes slipped off. My boots took a little more doing. After that, it was a race to nothing at all. I blinked stupidly at his Greek-god build. Muscles bunched along shoulders and arms. A sprinkling of dark hair circled both coppery nipples. Scars crisscrossed his stomach and chest suggesting many battles. Someday, I'd ask about them, but not just now.

He'd dropped the glamour and was in full Sidhe mode, his wings delicate and lovely, his ears rising to graceful points. I'd avoided falling into the real estate below his waist, but I finally peeked. Rising to curve against his flat stomach, his phallus stood proud. Thick and beautiful and enchanting.

"Amazing," I murmured.

"Nay, you're the amazing one. Men would fight wars over your breasts. And your ass is perfection."

"Mr. Golden Tongue."

"It's true," he insisted and opened his arms. I walked into them. Desire racked me as flesh touched flesh. Sex with other mages ascends to levels mortals can't even imagine. It was one reason I'd stuck with them for my few-and-far-between trysts: to make it simple to walk away.

My throat was dry. What was I opening myself to?

"Late in the game for that, darling," he rasped near my ear. Where before his touches had been on top of my clothing, now his fingers and tongue carved flaming paths everywhere they touched me.

Hours passed, or perhaps it was days. We took breaks for meals until we ran through my slender stores of food. Sharing the last of a box of cereal with a few drops of milk, I said, "One of us is going to have to break down and visit the market."

"Why?" He waved a hand and grocery sacks rustled into being, lined neatly on my kitchen counter.

"Next excuse?" Dark eyes twinkled merrily.

"I should at least look at my phone, and I bet you left a few things unfinished as well."

He pushed the bowls between us aside and laid a hand over one of mine. "Tired of me already, darling?"

"Not at all, but we have lives too."

"They can wait."

I licked lips that tasted of him. "True, but I need to find a way we can blend everything."

"I don't want to leave you."

The sincerity of his words seared me. I didn't want to leave him, either, but if I was going to close out my detective business there were ways to do it other than vanishing. People might be worried about me.

"How about this?" I smiled. "The nights will be ours, and if I have to work then, we'll swap our time for the next day."

"Promise?"

"Nothing is promised," I reminded him, "but I will do the best I can."

He stood, came around the table, and lifted me to my feet. His cock nested into my belly as he held me. "Once more," he crooned, "and then we'll let the world in."

I couldn't refuse him anything. The same ferocity driving him lived in me as well. "Once more," I agreed and batted my eyelashes, miming a coquette. "Maybe twice."

His lips crashed down on mine. He swept me into his arms and carried me to the bed. Aphrodite's age-old dance caught us in its web. Hours later, we were still kissing and loving and stoking the flames, our promises to rejoin the world forgotten.

I took care to shield my thoughts from Blake. Nothing this good lasts forever, but I'd love to be proven wrong.

You've reached the end of *Hands of Fate*, a novella length prequel to my Wayward Mage Series. Abria and Blake's story continues in *Jinxed,* which is available now. *Hunted* and *Salvaged* will be along soon.

JINXED, WAYWARD MAGE
BOOK ONE

JINXED

Wayward Mage Book One. Also includes the prequel, Hands of fate

ANN GIMPEL

Jinxed

WAYWARD MAGE BOOK ONE

An Urban Fantasy

By
Ann Gimpel

Tumble off reality's edge into a dangerous world fueled by lore and magic

Copyright Page

Book Description: Jinxed

Fitting in has never been in the cards. Not part of the hand Fate dealt me. My superpower is animals, magical and otherwise. They adore me. Birds and insects too. Back when the Celts still roamed the Highlands, I begged them to shed light on how I came to be since my power is unique.

You can guess how well that went. They're a taciturn, entitled lot. I didn't shed a single tear when they packed up and left Earth.

Other mages don't care for me. They don't trust my one-of-a-kind magic. On my more generous days I don't blame them. For now, I run a tiny private investigator shop in the Scottish Highlands. Mortals are quick to hire me because I always solve their problems. Using magic is cheating, but they'll never find out.

Most days, it's a delicate dance. If I get lucky, no other mage has it in for me. But I'm still stuck hanging onto enough of a glamour to fool mortals. Occasionally, I want to pack it all in and vanish to...well, to somewhere else.

No one to blame but myself when my life skids off the rails.

Books in the Wayward Mage Series

Jinxed
Hunted
Salvaged
Hands of Fate (a novella)

Chapter One, Abria

The shadows of a moonless night shielded me as I crept down a slimy cobblestone alleyway in Inverness. A small camera with a shit ton of pixels was slung around my neck. Addresses were hit or miss in the alley, but I'd already scoped out the part of the building that faced the street.

Like all back streets in big cities, this one stank of piss and vomit with overtones of shit. My night vision is excellent, or I'd have stepped in one of many rancid pools.

Tonight's objective was simple enough, even if it had been hodge-podged together at the last minute. A man had shown up at my teensy office in Nairn a couple of hours before. He'd seemed distraught, and I hadn't bothered to test his words with magic. No reason to. His request was commonplace for private sleuths like me: come up with proof his wife was cheating on him. He'd given me all the goods. Name. Address. Next assignation.

My footsteps faltered; I ground to a halt. If he knew all those things, why in the hell did he need me? He could have crashed their little tete-a-tete and demanded justice for his wounded ego. Drawing the night around myself, I took a shot at invisibility. I hated to return his thousand-pound retainer, but I liked walking into a setup even less.

I bit my lower lip, but not hard enough to draw blood. Suddenly, I had a surfeit of problems. The scent of blood—particularly blood tainted with enchantment—would be enough to draw things I had no interest in dealing with. Vampires. Ghouls. Dark Fae.

My magic isn't particularly strong, so my don't-see-me illusion had holes in it. Nothing a mortal could drill through, but even the weakest mage would have noticed me. Was my brand-new client on the up-and-up? Or was this one more shot to sabotage me? As in, I'd get to the appointed spot and run smack-dab into an ugly surprise.

I unclenched my jaw once I realized I'd been grinding my teeth. Paranoid isn't exactly my middle name, but it might as well be. Mortals have no idea magic exists, but those of us who wield it all pretty much know one another. Despite a few petty squabbles, most of the arcane get along and view one another as part of a brotherhood.

Somehow, that banner wasn't extended to me. I'm a one-of-a-kind sorceress, and the others don't trust me. Animals are my superpower. Insects too. And birds. Fish and sea creatures adore me. Not that it would do me any good in the alley. Sinking into a crouch, I put out a call to the rats. All urban sites have rodents to spare. Inverness was no exception.

A fat, gray fellow who must have weighed a good half a stone sashayed close with half a dozen more behind him.

Whiskers twitching, he fastened his beady reddish eyes onto mine. I didn't waste time with words. Instead, I sent a series of images into his head. He squeaked and chittered, passing my request amongst his troops.

As a unit, they spun and raced in the direction I'd been headed. Their task was straightforward. Find out what was waiting for me and report back. A pair of nighthawks circled; one landed on each shoulder, squawking their hearts out. Guess they'd sensed my unrest.

What was my problem? Usually, I was braver than this, but I still sported scrapes and bruises from my last go-round with a herd of Dark Fae who'd lured me out to celebrate Beltane. Bygones will be bygones, they'd promised.

Yeah. Right.

I hadn't fallen for their invite right away, hadn't even given them a firm yea or nay, but I'm a sucker for Beltane. It's my favorite of all the Wiccan festivals. Litha and Samhain run a close second. Of course, back in the day, those celebrations weren't linked to witches, but to the Celts.

One of the nighthawks shifted from foot to foot digging small holes in my shoulder. "What is it?" I asked him.

He didn't answer, but his shiny dark beak opened and closed as he scented the air.

I cast a seeking spell hunting for my forward guard: the rats. When I didn't find them, my stomach tightened into a knot. Animals follow my lead because they love me. All of them. Had I inadvertently sent a rat patrol to their deaths? The thought made me vaguely ill.

Rats are ubiquitous. No one should have paid them any heed. None at all. A sharply drawn intake of breath felt like I'd inhaled glass shards. It told me how dry my throat was.

The air thickened with an odd combination of power. Subtle, yet a distinct alteration from the way it had been a few moments before. I should leave, but I couldn't abandon the rats who'd willingly done my bidding. Adding to the symphony of my indecision, rain splattered down. What a surprise. Rain in Scotland. It's tough to cobble an entire day together without at least a few sprinkles, but gathering clouds suggested I was in for a deluge.

Only one choice left, and it wasn't anything I routinely did anywhere—especially not in the middle of a big city. Mortals would take note, and I'd have to be well and truly skilled to skate out from under their scrutiny. Opening my mind to my special magical frequency, I put out a call to any and all animals nearby.

Insects responded first, scurrying out of hidey holes in nearby buildings. Birds were next. More nighthawks and other raptors almost blocked out the dark sky as they hurried to my aid. It was starting to feel like major overkill, and the wolves and raccoons and squirrels and deer hadn't yet arrived.

Much as I'd done with the rats, I sent imagery and surged forward. The nighthawks on my shoulders took to the skies, joining their kin. Pounding of clawed feet on stone announced a local wolf pack. Their alpha, a large snow-white male named Obo kept pace with me.

"What do we face?" he asked.

"Not sure," I ground out feeling like an idiot. Just because animals always respond to me doesn't mean I ever take their loyalty and devotion for granted. Gah. Maybe I should have gone after the rats by myself and summoned backup later.

My original objective had been about a kilometer down the alley. The stones grew progressively more uneven and slimed with water, moss, and human waste. Clearly, no one with means trod this path—or at least not often. True to my prediction, the skies opened drenching me to the skin in minutes.

As if the rotten weather had been some kind of cue—or maybe whoever was orchestrating my latest torment was a weather worker—stones shot up all around us, hitting buildings before splatting back to earth. A snarl and a yelp suggested one of the wolves had sustained a direct hit.

I stopped cold, staring into the murk. What in the hell was happening?

The answer to my question swatted me in the guts as a wraith oozed from one of the holes the stones had left. Black on black on black, it had no form, but its breath was poison, as was its touch. If it got close enough, it could steal your soul through your mouth, not unlike Harpies.

"Do not touch them." My tone was sharp.

"How can we kill them?" Obo growled.

"You can't," I replied. Unfortunately, neither could I. Stronger power than mine was required to do away with most anything magical. Aw geez, those poor rats.

More wraiths emerged. They carry a stench ten times more potent than the worst rot you can imagine. I gagged. If I'd have had food in my stomach, it would have spattered on the stones.

I opened my mind voice intent on sending all the animals who'd come on foot back, but wraiths surrounded us. Wispy, insubstantial, and lethal, they formed an unbroken ring that had to augment their power.

"What?" I growled. Predictably, no one answered. I'm not even sure they have voices.

I didn't understand. I'd been the butt of many practical jokes, but this time someone wanted me dead. Breath steamed from my open mouth. Fear twisted my belly into a sour knot. If I didn't watch it, paralysis would set in. I'm not okay with dying, but I'm even less okay with anyone harming the animals who adore me, who've made me their queen.

The circle of wraiths was tightening. Soon, there'd be no choice but to touch them. I could not allow that to happen. A strangled yelp followed by a burned smell told me one of my honor guard had fallen. Snarls and outraged growls rose around me. They lit a fire under my indecision.

I dug deep, dredging power from the bottom of my more-or-less immortal soul. If anyone suffered lasting damage from this shit-show, it should be me. Buildings lined both sides of the alley. Centuries old, they sported even older rusting locks slotted through hasps on timbers that had seen better days. Apparently, no one worried about thieves entering their premises from this side.

Knowing Scots, they weren't worried about thieves at all.

I picked the rattiest looking door and sent power jetting toward its padlock. It was so covered with rust, if it hadn't had phalanges poking through a hasp, I'd never have identified it as a lock. With a creak and a clatter, it gave way, tumbling to the cobblestones below.

Almost as if the wraiths sensed I had a plan to elude them, they moaned and howled. Ha. Guess they had voices after all. The temperature, already chilly, dropped a good ten degrees, and the steadily falling ran turned first to sleet and then to snow. The weather here is pure crap, but it doesn't usually snow in the summer.

I judged the distance to the door I'd just unlocked. Not

far, but wraiths were bunching up between us and my safety hatch.

It left openings in the circle.

Nothing magical about the door I'd just freed up. The wraiths were stupider than I'd thought. But then, I'd never truly understood where they came from. They hovered on the edge between the living and the dead. Rejected by both heaven and hell, they roamed Earth on the hunt for anything warm-blooded they could glom onto.

I'd always suspected they were Harpy agents, but I lacked evidence to back it up. The animals around me were attuned to my every move. No need for words as I broke and bolted through a hole in the wraith line. Everyone followed me and flowed through another door where I blew the lock as I pelted toward it. For a moment, the door, swollen from centuries of Scottish rain, refused to budge. I hit it with magic and it shattered inward.

We swarmed through.

Nothing to slam in the wraiths' faces, but for some unknown reason, they melted back into the cobblestones. I'd been ready for a pitched battle in the doorway. It was far simpler than being beset from every side.

I blinked a few times to convince myself the wraiths were gone. All the raptors who'd been circling overhead fluttered to land on the cobblestones squawking their curiosity. Every species leads with a particular emotion. For birds, it's curiosity.

For wolves, it's outrage. Next to me, Obo growled in frustration.

One thing for certain, my bogus client had set a trap for me. I'd bet my last pound note his name wasn't Jerome

MacLaren. I really did need to start matching up ID with what people told me.

The scurry of claws on cobblestones was accompanied with squeaks and squeals of indignation as the rats I'd send on a mission returned en masse. Their leader bounded into the building I'd broken into and sat back on his haunches. *"Nothing there,"* he chittered.

"We checked all around where you said," another rat chimed in.

"And then when we tried to return, we ran into a barrier. We couldn't crawl over it or tunnel under it," the leader said.

"All of a sudden, it vanished," the other rat added.

"You did well," I told them and crouched to scratch furry heads and shoulders. "Now go while you can." I stood and made shooing motions toward everyone. We'd been given a gift, goddess only knew why, but I'd be a fool not to take full advantage of it.

"We will accompany you," Obo said.

"No need." I buried my fingers in his thick, white pelt. Water hadn't penetrated and he was dry near his skin.

Since no one would go anywhere until I did, I pushed out of the shelter and set a quick pace back the way I'd come. My car was at the end of the alley, and by the time I got there, the only ones still with me were Obo and two of his wolves.

"It really will be all right," I reassured them. "I'm going to dry off and drive home."

The wolves leaned into me. *"Call us if you need us,"* Obo said.

I shook my head. After tonight, his loyalty touched me. I'd have thought he'd be more invested in saving his own hide than protecting me. His fur held singed spots from wraith breath, and one of his wolves had fallen prey to them. I'd be a damn sight more careful before I summoned anyone to my aid after this, but no reason to tell him that.

After dredging keys from my pocket, I unlocked the door of my ratty old black Range Rover and found towels in the back, so I didn't completely drench the upholstery. The wolves retreated to shadows, but stood watching me drive away, tails pluming.

I started to shiver and turned up the heat, but the cold coursing through me had nothing to do with being soaked to the skin. I've had close calls, but tonight was the first time I'd felt certain I was sitting squarely in someone's gunsights. It felt downright creepy.

As I drove, I turned over and over in my mind who had it in for me. It couldn't be mortals. I helped them. Which left the arcane community. Like I said, they've always hated me, but it's a quantum leap between not liking someone and wanting them dead.

"Throw yourself a pity party, Abria MacLeone," I muttered and toyed with the idea of leaving Scotland altogether. Didn't take long for me to decide it was stupid. Mages are everywhere, and word travels fast in the magical world. If someone put a price on my head, a geographic wouldn't change a damned thing.

No closer to a solution than I'd been, I pulled into my usual parking spot next to the building that houses both me and my detective agency. Normally, I'd have jumped out of the car. Not tonight.

With all my doors still locked, I sent seeking magic in a 360-degree arc hunting for something, anything, that shouldn't be there. When I came back empty handed, I didn't trust it and scanned again.

It was only after the fourth scan I reluctantly left the safety of my car and scurried inside. The door had no sooner slammed behind me than I felt it, a presence that shouldn't be here. Fuck. Double Fuck. Triple fuck. Misfortune had found me, and I was more than done with it.

Chapter Two, Blake

❧

"Back here again?" a strident female voice grated against the island of peace I was doing my damnedest to cultivate in a distant corner of the *Dreaming*.

"Aye. What's it to you?" I snarled in a very old form of our Sidhe tongue. If the goddess was smiling—which rarely happened—Sybil wouldn't understand the dialect and get out of my way.

No such luck.

"You haven't darkened these parts in centuries, Elwyn Cardassier. I demand to know—"

"Demand?" I shouted. "I outrank you by many tiers. You forget yourself, Sybil. Do not speak my true name aloud. You know better. Or you should." I surged to my feet, loathe to relinquish the comfy spot where I'd been keeping an eye on the world beyond. A crack in the veil separating Earth from the *Dreaming* provided the perfect vantage point.

Sybil rolled silver eyes rimmed with bronze streaks. Tangled white hair floated around her head in full defiance of gravity. Like all my race, she was impossibly beautiful. Flawless face, long shapely legs, generous figure.

"Fine, Blake," she gritted through very straight white teeth. "No one is about to eavesdrop on your actual name. Or do you know something I don't?"

Progress. We'd moved from demands to wheedling innuendo. I made shooing motions with one hand. "Whatever you were about before you found me, I suggest you return to it."

She glided nearer and rested a hand on my shoulder. "I'm bored. How about a spot of...play?" Pheromones thickened the air around us redolent of ivy, bayberry, and vanilla.

My cock rose, thickening in automatic response. I told it to stand down, but of course it didn't listen. Before Sybil reacted to the musk that had to be radiating from me, I ducked from beneath her fingers. "Go. I'm engaged in critical matters. The best way you can help me is by leaving."

Her mouth formed a moue; her forehead wrinkled in dismay. Too late, I understood no one had ever turned her down before. Sex is meaningless to the faery folk. A pleasant way to pass the time. She'd laugh in my face if I told her I'd fallen in love with a mage outside our ranks. Thank Danu she wasn't peering into my mind.

"You may be occupied right this minute," she amended brightly. "I could easily return when 'tis more convenient for you."

Of course, she could. I switched things up. "Do you wish to leave the *Dreaming*?"

Her multihued eyes widened. "Why would I?"

I gave a slight shrug. "You've been here for a long while, and—"

She batted me to silence, said, "I like it here," and stomped off.

I exhaled long, slow, and noisily before retreating to the cushion I'd shoved into a corner. Sybil was gone for now, but not forever. Once she set her sights on a prize, she was as intransigent as a dragon squatting in the midst of her hoard. She'd return, probably buck naked and with a pheromone enhancer on board.

I wasn't under any illusions. She didn't care about me or anyone else, but the *Dreaming* lacked ready sources of entertainment. I'd bet my last pound note she'd run through every willing male in residence, and a few of the less-than-willing too.

Immortality drags on many of us. It's why we retire to this spot, a floating island between worlds, when we weary of everything our other life has to offer. Sybil assumed I was here for the same reason. It made sense. Why would I be any different? Fae blood was Fae blood and many of the Daoine resided here.

I've always viewed retreat as the worst kind of copout. Tired of being immortal? Buck up and deal with it. Big words. The whole reason I ended up at the head of the Daoine Sidhe was because I refused to give up or back down. Life wore on me too, but I'd never let anyone know.

Close to a year ago, I had a bit of a problem with one of our gateways. I could have managed it myself—at least, I told myself as much. But an unusual form of magic hovered not all that far from the gateway. I tried not paying it any heed, but it tantalized me. In the end, it drew me like a bloody lodestone and turned into all I could think about.

One day when I couldn't stand it any longer, I set spells to guard my broken gateway and ventured into Nairn, following the track of the magic I couldn't figure out. I'd already determined the owner had to be female, but I'd expected something truly obscure like an ogre or a troll. Instead, the trail led to an innocuous building that must have been standing for centuries judging from its architecture. Naturally, it had been remodeled several times, but its roots ran deep into the Highlands mingled with the same arcane power I still couldn't identify.

On the door sat a sign announcing *Abria MacLeone, Detective for Hire*.

After that, it was simple enough to manage an accidental meeting. She was riding a unicorn in a madcap dash through nearby farmlands. Mortals saw a horse between her exquisite thighs, but I can drill through virtually any magical disguise.

Abria and the unicorn saw through mine quick enough, too. Not such a bad thing. Good to level the playing field.

Once we'd gotten the meet and greet out of the way, with me keeping mum about the unicorn, I hired her to help with the gateway. Turned out she was extremely useful. Her and her entourage.

Who would have thought she was an animal mage? In the dim recesses of my memory, I'd heard of one long ago, but never taken the reports seriously. We all have some affinity for animals, but her power ran far deeper than that. They adored her, revered her, and made it their personal mission to protect her.

And me? I was a lost soul before I even laid eyes on her.

The long red hair, greener-than-green eyes, and lithe, athletic build sealed the deal. She was a knockout in a far more "real" way than the Sidhe, whose beauty carries an ephemeral aspect.

We became lovers, and I was having a fine old time. Until she kicked me out. I figured she was teasing when she said it was past time for me to leave, but no. She was serious. Confused and heartbroken—something I'd never reveal to anyone—I left.

But I didn't go far. After lurking around Nairn behind carefully constructed wards, I located a wing of the *Dreaming* that allowed me to keep a close eye on Abria. I had to operate on the QT. She has a lot of pride, that woman, and she'd have been horrified to know I hadn't truly reverted to one of my many lives as the Earl of Galloway. I'd never shared my true name with her, but tit for tat. In retrospect, she'd kept a few secrets of her own.

Like the extent of her power, for one. She frequently bemoaned how weak her magic was, but I caught flashes of incredible power when she was convinced I wasn't paying attention. I'd been closing on offering her a trip to our primary library to research her lineage—an unheard of honor for a non-Sidhe—when she sent me packing.

Maybe I should have spoken up sooner, but I refused to grovel once I understood she meant every word about me leaving. Fool that I am, I needed her to want me for myself, not for the side benefits I could offer.

Months have passed. In the first few weeks, I kept expecting her to call me, say she'd made a mistake.

Never happened.

If another man had popped up, I'd have struck him dead

on the spot. Even if he'd been magical, my power overshadows nearly everyone's. That never happened, either. Nay. Abria went her merry way, solving meaningless human problems and communing with one animal or another. She loved them all, and they adored her in return.

Maybe that was it. Her heart was already so full, there hadn't been room for me. Except I didn't believe it. How could I have been so taken with her, so smitten, only to have her throw me over?

What had passed between us was significant, earth-shattering. I'd never opened myself like I did with her, never shared as much of who I truly am. To reveal so much and be spurned stung. A lot.

I'd been gritting my teeth, so I relaxed my jaws. And my fists.

Maybe it was time for me to pop back into her life. Nothing heavy or demanding. I'd make a point of staying out of her bed—if I could summon the willpower.

Perhaps if we could share a meal or two, laugh together, it might rekindle the special spark I was certain we'd shared. Raking through my memories once more, I tacked down the event when the tide had turned. She'd said she had to get back to work, and I'd told her I'd take care of her.

Words that should have soothed had turned sour fast. Within the next couple of days, she withdrew more and more until I found myself walking out her door for the last time.

Could it be that simple? I'd infringed on her unfettered nature? Hard to believe she'd have walked away from the inferno blazing between us for such a tiny thing.

Except it wasn't tiny to her. To Abria, her independence meant everything. Back on my feet, excitement raced through me. I'd knock on her door and reassure her I'd never threaten her spirit, her autonomy. I wouldn't beg, not exactly, but neither would I take no for an answer.

It might be hubris on my part, but I couldn't believe she didn't care about me. Not with how deeply I'd fallen in love with her. My nostrils twitched. Doubling up a fist, I punched the air. Sybil was on her way back for round two. I cast a hasty journey spell, taking care to mask my destination. The *Dreaming*, ancient bastion for burned out Sidhe, dissolved around me. I doubted Sybil would try to follow, but I didn't want to take that chance.

Nothing like knocking on Abria's door only to have Sybil teleport into the cottage and wreck everything. It was late evening on Earth. The *Dreaming* lacks day-night cycles. It's always the same there. My kinsmen find it soothing, but I understood Sybil's boredom all too well.

Late evening was a plus since no mortals milled about. I'd keyed my spell to come out in copse of trees not far from Abria's home. The only ones I startled were a couple of drunks snoring under the thick canopy of leaves and branches. After spelling them back into a drunken stupor, I walked to Abria's cottage.

I knew right away she wasn't there, but I'm the best of trackers. I started after her, but reined myself—and my enthusiasm and errant erection—in. She was probably off doing detective work. What would I say when I popped into the middle of an investigation?

"Hey there, darling. Could you use a spot of help?"

I made a face. It sounded sappy and contrived. Far better to—

Every sense I had hit mach 10 from a full stop. Abria was

in trouble. I could feel her fear and angst even across however much distance separated us. So much for looking like an ass. She needed aid. I'd provide mine whether she wished it or no.

After dragging a cape of invisibility around myself, I set a tracking spell in motion. Rather than teleporting, which would remove me from Earth, I chose to skim along keeping a careful eye on everything. I'd reached the intersection leading to Inverness when I felt her drawing nearer.

The terror and anguish that had alerted me were receding. Damn it. I wanted to be the one to rescue her. Or maybe she'd managed to get herself out of a jam with help from her animals. She welcomed them into her circle. Why not me?

Another scan reinforced that she was definitely on her way back. Only one thing to do. I wasn't about to risk her slamming the door in my face. Nay. I'd teleport inside and she and I would have a talk. A good one. We'd hash everything out. At the end of it, I'd lift her in my arms, crush my mouth on hers, and carry her to bed.

My cock throbbed where it curved against my belly. The old chap's way of letting me know my plan had earned his total endorsement. And then, I rebuked myself soundly. This wasn't about me. It had to be about her. Whatever had happened tonight had shaken her badly. Otherwise, I'd never have sensed her anguish across the distance separating us.

I slipped inside and hid in the washing alcove on the main floor. She'd be angry I was here without her leave, but maybe whatever had transpired would take precedence and she'd welcome a loving ear.

Eventually.

I crouched in the dark, masking my presence. The crunch of tires on gravel told me I didn't have long to wait. The feel of her so close was intoxicating, but I had to downplay my intense need. If she had a problem with the magical realm, I'd solve it.

And then we'd see if we had a future.

As settled as I was likely to get, I waited for the door to open.

Chapter Three, Abria

"Show yourself," I shouted beyond pissed someone had broken into my home and too overwrought to use magic to figure things out. "For fuck's sake, show yourself."

What little enchantment I had bounced from one outstretched palm to the other, and I readied myself to annihilate whoever had breached my sanctuary. The house is old, rooted in tradition dating back to the Crusades. Because it's been mine forever, I linked to its intrinsic magic.

The lightning bolts arcing between my hands brightened considerably. I girded myself to kill first and ask questions later.

"What's got you so riled up?" a familiar voice inquired with the barest hint of dry humor laced into the question.

"Show yourself," I gritted. Just because the voice sounded like Blake Townsend, a Daoine Sidhe I'd met several months before and had a short-lived torrid affair with, it could be someone impersonating him. After tonight, I didn't trust anybody as far as I could see them. And we've already established whoever was in my home was skulking behind a ward.

"Are you going to spear me?" The dry humor deepened.

"Not if it's really you." Frustration burned a track through me. I kicked a nearby table leg. I'd have punched the wall, but both hands were occupied.

"Who in the hell else would it be?" His rich, melodic voice with its upper-crust British accent held a calming spell.

I warded myself. I'd been suckered once today. I'd be damned if I'd be anybody's doxy a second time. Fuck Jerome MacLaren. I'd keep his thousand pounds. If he had the nerve to show up requesting a refund, I'd batter him to pieces and feed the remains to my pet ravens.

"Abria?" Blake's voice—if it really was him—broke into my revenge fantasy. "I'd like to drop my warding."

I wrestled with telling him to get the fuck out of here. I hadn't seen him in the last four or five months, and I did not believe in coincidences. "Why are you here?" I growled.

"To help if I can. I felt your unrest through the connection we have."

The words were so sincere I almost believed him. I'd been the one to kick him out. Not because I didn't care about him, but because we spent all our time in bed, and my private eye business was dying on the vine. Blake is loaded. I'm not, and I had no intention of sponging off his generosity.

I might not have had intentions, but I'll admit I'd been tempted. So tempted my only avenue had been to nudge him out the door. Because my attention had wandered, one end of the lethal magic I'd been hanging onto singed my hand.

I swallowed a yelp.

"Drop your ward and stand where I can see you." Blood from my abraded skin dripped onto the floor. Oops. Not good. Blood gives anyone magical power over you. So do other bodily fluids. Blake had neutralizing spells. Me, not so much.

Across the room, a patch of air shimmered and undulated. When it quieted, Blake took a step toward me, the characteristic twang of his Sidhe energy palpable. No human glamour today, but his jewel-toned black wings added to his exotic good looks. Slightly over six feet tall, sleek, and graceful, he had the same broad-shouldered, slim-hipped build of all his race. Tonight, he was dressed in a tan corduroy jacket, a cream-colored linen shirt, and brown pants. Polished wingtips peeked from beneath his trouser bottoms. Inky-black hair had been layered and reached collar level. With a high forehead, sculpted cheeks, a square chin, and dark eyes surrounded by eyelashes any woman would gladly kill for, he was quite the vision.

No one could impersonate him—or the feel of his essence—this well, so I lowered my hands and released the magic that had stung me. "Unrest, eh?" I made a face. "So you felt *unrest?* Hell, Blake, someone tried to kill me and damn near succeeded."

He tilted his head to one side and frowned. "Yet, you're still here. Perhaps they were only trying to scare you?"

I waited but he tactfully refrained from pointing out my *persona non grata* status in the arcane community. Or how pathetic my actual magic was. Good. I didn't need reminders I'd been jinxed from my making. Or my birth. My memory is blank where my origins are concerned, as if someone wanted to make damn good and sure I never found out. My earliest memories are of being an orphaned beggar girl on the streets of London around 1400. Not the nicest recollections. Mostly, I hid in any alcove I could find and scrounged food with a magical assist from rats and birds who always came to my aid.

It took me a while to put two and two together. For the longest time, I figured the animals were just being kind—

"Abria?" Blake spun one hand in a come-along motion since I hadn't answered him.

"I was set upon by wraiths," I admitted. "Me and the animals who heeded my call. Wraiths killed one of the wolves, so yeah, I believe they were serious."

His dark eyebrows shot up. "Wraiths, eh? Been centuries since I've seen one."

I nodded, muttering a noncommittal, "Uh-huh," while my mind raced at a feverish pace.

Fuck. If Blake hadn't laid eyes on one in that long, someone must have summoned them. They didn't show up on their own. Hooking a foot around a chair leg, I dragged it into position and dropped into it. I'd have sold my soul for a cup of tea, but I was too wiped out to get up and put the kettle on.

He glided forward and pulled out a chair, positioning it across from mine before sitting. "Did anything happen before the wraiths? Or did they materialize out of nowhere?"

Nodding tiredly, I filled him in on Jerome's visit. As I talked, Blake drew his brows into a thick, worried line. I knew what was coming next, and he didn't disappoint me. "You know better, Abria," he said in a mild tone.

Defensiveness left a sour taste in my mouth. "So sue me. Most mortals are harmless. Why would I suspect this one?

He appeared genuinely flustered and furious his wife was cheating on him."

Blake shrugged. "You spend more time with humans than I do."

"Not true," I shot back too tired to be diplomatic. "Mister Earl of Galloway. You spend untold hours hobnobbing with mortals while you pretend to be one."

"That's different," he protested. "They look to me for direction. And I provide it."

"Not all that different," I muttered. "Mortals come to me for help—and I provide it."

He scooted his chair close enough to lean forward and place a hand on my thigh. Heat jetted through my damp jeans, reminding me of my wet clothes. I'd had them on so long, I'd stopped noticing. His touch brought scorching scenes of being naked with him front and center. Along with them came an almost irresistible urge to stand and strip off my garments.

If I did, we'd end up right back where we left off. Drenched in torrid desire that had no beginning nor end. I couldn't afford that. Not now when a malevolent someone—or someones—had it in for me.

"Tea," I mumbled and hoped he'd take the hint. I lacked the willpower to remove his long, tapering fingers from my leg.

After a few more circular strokes that made me wish his hand was sitting atop my sex, he stood and snatched the kettle from its usual spot on the stove. "You should get out of those wet clothes," he said brusquely. "By the time you're changed, I'll have a nice cuppa together for us."

I pushed upright. It took way more effort than it should

have. I'd known I was close to the end of my reserves, but this clinched it. "Put something alcoholic in mine," I said as I stumbled out of the room.

Mounting the stairs to my spartan living quarters, I started removing my sodden garments along the way. By the time I got to my bedroom, I was down to a soaked sports bra on top. After hanging my jacket and top on hangars and arranging them near the heat vent to dry, I bent to unlace my boots. Once they were gone, my pants followed and then my underwear.

My skin wasn't wet, but I rubbed myself with a rough towel hoping for a return of energy. I'd wrapped myself in a robe before it dawned that wasn't such a hot idea—unless I wanted to get laid. Sex was a luxury I couldn't afford until I sorted through who was after me.

Robe back on its hook, I donned sweats and an old pair of sheepskin slippers before padding back downstairs. The scents of mint and anise met me before I reached the kitchen.

"You're more than just another pretty face," I said and scooted into a chair in front of a steaming mug of hopefully spiked tea.

"Coming from you, that's high praise." Blake plopped down across from me and tipped his mug to his mouth.

For the next few minutes, we sipped tea in silence. The frantic feeling left over from my narrow escape was dissipating, but slowly.

"I put out some feelers while you were upstairs," he began.

I'd been slumped in my chair, but I straightened my back. "What kind of feelers?"

"To see if anyone knew anything about what went down tonight."

"And?" I was pretty sure I knew the answer, but I asked anyway.

"I didn't find much," he admitted.

"Why would you?" I locked gazes with him trying not to notice his kissable mouth with its well-formed lips.

"What do you mean?"

My turn to shrug. "I'm not exactly at the top of anyone's favorite mage list. Presumably, that includes the Sidhe."

"My people did not have a hand in your current troubles." He sounded offended.

"How could you possibly know?" I countered.

"They couldn't keep such a thing secret from me," he insisted.

Um, sure they could.

The more I thought about it, the less I liked the answers that popped up.

"It's possible some of the other Sidhe didn't approve of you, uh, slumming with me. So they hatched a plan to take me out of the equation."

"But we haven't seen one another in months," he protested.

"Good point. Maybe they decided it was as good a time as any. If they'd offed me in the middle of our..." I faltered, not sure how to label what had passed between us.

"Affair?" he suggested dryly.

"Sure. Affair." I latched onto his word choice. "Anyway, you'd have been..." Again, words failed me, mostly since I had no idea how he would have taken my demise.

"I get the picture," he cut in. "If you'd died when it

appeared I was still enamored of you, I'd have gone on a hunt for the perpetrators."

"Exactly." I piggybacked onto his explanation and added to it. "You'd have figured out who did it and ended them. Or had a unicorn do the dirty work. But now, when it seemed we'd drifted apart, no one wanted to risk us getting back together."

"It's one possible explanation," he conceded. "There are many others. But I will get to the bottom of this, and—"

I held up a hand. "No. I'll figure it out. I really don't need help."

"Not how it looked a couple of hours ago."

I winced.

"I was on my way to where I sensed the disturbance in Inverness, but then I felt you traveling this way. You had to be heading home, so I came inside and waited."

I set my mug down. It was empty. Somehow, I'd finished the tea without noticing what I was about. "It's kind of you, but I can take things from here."

"Can you?"

The question hung between us. I tried running a mental list of pros and cons, but my mind ran in tired little circles like a hamster on the wheel to end all wheels. "I need sleep," I muttered. "Can we continue this conversation in the morning?"

I clapped a hand over my mouth as I realized my turn of phrase suggested he'd still be here in the morning.

He was too quick for me in my current state. Already on his feet, he drew me upright. "Wonderful idea," he purred. "We'll go upstairs and lie down. I'll wrap you in a calming spell and watch over you, so no harm intrudes."

I opened my mouth, but the "thanks, but no thanks," I meant to give voice to never happened mostly because warm tendrils of magic snared me, soothing my fears. Blake wasn't in the taking no for an answer mood, so he'd stacked the deck in his favor.

Or maybe in my favor. I wasn't thinking clearly. Having him stand guard was appealing. Nothing I might summon as a ward would be foolproof, and both of us knew it. Strong arms lifted me as if I weighed nothing. He cradled me against his chest and started up the stairs.

"No sex," I blurted with my head tucked between his neck and shoulder.

"Not until you're ready," he agreed cheerfully. Too cheerfully.

Beyond understanding how pathetic my magic was, he knew the effect we had on one another. Drawn like moths to a flame, we'd spent months locked in one another's arms. I'm sure the good citizens of Galloway had wondered what the hell happened to their Earl.

We'd reached my room. A jet of iridescent magic tugged the coverlet off the bed. Blake placed me on the mattress and then curled his body protectively around mine. Feathery wings snared me in their folds, promising nothing would happen to me—not on his watch. The four directions come alive at his behest, and a spell rose around us. Warm and shimmery, it bathed me in a pale violet glow.

"Sleep, darling." Blake kissed my forehead.

The touch of his lips was the last thing I remembered before darkness rose up to meet me.

Chapter Four, Blake

Abria finally relaxed against me. It took her a while to accept my embrace. When I first tried to hold her, she was stiff and uncomfortable. Only after I added my wings, tucking her into them, did she truly let go. Exhaustion carved deep into every cell of her body. Her distress smote me. I deepened her relaxation with a smidgeon of calm. Between that and the wings, she fell asleep, her breath warm on my skin.

So far, so good. I was still here. She hadn't shrieked in my face or forced me out the door. I'd resisted clucking over her, at least not too much.

It wasn't easy. She looked like hell with dark smudges under her eyes that hadn't been there before. A savage need to protect her battered me, but it was the wrong approach. She didn't believe she needed protection, and she'd dismiss my Sir Galahad routine out of hand.

She had to recognize me as an elemental part of her

defense against whatever had trapped her tonight. The best way to accomplish that would be to identify exactly what she was up against.

I considered her theory about other Sidhe being behind tonight's near brush with disaster. It was possible, but unlikely. I might run the Sidhe council, but it wasn't as if I were a prince or anything. Some say the Daoine are Sidhe royalty, but it's not true. We're the original strain of Sidhe. Very few of us remain. Tough to keep one's blood pure when there are so few. Doesn't take much for a stray sperm here or an errant egg there to create mages who are only half Daoine. It's how the rest of the Sidhe lines were created.

Back in the day, the council—and the Daoine—played a far more active role. I wasn't even certain why we maintained our council structure, other than to pay lip service to our long, rich history.

Abria rolled over in her sleep, pressing a shoulder against me. I tucked her close listening to the ragged ebb and flow of her breath. If she'd been having problems, why hadn't she called me?

Because she never asks for help. An inner voice stated the obvious. After tonight, I bet she'd think long and hard before even involving the animals. They'd lay down their lives for her, but she didn't want their sacrifices any more than she wanted mine. Not that protecting her was a sacrifice. More like a welcome task.

The sad truth was I wanted her to need me.

If it took an external threat to open her eyes to how vulnerable she was on her own, I was all for it. Over the course of working together, maybe I could find a path back into her life. We'd made a decent team resurrecting the gateway. It could happen again...

Having her so close, body warm and soft with sleep, wasn't conducive to rational thought. All I could envision was her, but coming up with ways to make her recognize how valuable I was wouldn't work. She might reluctantly admit she couldn't go it alone right now, but she'd end up hating me if I took advantage of her situation. I nodded to myself. I'd stand by her, marshal every resource at my disposal to ensure her safety, but my aid wouldn't come with any expectations. We'd see where we were at the end of this.

If she still rebuffed me, I'd respect her wishes. Never mind, she was the only woman for me. I'd known it the moment I scented her unique magic. But I was getting ahead of the game by leaps and bounds. First, we had to identify who'd set her up tonight.

I don't need much sleep, so I decided to do a spot of sleuthing. Two of us could play detective.

Careful not to disturb her I withdrew the wing from beneath her and quietly stole from the bed. Jerome had been here and not all that long ago. Perhaps traces of what he was would linger. It was as good a place as any to start. By the time Abria woke, I might have an answer or two.

Moving with the silence inherent to the Sidhe, I made my way down the stairs and into her office. Extending my magical antennae, I searched for what had to be there and came up with a blank. Even a mortal would have left bits of their essence behind. For there to be nothing pointed to Jerome not only not being human, but to him being exceedingly well warded.

If not by him, then by whoever was masterminding this project.

A quick search of her bookcase yielded a telephone directory. Lots of MacLarens, but no Jeremy. Not much of a surprise. Anyone who'd take such pains with warding themselves would have used an alias. His cheque sat in the middle desk drawer. I didn't get any more of a hit off it than I did the rest of her office.

No one but her had been here in days.

Except it wasn't true. The cheque was proof positive to the contrary.

I'd hoped for something simple, but it wasn't shaping up. The deeper I dug, the murkier this whole mess grew. Closing my eyes and extending my arms, I quieted my mind and soaked in the feel of the still, dark air. At first, I felt nothing, but after a time the faintest tinge of wickedness washed over my wingtips.

Or I thought it did. When I moved from purely passive mode to an attempt to latch onto the rottenness, it was gone.

Nothing further to be gained here. Tomorrow, I'd be fresh. Surely, I'd work things out then. I've never run up against a magical problem I couldn't solve.

This wouldn't be the first.

Determined to break the world if I had to, I glided back up the stairs and joined Abria in her bed. She murmured in her sleep as I placed a protective wing over her and cuddled close. I took it as a good sign. When she wasn't invested in defending her independence, a part of her still cared.

Chapter Five, Abria

Light spilling through the room's wavy leaded glass panes woke me. For a moment, I recoiled at Blake's lanky form with a wing tossed over me, and then the previous night came flooding back. He'd cared enough to show up at my house.

He must have been close, an inner voice piped up. True enough. Geez, I should have made that association a few hours ago.

We did have a connection, but not one that would span the length of Scotland. Taking care not to move much, I studied his face. Sleep had softened the harsh planes, lending him a young and carefree appearance. Never mind he was neither. He'd never told me exactly how old he was, but there hasn't been a new Daoine Sidhe in the past thousand years. They're royalty, and apparently adding to their ranks didn't appeal to them.

I'd always assumed they argued incessantly among

themselves, but it was conjecture on my part. Blake was the first one I'd known on more than a cursory level. If I've harped on the fact others with magic spurn me, it's because it's true. The direction of my thoughts brought other reflections crashing back.

Blake's associates, the other Daoine, couldn't have appreciated his connection with me. Last night's attack felt different than the practical jokes other mages liked to toss my way: deeper and far more deadly, suggesting someone powerful had to be behind it.

Had any animals beyond the wolf died? I sent a hasty prayer to Danu asking her to take good care of their souls. In the future, I wouldn't be so hasty about summoning help, but my reticence probably wouldn't matter. Animals are attuned to me. Once they sensed unrest, they'd hustle to my side.

I'd just have to do a better job of cloaking my emotions, making certain nothing leaked out. Next to me, Blake stirred. Opening bottomless dark eyes, he murmured, "Up already?"

Nodding, I untangled myself from his wings and scooched to the side of the bed. As I rolled into a sit facing him, I noticed my sweats from the previous night were still in place. I smothered the tiny sigh of relief that wanted out. Okay, maybe there was a smattering of disappointment mixed in, but I couldn't go there.

So far. So good. We'd managed a night together without dissolving into lust-crazed maniacs.

"You were already close to Inverness," I said, not couching it as a question. "Why?"

His full mouth split into a grin. He stretched his arms over his head, muscles tensing and relaxing beneath the clothes he hadn't removed. After tucking his hands beneath his head, elbows akimbo, he latched onto my gaze.

I hadn't realized I was staring at him until then, but I didn't look away. I'd be damned if I'd back down. Or let him know how his proximity affected me. Not that he didn't already know. My elevated heartrate probably lent a flush to my normally pale cheeks. My clothing was loose enough to camouflage other evidence of his impact on me.

"Do I need an excuse for my comings and goings?" His expression turned from teasing to guileless.

"Of course not." My tone was testy. "Do you usually cruise by Inverness?"

His next words surprised me. "Aye. Now that you mention it, I do check on you from time to time."

My eyebrows shot up; my voice came out in a squeak. "You've been close but not told me about it?"

"What's it to you? As I recall, you instructed me to leave and never return."

"Pfft. See how well that turned out."

"Better than expected," he ventured. "You needed someone last night. It's fortunate I was nearby."

I pressed my fingertips along my forehead, urging rational thought but not getting very far. When I dropped my hands into my lap, I conjured a primitive truth spell. It clanked into place around both of us.

"Was that really necessary?" His question held sharp edges.

"I thought so, or I wouldn't have bothered," I retorted.

The next question, one I felt compelled to ask, made my chest tight, but I choked it out. "Did you put some of the other Sidhe up to terrorizing me, so you could sweep in and play Sir Galahad?"

Blake moved from prone to standing over me so fast I couldn't follow his movements. "Do you truly think so little of me?" he ground out. Fury turned the air around him a hazy red, and he locked his hands together. Maybe to resist funneling magic through them to break something.

Pushing past him, I stood toe to toe looking up. My spell clattered a bit as it regrouped. "What I think or don't think of you isn't what I asked," I went on. "Answer my question."

He batted at the strands of my spell. "As if this pathetic weave is going to tell you shit."

Straightening my back, I gritted. "Answer me or leave right now." I struggled against an inane desire to burst into tears. Or apologize. Sheesh, what was wrong with me? I may have told him we were done, but if he'd been the force behind the wolf's death and my near miss with disaster, I'd be devastated.

"It wasn't me," he said. His words rang true.

Not satisfied, I prodded, "Did you know about it? Or have any role to play?"

He shook his head.

Breath rattled from between my teeth. "Words. I need words. My spell can't interpret movement."

Heavy hands dropped onto my shoulders, squeezing hard. For once, they didn't feel the least bit seductive—or warm or supportive. He angled his head until I had to look right at him. "I had nothing to do with your mishap last night. Not overtly or covertly. There. Satisfied?"

A little trill verified his assertion. He'd already said my spell wasn't worth the magic it was woven with, but it was the best I could come up with. Because it was draining me, I dismissed it.

A muscle danced beneath one of his eyes. He removed his hands from my shoulders. "Now can we get back to my question? Do you truly think so little of me?"

Suddenly, I was as tired as if I hadn't slept at all. "I don't know what to believe anymore," I said dully. "Someone has it in for me, and I can't think of anyone beyond your kinsmen who would hate me that much."

He glared beneath lowered brows. "If it was one or more of them, I wasn't privy to their plans. I'd have pulled the plug forthwith, and if you don't know that, Abria, without summoning truth spells, we truly are finished."

I blinked a few times, but my murky thoughts didn't become clearer. "I assumed we were done a few months back," I mumbled. "No percentage to a relationship where we were shackled to my bed."

A corner of his mouth twitched downward. "I rather enjoyed our...activities. And you put up one hell of an act."

"It was not an act. I liked what we did, how we were together, but the rest of my life vanished into oblivion."

"What's wrong with that?"

After crossing the room, I sank into a chair. This was the same conversation we'd had the day I told him he had to leave. Somehow, I'd summoned the strength to repeat myself enough times he'd actually gone. Once the door had shut between us, I'd cried buckets before picking myself up and moving forward. No reason he needed to know that little tidbit, though.

"Thank you for standing vigil last night," I said with as

much dignity as I could muster, "but your job is done. You can leave now."

An unreadable expression crossed his face just before he shoved a fist through the nearest wall. Plaster rained down. Great. Just peachy. I'd have to find one of the village lathe and plaster masons to repair it. Money was tight, even not factoring in unexpected repairs.

"I am not going anywhere," he ground out inserting spaces between the words. "Not until we determine who was behind last night's shenanigans."

"It's really not necessary," I began.

"Aye, it is." Muttering under his breath, he stomped down the stairs. I heard the cottage door open and then slam behind him. Before I could congratulate myself on him changing his mind and returning to whatever his life looked like in Galloway—or wherever he spent most of his time—his voice filled my head.

"I've gone to seek lodging in town. Do not leave the premises without me."

My turn to double up a fist, except I had nothing to punch. Telepathy wasn't one of my strong suits, and he knew it. Out of my chair like a shot, I crossed the room and tugged up a window.

"Had to have the last word, huh?" I shouted after him, heedless of what the neighbors might think of me. They'd already labelled me a fallen woman during his last stint in residence.

He had to have heard me, but he didn't even turn around.

Nervous energy burned a track through me, so I grabbed a broom and rubbish bin and swept up the plaster mess. The hole didn't go all the way through to the outside. Maybe I could patch it myself.

Running on autopilot, I showered and dressed in dark slacks, a white blouse, and a multicolored sweater. After shoving my feet into flats, I clattered downstairs. A futile hunt for my handbag made me figure I'd left it in the car.

Keys in hand, I violated Blake's order and left my house, locking the door behind me. Not that it would keep him out, but I had things to do. Like cashing Jerome's thousand-pound retainer.

No one was more surprised than me when the bank verified the funds and transferred them into my badly depleted account. He'd no doubt assumed I'd be dead and not in any shape to force him to make good on his draft.

"Go ahead," I mumbled, inviting him to darken my door again. If he was stupid enough to show up, we'd have quite the little showdown. My next stop was the hardware store. I bought a bucket of plaster and two spatulas. Paint would have to wait until I brought in a sample.

I'd halfway expected Blake to show up and chastise me. He didn't.

I was back in my kitchen brewing tea and boiling oatmeal when he stomped through the door. As I'd suspected, the fact I'd locked it didn't even slow him down.

"Thought I told you not to leave without me," he growled.

"How do you know I did?" I inquired sweetly and stirred the porridge.

He pointed at the plaster tub I'd placed next to the door. Breath hissed through what were probably clenched teeth. "What part of our connection escapes you? I know precisely where you are."

"Bully for you." I spooned porridge into a bowl and poured cream into it along with raisins and sugar. "Besides, it's hardly *our* connection since I haven't the faintest idea where you are, ever."

"Have you looked?"

His question caught me by surprise. "Erm, no. Why would I?"

Snatching up the plaster, he clomped up the stairs.

"I was going to fix that," I called after him. He didn't answer. Crap. If this was going to be our new normal, I didn't like it at all.

My tea was ready, so I carried it and the porridge to the table and ate while I scrolled through my tablet catching up where I could. Cursing from upstairs suggested plastering wasn't as straightforward as I'd assumed, but then the Earl probably had a flock of underlings to do menial labor.

He came back down about the time I was done with my breakfast—or maybe it was lunch at this point. His dark hair was dotted with white dust, and a streak of plaster cut across one high cheekbone. After shaking the teapot, presumably to ascertain if I'd left any, he poured himself a cup and sat across from me.

"We need to talk," he said, sounding more tired than autocratic.

I resisted the urge to give voice to the "ya think?" rattling around in my head.

"You have enemies," he went on. "I am not one of them. By Danu's tits, why can't you see that?"

"You have ulterior motives," I said.

He shook his head. "Nay. No longer. You've made your position abundantly clear, but it doesn't mean I won't help you dig your way to the bottom of this dung heap and identify who wants you dead."

Something like guilt smote me. "You really don't have to. I'll work things out."

Emotions flickered in his eyes. Caring. Regret. Concern. Guilt pricked deeper, but I'd taken a stand. I'd be damned if I'd back down. I was weak where he was concerned. It wouldn't take a whole hell of a lot to fling myself into his arms.

"Open your magic," he invited. On his feet, he extended a hand. "Come outside. Let me help you sense what I do."

His tone was sincere, not seductive. I rose, ignored his hand, and headed for the door. Following on my heels, he said, "Take my hand. I can't strengthen your ability any other way."

At least, he was being diplomatic. We both knew my magic, such as it was, held all the panache of dirty dishwater. I grasped his hand, and we stood under the eaves of my cottage. It had begun to rain, the skies gray and menacing.

He titrated magic into me bit by bit. Once he was satisfied, he murmured, "Open yourself to what's around you."

Trusting nothing would have changed, I cracked my power tentatively. Linked with Blake's it swelled to fullness, and I sent a tracking spell outward. My easy breaths froze as something ancient and threatening surrounded not just me, but my cottage. Even my battered old car wasn't immune.

I took a step toward where I sensed the wickedness. Blake grabbed my arm. "Uh-huh."

"Why not? I want to know what it is." I tried to jerk free, but I may as well have been chained to a boulder.

"You only think you do." He reeled in his magic, and mine

along with it. Next, he turned us around and led me back inside.

Meanwhile, I'd begin to shiver. Teeth chattering, I lurched to the wall heater, holding chilled hands to its warmth. "Why'd we do that?" I managed between shudders.

"So you'd understand the complexity of what's arrayed against you."

"But I don't, not really," I protested.

"I do. It's all that matters. Like it or not, you need me."

Something about his tone grated. "Look. It's not as if I've been jinxed or anything. No worse than before, anyway."

He nodded sadly and reverted to Gaelic. "Och, 'tis far worse than being jinxed. Ye've been cursed, lass, and by the blackest of black magic. Were the Celts still here, ye might have appealed to them. They aren't. We must fix this, lass, afore fearsome harm befalls the whole of the Highlands."

"You're talking in riddles. What earthly connection do I have with the rest of the Highlands?" I managed before a sense of impending doom rose through the floorboards into my feet and swept through my body. It felt as if I were freezing from the inside out. I opened my mouth to scream, but an enormous weight bore down on me. Legs suddenly useless, I sprawled on the floor.

Chapter Six, Blake

amn her, anyway. How could she be so bloody appealing and so prickly at the same time. Somewhere, a portal to Hell was propped open, nothing else could feel as bleak or as evil. The night may have gone well, but this morning we'd reverted to snarling at one another like a couple of Brownies defending their respective hearths.

The attraction between us hadn't gone away. A time or two, I'd caught unleashed longing sheeting from her, but she'd sheathed it damned fast. I still couldn't believe I'd punched a hole in her bedroom wall. My loss of control was appalling, something I needed to get a handle on and damned fucking fast.

I'd specifically told her to stay within the walls of her home. Its foundations were firmly attached to the ambient magic of the Highlands. It's far from accidental that so many tales began in Northern Scotland. It's where magic first touched Earth, and it may well be where it breathes its last.

The specter wasn't comforting. Absent Earth, magic-wielders would repair to other worlds... My thoughts were ranging too far afield. Backtracking, I'd told Abria to stay here. She'd thumbed her nose at my request. I'd felt an alteration the moment she walked outside.

Once she was visible, the forces that wanted to flatten her developed new life, became energized. I hadn't planned on returning to the cottage. Not today, but her little stunt forced my hand. As long as I was here, I fixed the mess I'd made upstairs. It was either that or stay on the ground floor, grab her by the shoulders, and shake her.

She'd have been outraged. She didn't listen very well as it was. Or perhaps she listened selectively, tuning out messages she chose not to hear. I dragged her outside and fed power into her, so she'd develop a healthier appreciation for her foes.

And then, I felt like the worst kind of cad. Color had leached from her face, and her eyes had looked like mossy pools sunk into the bony orbits surrounding them. I warded the door—and made certain to both open and shut it fast—but the other side was quicker.

They didn't require the door. I felt wrongness follow us through the walls and the floor. It should have put me on high alert, but the bastards understood full well I was standing between them and Abria—or they should have. The next part isn't terribly clear. We walked back inside, and the air turned fuzzy, hard to see through.

She was shivering and held her hands out to the heat. I felt the cold too, but it wasn't aimed my way. She asked for details, but I wasn't willing to voice them. Some entities draw power from being named, and we were on a slippery slope as things were.

I answered her as best I could in Gaelic, but I was vague. I'd have preferred to use the Sidhe tongue, but I feared she wouldn't understand it. So much I didn't know about her. It floored me since I loved her so much it was all I could do not to whisk her away to a safer place. Underhill would do. Nothing evil has ever penetrated its boundaries.

The haze around me was thickening. She asked me something about the Highlands, but I couldn't make sense of it. The *thunk* of her body hitting the floor broke through when nothing else could.

Fear tightened my belly and added a metallic taste to my tongue. Was I too late? Had demonspawn incapacitated me enough to kill Abria? Crossing to her, I began to chant.

They would not take her. Never!

I'd drain every molecule of magic at my disposal to wage war against the dark forces hovering around Abria. Power poured from me as I gave voice to our ancient battle cry. Next, I drew a circle around where she lay on the scarred wooden floor, first with magic and then with a dirk I always carry. Comes in handy for a whole lot of things.

Darts stabbed my back as I worked. Or it felt as if they did. When I looked later I couldn't find a one. I snatched the pain and funneled it into my casting to strengthen it. Abria wasn't dead. Her life essence pulsed, but far weaker than I'd have liked.

Our first lesson would be on wards. She couldn't go anywhere without one ever again. A putrescence filled the room, ebbing and flowing. It pushed against me and my circle. I pushed back. Maybe I was more driven than whoever had laid siege to the cottage because eventually my task grew easier.

My earth eyes were shut. My third eye showed an undulating backdrop, illuminating it in bas relief as if I wore night vision glasses. It also pinpointed weak spots. I juggled two spells. One to keep the circle intact. None could pass or get to Abria while she lay within its confines. Keeping her safe was my number one priority.

The other casting was pure offense. I sent as much lethal power as I could muster to vulnerable spots in the weave surging around us. Shameless in my need for an inexhaustible source to feed my flagging magic, I tapped into the cottage.

It held surprises, good ones.

I settled into a rhythm. Two beats of protection, one of defense. It worked. I could keep this up for as long as I needed to. I hoped. Power is a jealous taskmistress. When I'm sunk in wielding it, not much else remains.

Abria's power crashed into mine. With a shock, I realized she'd left the circle. Stupid, stupid woman. Didn't she want to live? "Back. Go back," I panted, surprised by how raw my voice sounded.

"Whatever wanted us left," she mumbled. Her voice was rusty, as if she'd forgotten how to talk.

Had they? Whose side was she on? Before I said something I'd truly regret, I culled through the layers of enchantment keeping my spells alive and hoped to Danu I wouldn't regret it.

Chapter Seven, Abria

A circle formed around me, the thinnest margin of safety. Blake had bent, scribing something on my scratched kitchen floor. I felt its edges—and pure evil on the other side intent on finding a path through. The sound of Blake chanting made its way past the barrier in fits and starts. Whatever he was invoking wasn't a spell I'd ever heard before.

Neither was the language.

Rather than rich and mellow, his tone was harsh, strident. When the resident mice flowed through holes that led under the cottage, I remembered too late to build walls around my panic.

"Go back," I told them.

"But you're in danger," one of the mice argued, his whiskers twitching with worry.

"Go back," I repeated.

Animals obey me, so they retreated; I breathed a sigh of

relief. No more casualties on the altar of my misfortune. Not today, there wouldn't be. The pressure against the circle lessened. I heard Blake more clearly now. Sweat tracked down his face; small wrinkles spiraled out from the corners of his eyes. Whatever he'd conjured was draining him.

No one's magic is limitless. Not even his.

I rose to my feet, grateful whatever had knocked me down didn't try for an encore. My power might be puny, but I'd be damned if I'd let Blake run himself down to bedrock on my behalf. The immediate danger seemed to have withdrawn, so I stepped across the rough line scribed on the floor and linked my magic to his.

He didn't seem to notice me until our power clinked together. The glazed look left his eyes. "Back in the circle," he panted. "I can maintain it."

"You don't have to," I told him. "Whatever wanted us left."

He shook himself. Bits of plaster fluttered to the floor. When he looked at me, his eyes were haggard, and his handsome face held a drawn look. "Hate to admit it," he muttered, "but you're right. I was so deep into holding two spells together, I hadn't noticed. We should leave. Now, while the getting is good."

"And go where?"

He put a finger over his mouth in the universal sign for silence and reverted to telepathy. *"For once in your life, don't argue with me."*

I resisted a childish urge to stamp my foot and say I wasn't going anywhere until I had more details, but a wiser part sprang to the fore. Whatever had thwacked me across the back meant business, and the force or spirit hadn't even been inside. If they could command that level of power from a distance, maybe I should leave.

Now. While it appeared we still could.

Nodding, I dragged the strap of my shoulder bag across my body and walked to his side. Power jetted from him as he sealed doors and windows. At least I recognized the enchantment. Before I could ask how we were going to leave —since he'd shuttered every exit—he draped an arm around me.

The scent of his magic, rich with damp evergreens and ocean brine, surrounded us, and the walls of my kitchen shimmered to nothing. When they cleared, we stood in the abandoned courtyard of Rait Castle. It's not all that far from Nairn, under four kilometers.

The ruined castle, dating back to the 1300s, was how I'd met Blake. He'd hired me to help him with an incursion of Hellspawn. We'd made short work of them, retired to my bed, and not surfaced until I booted him.

"The gateway," I murmured, remembering the castle held a portal into Faery and other worlds as well.

"Ssht." He said and took off at a fast clip.

For one defiant moment, I considered not following him, but then I reconsidered. He'd been right about one thing. I had enemies, and he wasn't among them. Or if he was, he'd put on quite a convincing show to the contrary.

"Abria," rustled through my mind.

Being summoned rubbed me the wrong way. If his plan was to take us both into Faery, I wasn't sure I'd agree. Beyond my curiosity about Underhill or whatever the Sidhe were calling their home these days, I'd never lusted after a visit beyond the time he'd dragged me there. For one thing, the myths all warned of endless labyrinthine corridors designed to trap those who didn't belong.

Like me, for example.

I'd believed the part about the labyrinth but not that the Minotaur still roamed, plucking off the unwary to sustain himself. My pace had slowed, but Blake didn't call my name again. When I reached him, he stood at the top of a hole in the ground. Power shimmered around it, turning the air silvery-blue.

Before he could grab my arm, I held back and said, "I don't belong there."

A curt nod was followed by, "Agreed. You'll be under my protection just like last time, or I'd never consider this."

Surprise rocked me. I'd expected him to tell me I was full of shit. I crossed my arms beneath my breasts. "Then I'm definitely not going."

He'd been half turned toward the pulsing gap in the earth. After swinging an arm downward, the breach vanished. Residual power still swirled tinting the air blue, but the opening was gone.

"It's the only safe place," he argued, but the words lacked his usual forcefulness.

I shrugged about the time he ended up facing me. "Safe isn't part of my path." My voice wasn't as firm or convincing as I'd hoped, but I forged ahead anyway. "My journey isn't yours. Like I told you earlier, leave and let me untangle this."

"Have you ever been to Faery beyond the time I took you to Underhill?"

I shook my head. "Now's not the time to start, either. Your kinsmen never cared for me even before you and I, um, hooked up."

A corner of his mouth twitched. "Is that the modern term for it?" Before I could answer, he flapped a hand my way. "You cannot return to your home. Where will you go?"

I bristled at being told what to do. I may look young, but I'm hundreds of years old. "I have to go back long enough to collect a few things. And my car."

"Not wise."

"Maybe it isn't, but I'll do better if I'm not on foot."

"This place"—he swooshed an arm to one side—"contains portals to many worlds, not just Faery. How about one of the other ones?"

"Uh-uh. Who know what I might run into."

"I'd go with you. To ensure you have sufficient magic at your disposal to move from one spot to another."

"Presumptuous of you," I muttered.

He arched his dark brows. "How about thank you?"

I dropped my arms to my sides, both hands curled into fists. Him planning out my life—as if we'd never stopped seeing each other—infuriated me. Anger's always been my go-to place. No wonder I've never gotten along with the other mages, never had any truly close friends.

He was looking at me expectantly, waiting for me to see the light and glom onto his offer of help. It came with strings —big ones—and we both knew it. Standing around talking wasn't smart. Eventually, he'd snare me in some sneaky acceptance casting.

Reluctantly, I withdrew my gaze, focusing on the damp earth under my feet. I'd never be able to build a transport spell and loose it without him noticing, so I made a grab for the moral high ground and told him what I planned.

"I'm leaving," I said with as much dignity as I could gin up.

Shock tightened his mouth and scribed lines in his high forehead. Clearly, he hadn't expected me to say anything of the kind.

"Do you have a death wish?" he inquired dryly.

My temper had been on a short leash. It jumped the gate; I funneled anger into my fledgling teleport casting. "Do I look dead?" I ground out.

For once, magic jumped to my call. It's rare in my experience, but perhaps the innate power of Rait Castle helped. He was yelling something at me—guess I'm not the only one with a temper—as the rear of the crumbling castle dropped away. Moments later, I popped out next to my car. Luckily, no one was out and about because of the weather.

The earlier drizzle had ceded to a punishing downpour. Congratulating myself for having the foresight to still have my bag slung across my shoulders, I rummaged for my car key. Once the door was open, I tossed my bag inside, relocked the car, and tried to get into my house.

Tried being the operative term. Blake had it battened down with magic. His magic. Nothing I could do—including teleporting—got me past his iron-clad warding.

Fine.

I'd only meant to bring a change of clothes. Power fades when it's not actively tended. Perhaps by the time I returned, I'd find a way through his wards. Meanwhile, they should keep everyone else out too.

Back in my car with the windows turning steamy, I considered my options. Not that I had many. My enemy was magical. It meant nowhere I ran would be far enough to stymie its efforts to locate me. Since I had a moment, I searched for the dark oppressive energy that had sent me running.

Not there.

Had it followed Blake and me? Was it regrouping back at black magic central? I needed help, and I'd just spurned the most likely source. I pounded the flat of my hand against my forehead. Telling Blake to pound sand hadn't been my brightest move, but I couldn't undo it.

Eh, probably I could since he claimed to have an evergreen link with me, but all the reasons I'd left him standing next to the castle were still alive and well. Relationships have to be more or less equal, and ours had always been lopsided. He'd never lorded his superior ability over me, but it still stood there, silent sentinel to all our cavorting in bed.

He'd never given me a reason not to trust him, but I didn't. I'd always figured he'd tire of me, and that would be that. Maybe me kicking him out had been a preemptive move. Something to forestall the inevitable, and with less pain on my side.

The car windows turned opaque from the warmth of my breath. I had to go somewhere, so I tapped the ignition and started the defroster and wipers. Once I had marginal visibility, the car rolled forward. I wasn't paying particular attention to where I was going, but I wasn't surprised when a short drive north out of town landed me at Birgit's cottage.

Actually, it was more like a cave. The cottage part formed a door and an entry leading into a deep hillock. She's a witch and the closest thing I have to a friend, which isn't very close at all. What I mean by that is she'll talk with me, if she's feeling kindly disposed.

Uncertain why I'd ended up here, I drove past her home a short distance and killed the engine. Should I go inside? My mouth curled into a wry expression. The question was if she'd invite me in. Hell, for all I knew, she wasn't even at home. Mortals may scoff at magic, but Birgit made a good living selling charms, presiding over births, and removing bad luck.

No one ever admitted to hiring her, but she was busy.

My intuition had plopped me here for a reason. Worst thing that could happen would be she'd tell me to go away, and then I'd be back to square one. Needing safe haven without the first idea how to find it. I'd been quick to tell Blake safety wasn't part of my current gameplan. I'd been flip about it, not fully cognizant of the consequences of spurning his protection.

He might care about me, but his tolerance wasn't bottomless. After my performance today, I wouldn't blame him if I never saw him again. It shouldn't bother me, but it did. I couldn't figure out why. I'd barely thought about him until he popped back into my life last night.

Well, maybe something more than barely, but he'd quit being a standing fixture in my thoughts.

My windows had fogged up again. Resolute—after all, I'd ended up here—I got out of the car and walked along a well-beaten track next to the roadway. No other cars had come along. It seemed odd since this was the main throughway out of Nairn, but I plodded along intent on at least knocking on Birgit's door.

Rain soaked through my jacket and trousers and ran down my neck. I ignored it. You can't live in Scotland and pay much heed to the weather. I felt Birgit's witchy enchantment before I reached the whitewashed planks that served as her front door. A welcoming banner wrapped me in warmth. I took it as a good sign. If she didn't want to be bothered, that same magic felt considerably more prickly.

I reached the door and raised my hand to knock. Before I could, the rounded entry swung inward. I blinked at it. This had never happened before. Usually, she stood in the doorway looming over me with a frown as if to ask why I'd had the gall to disturb her.

Rain ran off the sod roof in rivulets as I stood staring at the open door. My mind pedaled in slow motion. Whatever was wrong with me? I took a step forward about the same time Birgit's hand shot out and grabbed hold of my soaked jacket yanking me inside.

"Get in here," she hissed.

I tried to jerk out of her grasp, but she was stronger. The same pressure to run that I'd felt with Blake at Rait Castle filled me with panic. My heartrate sped up, and sweat dribbled down my sides.

"Stupid twit." Birgit chastised me and dragged me inside, shutting the door with a resounding slam.

"I shouldn't be here," I moaned.

"Probably not," she snarled after releasing her iron hold on my arm. "Now you've gone and involved me too, but we'll deal with it. Get out of those wet clothes."

"No." I wrapped my arms around myself, wet fabric squishing against my body.

"Abria." Birgit's tone softened as if she were dealing with a child. "You've been jinxed, woman. It's possible there's something in your garments. I won't know until you've removed them."

"What do you mean, jinxed?" My teeth had begun to chatter.

"The meaning is clear enough." She stood in front of me. About my height and wraith thin, she'd always reminded me of a raptor wearing human skin. Her hair was white and plaited into two thick braids that hung down her back. Ice-blue eyes regarded me from beneath white brows. Her face was all planes and angles with a sharp beak of a nose and a thin-lipped mouth.

Rumors had circulated she'd been in this part of Scotland since the island rose from the North Sea, but those were tales told by mortals unfortunate enough to catch a glimpse of her.

Her voice gentled still further. "Let me help you."

Somehow, my jacket ended up on a hook along with everything else. Puddles formed beneath my garments and my sodden boots. All that remained was my underwear, so I skimmed out of it too.

Birgit snapped bony, long-nailed fingers. A robe materialized, and she draped it around my shoulders. At least I'd stopped shivering. While I watched, she searched my clothes with a combination of magic and nimble hands.

"Ha!" She extracted a long, thin bit of what might have been wood from the weave of my jacket.

I moved close. "What is it?"

"Hawthorne," she said, "sacred to the Sidhe."

Chapter Eight, Abria

"Blake," I stammered, my stomach twisting sourly. "Aw crap. He was behind all of this after all."

She dropped the bit of wood, grinding it beneath the heel of a stout boot before setting it on fire. It burned far longer than it should have. "Who's he?" she inquired.

"A mistake," I mumbled.

"Come along." She crooked a finger. "I'll set some tea to steep, and you can tell me all about this...mistake."

Maybe not him. He'd not the only Sidhe in the world, an inner voice murmured as I followed Birgit.

"Wishful thinking," came out aloud, earning me a penetrating glance over one bony shoulder.

She shooed me to a small, rickety table. Earthen walls meant we'd moved deep into the hillock behind the front door. While I huddled in a chair, she stoked the fire in a potbellied, cast-iron stove and set a shiny silver kettle on its flat top. The cozy space filled with the scents of mint, rosemary, and anise with something I couldn't readily identify mixed in.

"How long have you lived here?" I tried for inconsequential conversation to loosen the knot in my stomach.

"What does it matter?" Birgit didn't even turn around.

"It doesn't. I was just curious."

"Don't be. You're the first person I've invited beyond my entry space in a very long while. I didn't do it to chatter about myself, so don't make me sorry."

All right, then.

Closing eyes that felt gritty, I cleared my mind of everything. A raucous purr jerked my attention to my feet where a very large, very ragged black tomcat was rubbing against my ankles. Instinctively, I reached out my hands. He jumped into my lap, curling into a ball and burrowing into the robe's soft fabric.

"Mistress likes you." He purred louder.

I scratched behind his hears. *"How do you know?"*

"Jethro. Hush," Birgit chided. Gliding forward, she set a cream-colored ceramic mug in front of me. Another matching mug in hand, she settled into the only other chair. "If you want cream, you're out of luck."

I sipped at the fragrant brew. "This is lovely as it is. Thank you."

"Tell me," she urged. "Everything."

I started with how I'd met Blake when he'd hired me to help with the Rait Castle gateway. After glossing over our torrid affair, I simply said I hadn't seen him in months until I ran into trouble chasing down work for a client who'd clearly been a decoy. If Jerome even had a wife, I'd burn down my cottage.

Birgit had been silent. She held up a hand, so I quit talking. "And so, Blake just conveniently showed up at your home after your travails in that alley in Inverness?"

I nodded.

"Didn't you find it strange?"

"Yeah, I did, but he said he'd been through Nairn many times to check on me."

"Without stopping in?" She frowned. It brought her white brows together into a thick, bushy line.

I cleared my throat. "I, um, kicked him out. Said we had no future together."

"I see." She tilted her head, adding to her bird appearance. "You left out a few things."

"Um-hum. No need to share all the dirt."

At that, she shrugged. "Makes it easier to help when you're honest."

"I have been," I protested. Thank the goddess she didn't launch into a dissection of sins of commission versus sins of omission.

She drank from her mug. I did too. Something about the tea was both calming and invigorating at the same time. Must be from the herb whose scent I couldn't identify.

"What makes you think this Blake person is behind the attack?" Cup back on the table, she stared at me.

I resisted flinching under the weight of her gaze. "I'm far from certain," I admitted, remembering how he'd shielded me with his wings and offered the illusion of safety.

"Why would any other Sidhe have it in for you?"

Good question. My cheeks grew warm. "Other mages have no use for me," I stammered.

Before I could go on, she quirked a brow in amusement. "Join the club, sister."

"But there are other witches," I argued, "and only one of me."

"The last coven in these parts disbanded almost seventy-five years ago." She flapped a dismissive hand. "Good riddance. None of them had anything in the way of true power. What does your lack of mage companionship have to do with the price of tea in India?"

A reluctant smile parted my lips. "It's China," I said and chose my next words carefully. "My first thought—and I ran it past Blake—was a bunch of his kinsmen wanted to make damn good and certain he and I never resurrected our, erm, whatever it was we had."

The quirked brow edged a bit higher. "What exactly lay between you?"

"A whole lot of epic sex. We never got out of bed long enough to see if we had a future as anything except lovers."

"Sounds idyllic," she murmured. "And you kicked him out why?"

"The rest of my life was falling apart. My business was going down the shithole. I had too much pride to accept his assurances he'd take care of me."

"Sounds rather more serious than you let on."

I nodded mutely.

"Mmph. Probably shouldn't have destroyed the hex stick. But I couldn't very well have left it intact. Would have led whomever right to us."

"Doesn't that work two ways?" I ventured.

"Aye. There are spells to identify the person who placed the charm. Since they require utilizing the charm, they can be quite dangerous because the mage on the other end would sense my presence."

"Won't they know you found it?"

She curled her lips into a frown. "They might have missed me moving it, but they'll notice its absence. Do you always wear that coat?"

"No. I have several."

"We need to check them." Her tone was grim.

I drained the rest of my tea and stood, prepared to get back into my sodden clothing. Jethro, who'd still been curled in my lap, hissed from his new position on the floor. *"Sorry,"* I told him, but he stalked off, ears back and tail fluffed with outrage.

Birgit patted the table with the flat of one hand. "Sit back down. We're not done here."

Feeling like a child who'd misbehaved in school, I plopped back into my chair. "But don't we need to hurry?" The specter of someone breaking into my home and mucking around in my closets planting tracking devices—or whatever they were —made my head hurt. At least, the tea had settled my stomach.

"Your cottage is only a ten-minute drive," she pointed out.

"Less than that," I mumbled.

"See?" She offered a smile that was all teeth and no warmth.

I didn't, not exactly, but I nodded. Discovering I was the target of goddess only knew who was damned unsettling. Not that I hadn't suspected before, but the sliver of wood clinched it.

"You left Blake at Rait Castle?" she prodded. "Why?"

"Well, I didn't want to go into Underhill. Leaving for another world seemed unwise."

"He said he'd go with you. Why not take him up on it?" She'd glued her eerie blue gaze on me again.

I opened my mouth, shut it, and then blurted, "Because I do not want to be beholden to anyone, let alone him. Our relationship was so lopsided magicwise, it never had much of a chance."

"Knowing as much, why'd you—"

I held up a hand, palm outward. "Stop. No one likes their nose rubbed in their mistakes."

"I'm not so certain he was a mistake," she mumbled half to herself.

"He did say if a Sidhe was behind this he'd hunt them down." The words popped out before I could stop them. For some enigmatic reason I felt the need to rise to his defense.

"Aye, you already said that." She paused to take a measured breath. "It's significant because they're very close-knit. Like a heard of yaks. The Sidhe keep their secrets in the center and circle the wagons against dangers from the outside. You said he was Daoine, which means he's part of their royalty, so he'd be even more invested in defending the status quo."

Yaks, eh? This conversation had definitely developed an odd twist or two.

"Your point?" I picked up my cup, realized it was empty, and set it back down.

"For all their conceit and faults, the Sidhe cannot lie. If he told you he'd make a point of ensuring none of his kinsmen were to blame, he meant it."

I hadn't known that, about the inability to lie part, but I'd be damned if I'd admit it. Instead, I rose again. "We really should leave. There's one teensy problem, though."

Birgit stood too. "What might that be?"

"Blake warded my home. Eventually, the magic powering his spell will weaken, but when I was just there, try as I might I couldn't break through it."

"Not a problem at all," she retorted. "In fact, it's a plus. It will give me a feel for his magic, and I might be able to rule him out as a suspect. Assuming we locate more wood slivers."

"But how will we get inside?"

She shot me such a pained look, I shut up. Nothing like being reminded how pathetic my power is. Again. I trudged back through the long, rounded hall to the entry where my clothing still hung from several hooks. Miraculously, it had dried. Shucking the robe, I dressed quickly. Once my boots were laced, I placed the robe on one of the empty hooks.

Birgit joined me, a leather satchel in hand. "I took the liberty of gathering a few items that might shorten our search," she explained.

I slung my own bag over a shoulder, considered asking what was in her satchel, and then deciding it wasn't worth it. Even if she told me, I wouldn't have the foggiest idea what the items were for. Because of my one-of-a-kind skillset, I never found a teacher. Despite that handicap, I've slogged along as best I could, but I'd never employed aids. Perhaps I should have. They might have helped augment my ability, such as it was.

She spoke a word; the door opened on velvety darkness. Whoa. Time had certainly slipped past. I'd had no idea we'd been in her kitchen for hours. The rain had stopped. Par for the course. The driest hours in Scotland always happen at night.

"My car's this way." I crooked a thumb to the left.

"I'd prefer to travel on my own," the witch informed me. "Meet you there." The air around her developed a glistening quality. When it cleared, she was gone.

She'd never visited me, but I trusted she had ways of making up for that impediment. The power Blake had splashed around my small building would light up any mage's senses. I walked toward my Range Rover feeling more hopeful than I'd been earlier. No reason for it. Not really. None of my problems had seen anything approximating resolution.

An unwelcome epiphany crowded close. I felt better because I wasn't as alone. I'd always told myself the plethora of animals surrounding me made all the difference, that I didn't need anything—or anyone—beyond their company.

"Fools make excuses where angels fear to tread," I mumbled. It didn't exactly fit my situation, but neither was it far off the mark. I'd made the best of a difficult situation. No one likes being shunned for what they are. It hadn't been as noticeable a few centuries before when magic was common and mortals far fewer.

In those days, their belief strengthened all things magical, and my fellow mages weren't as critical of my abilities. The every-mage-for-himself philosophy hadn't shown up until science seduced humans away from their rituals and belief in those like me. Eventually, the arcane who chose to remain on Earth had been forced to don false mantles.

Rather like me with my private detective agency.

I had to survive, and I couldn't manage any other way. I'd tried to make a go of it as an animal trainer, except it went against the grain. I believe animals should be free to do as they will, but then I have an edge. I can reason with them, whereas the average human is clueless.

My car loomed out of the darkness. Being black, it blended right in. I unlocked it, executed a highly illegal U-turn, and covered the short distance to Nairn. By the time I pulled up at my cottage, lights blazed from the windows.

Mmph. Guess Birgit had managed to let herself in without any trouble. Longing for her ability filled me; I dragged myself out of that pit fast. Wishing for the impossible was a total dead-end.

Out of the car, I collected my shoulder bag and walked to the front door. Unlike my last attempt, it opened easily enough. The sound of voices reached me and stopped me in my tracks. Goddamn it all to hell. Blake was here talking with Birgit.

Did they know one another? Made sense if what he'd told me about passing through Nairn to check up on me was accurate. No reason it wouldn't be. I pulled the door shut, dropped my bag on a bench, and forced myself forward. My first instinct had been to double back to the car and drive like a bat out of hell to anywhere but here.

My spine creaked with the effort of holding it straight. I'd be damned if I'd let Blake drive me out of my own house. He had Underhill, and maybe a castle or two in Galloway to retreat to, but I was stuck here.

"There you are." Birgit beamed at me as I crossed under a lintel and into the kitchen. At least she was kind enough not to ask why I hadn't hustled right in.

"Here I am," I agreed as I headed for the kettle, intent on adding water if there wasn't enough for tea. Birgit must have filled it, and it was steaming, so I added herbs to a tea strainer and poured water over everything.

While my brew steeped, I turned to face them. "What are you doing back here?" I asked Blake.

He gave a guilty shrug. "Occurred to me you'd be barred from you own dwelling. I stopped by to render my wards useless. Against my better judgement, mind you."

"I told him about the wooden sliver," Birgit cut in. "And since he's here, I have a snootful of his magic. He's not who crafted the bit stuck in your coat."

"Too bad you destroyed it," Blake said sourly. "I'd have liked to examine it."

Breath whooshed from my mouth. I did my best to cover my relief, but it had to have been obvious. Each magic wielder's workings hold a particular scent. Even I, humble animal mage, possess my own unique magical signature. Had I been stronger, I'd have been able to rule Blake out as a suspect back in Birgit's entry hall.

"Did you go through my other clothing?" I asked her.

She shook her head. "Not yet. I'd only just dismantled Blake's warding when he showed up to do the same thing. I invited him in—once I determined he wasn't your bad guy—and we've been comparing notes over tea."

"I can leave if you'd like. I will anyway once we check for other Hawthorne twigs." Blake's dark gaze zeroed in on me.

My cheeks grew warm. Damn it. Why did I blush so easily? "I'll look," I mumbled and headed for the narrow stairwell, mug in hand.

"Better if I do it." Birgit slipped past me and mounted the stairs clutching her satchel.

I stared after her, feeling at loose ends. Of course, it was wiser to allow her to hunt. She possessed sufficient power to find dark magic. Clearly, I didn't, or I'd have ferreted out the Hawthorne on my own.

"What did I do to alienate you?" Blake's deep voice held a forlorn note.

My eyes grew hot and prickly. After blinking a few times to ensure I had my tears well in check, I turned and walked toward the table. "This isn't about you, not really," I said, pleased my voice didn't quaver.

"I don't understand. I could scan your thoughts, but it's rude. Why not just tell me?"

I waved both arms to the side. Tea sloshed out of my mug, wetting the wooden floor. After setting the mug on the table, I splayed my hands on its surface and leaned on them. This wasn't a conversation for sitting down. "We're not well matched," I explained. "My power is a hundredth of yours. Maybe less than that. Eventually, you'd have tired of me, so I hastened the inevitable."

There, it was out. I silently dared him to refute what I'd said.

"It was never about your magic." His gaze lured me in. "'Twas you I wanted. Besides, you're wrong about your power. It's different, not weaker."

"Thanks, but you're full of shit. I know exactly what I can do—and what I can't."

Blake got to his feet and came around behind me. I shouldn't have let him touch me, but when he closed his arms around my shoulders, I relaxed my grip on the tabletop and leaned against him.

"One of the things I've spent the months we've been apart doing is researching your magic."

"How? I'm the only one."

"Now you are," he agreed, "but such wasn't always the case."

Chapter Nine, Blake

S he was allowing me to hold her, not struggling to escape. I savored the feel of her back pressed against my chest. Her rounded ass was divine where it nestled over my hips. I could hold her this way forever and never tire of the sensation and her luscious scent. The sound of rustling and footsteps from above reminded me the witch was on a hunt for more of the insidious tracking devices. No wonder Abria had been easy to find.

Hopefully, Birgit would locate at least one more, so I could douse it with magic and discover who'd made it. Hawthorne is sacred to the Sidhe, but I couldn't accept that one of my kin, a mage I'd probably known for hundreds if not thousands of years, would be so unprincipled. Not that we don't kill. We do, but always for sound reasons. Abria was innocent. The Sidhe shouldn't even have known about her existence. I certainly hadn't until I stumbled across her by accident.

Jerome may have set her up, but those behind this weren't taking any chances. If she'd have gone anywhere other than where he'd indicated his wife was meeting her lover, they'd still have located her.

"You can't drop a bombshell like that and clam up." Abria's melodic voice drew me back from my musings. Sometimes she sounded like harp music or bells. She still hadn't made a move to disentangle her body from mine. She may have forgotten my arms clasped around her, but I hadn't.

"If you'd like, I'll accompany you to our library. You're welcome to read the source documents for yourself." I kept my tone neutral. It was the same invitation I'd been about to offer before she'd decided we were done, ostensibly because of her lack of magic.

"You didn't exactly shed any light on my beginnings." She twisted in my embrace until she faced me, green eyes ablaze with hope and curiosity mixed with more than a little trepidation.

"Fair enough." I opened my mind, allowing her to search and probe. While she did, I murmured, "You resulted from a longstanding dispute amongst the Celts. Ceridwen argued long and loud about needing a mage specific to animals, birds, insects, and sea life.

"Arianrhod agreed. The others saw such a development as redundant and unnecessary. Ceridwen presented vision after vision, courtesy of her cauldron. Finally, she must have tired of being shot down because she and Arianrhod and the Morrigan—"

"The battle crow?" Abria cut in. "I always assumed she worked for the other side and was pure evil."

"Not always. She developed a reputation in her later days,"

I clarified. "But she was elemental to many major battles. No one could replicate her triple nature or her ability to shapeshift into a crow. A falling out with dragonkind was her eventual undoing, but your making happened long before that."

"I'm listening." Abria nodded solemnly.

"The lore was murky on exactly how they accomplished your making," I went on. "Your essence was drawn from the bones of the earth with spirits from every bird, animal, and fish imaginable woven into the brew. They may have used Ceridwen's cauldron, or something far better hidden from view.

"The process took years. They started over a few times before they were satisfied. Once you emerged fully formed, the other Celts were furious at being duped. They demanded you be unmade. The three goddesses refused. In a burst of prudence, they hid you away for many a long year for tempers to cool. During that time, you were kept in a trance."

I stopped and tipped an index finger beneath her chin. "One day when they visited the spot where you'd been sequestered, you were gone. Do you remember how you escaped?"

Tears sheened her eyes, and she nodded once. "I woke in the dark surrounded by animals, mostly rodents, but wolves and coyotes and deer too. One of the wolves bit through the chains that bound me in place, and then the animals made a bier and carried me away.

"I traded one cave for another and spent the next span of time terrified my captors would hunt me down. They never did. Finally, I felt safe enough to venture outside, but not safe enough to stay put. The animals accompanied me, some of them, as I fled to the south and then farther still."

I had questions, but they would keep. I didn't want to break into her concentration. Or her determination. I suspected this was the first time she'd talked about her early years with anyone but animals.

Her eyes developed a pinched look. "Along the way, I discovered I commanded magic, but not very much. Everything I tried that worked was linked to animals in some way, shape or form. Mostly, I kept away from everyone. A century passed, and then another. As time frittered by, I found ways to make money and feed myself."

She paused. "Thank you for letting me tell things in my own way. Your information was interesting, but it doesn't say much about my power—or lack thereof."

"You never had anyone to teach you," I pointed out. "Those who made you were negligent. They could have entrained the magic they poured into you, yet once you were gone not a one of them lifted a finger to track you down."

Anger raced through me like high voltage electricity until my skin felt two sizes too small. It rivaled the fury I'd experienced when I first discovered what they'd done next. "Rather than locate you," I gritted, "they began anew."

Her eyes widened; she took a step back but didn't leave the circle of my arms. "And?"

"For whatever reason, they couldn't replicate the process that created you. Perhaps they didn't try very hard since the other Celts pitched such a fit when you were presented to them."

"I don't remember that part," she muttered. "Or I'd never

have approached them at all before they left Earth for good. No wonder they treated me like yesterday's garbage."

"You wouldn't remember your making. One thing they eventually agreed on was wiping that event out of your memories. They haggled like a bunch of fishwives over it." I cleared my throat. Good thing they were gone. They wouldn't have appreciated my editorial commentary.

"In any event," I went on, "they switched up the template and their next two animal mages ended up in Underhill because their magic was closer to ours than anyone else's."

"So you've known about me for a long time?"

I shook my head. "Not until I made a point to troll through the lore. And I didn't do that until after I'd met you. You remember the Celts. They'd have moved heaven and earth not to be reminded of their failures. I had to dig deep to find the scroll that memorialized your making. It was hidden beneath many spells."

"What happened to my, erm, siblings?" She arched a russet brow.

"They're in the *Dreaming*. They were never strong enough to withstand much. Oddly enough, animals never cared much for them."

"Can I meet them?"

I thought about the logistics of introducing a non-Sidhe to the Dreaming. "Maybe. I'll do my best to work it out once we get through this next part."

"Figuring out who wants me dead?" A corner of her mouth twisted downward.

"Exactly."

Chapter Ten, Abria

"Looks like you two made up." Birgit's contralto jerked me out of Blake's arms.

"We were just talking," I stammered.

"Whatever. Took me long enough to find these." She strode close and dropped two more of the Hawthorne twigs onto the table. Power wafted from them, adding a blackish tinge to the air and making me vaguely sick to my stomach. I backed away from the slivers. How in the goddess's name could innocuous items have such an effect?

Blake's attention shifted to the tabletop. His palms hovered over the wood. "Nice work," he told Birgit.

She dusted her hands together. "I thought so. Do you know who made them?"

"I do, more or less, but it's...curious."

"What is?" I ground out, disappointed he hadn't teleported away to make short work of my tormentors. I gave myself a solid mental shake. He wasn't mine to command, and even if he were, these were his kinfolk.

He turned toward me lips pressed into a thin line. "There are many types of Sidhe. Sparing you an explanation about how the Unseelie Court is structured, those twigs were fashioned by one of the Merrow."

"How?" Birgit sputtered. "They live in the sea."

"Not many Hawthorne trees there." I aimed for a more neutral tone. I'd heard of them a time or two, but always lumped them in with Kelpies and the Kraken and other magical creatures who inhabited the oceans. How would they even know about me? And why be bent on my destruction?"

Something about my face must have alerted Blake because he asked, "What?" and spun one hand in a get-on-with-it gesture.

"They must be working with someone who needed to cover their own magical mark."

"Seems logical," Birgit agreed and addressed her next words to Blake. "Where do we begin hunting?"

"We?" He raised both dark brows.

"Aye." She tossed her head and set her chin at a defiant angle. "I'm in this up to my hipbones. Not walking out now."

"I want in too," I announced, not exactly believing I'd volunteered until the words left my throat. In a perfect world, I'd retreat to a forest glen and bury myself in as many animals as I could. Riding a unicorn held appeal too. One, Becca, was a special friend, but it wasn't relevant.

I refocused on what was unfolding in front of me.

Blake swallowed. Next, he narrowed his eyes. Fascinating, I'd never seen him uncomfortable before. "Might be simpler if I handled this on my own," he said sounding uneasy.

Birgit was close enough to jab him in the chest with a long-nailed index finger. "Bullshit. What you're not saying is that your precious Sidhe won't want to hobnob with the likes of us. I have ways around it."

"Love to know what they are," I said and rounded on Blake. "This is precisely why you and I have no future. You're ashamed of including anyone who's not like you." I warmed to my tirade and did my own spate of finger poking. "This is about me. I'm the victim, and it's a sad day if you won't include me."

Never mind I'd had no intention of going until a couple of moments before.

"Nice job, sister." Birgit hip-butted me.

"Thanks."

The corners of Blake's mouth twitched. After what was clearly an internal struggle, his lips formed a hint of a smile. "Fine. I can see I'm outnumbered. And I am not ashamed of you," he added. "Even though I can see how you might interpret it that way."

"Save it for later," Birgit snapped. "We have work ahead of us. You two can sort out the state of your non-relationship later."

My practical side swam to the surface. "Don't know about you two," I said, "but I'm starving. If we're going to do battle, we need food." Hands on hips, I faced Blake. "Are we?"

"Are we what?" he countered. "Food sounds good."

"Not what I meant. Are we a team? Or are Birgit and I going to solve this without you?"

The smile turned into a hearty laugh. "Outnumbered to the max," he got out between gouts of laughter. "I know when I'm beaten. We'll figure this out together. On a more serious note, it's better than the two of you setting out on your own and me doing individual sleuthing."

"Oh really? Why?" I snarled.

"Gods you're gorgeous when you're angry."

I recognized the lustful sheen to his eyes. Shocked by how deeply it still affected me, I said, "Shove it. You didn't answer my question."

"Battle strategy 101," he replied. "We're after the same enemies, so we need a unified approach. If we go into this from two fronts with no communication between us, we have a far greater chance of alerting our target."

"Giving him—or her—more of a chance to elude us," Birgit broke in.

"Exactly." He nodded.

I told my temper to take a hike. Along with my desire, which hadn't abated in the months we'd been apart. To avoid dealing with either, I opened the cold box, surveying its contents. Luck was with me, I had enough to make a hearty vegetable soup. Birgit tossed biscuits together.

Over a midnight supper, we hatched up the beginnings of a plan. I'd slip into the North Sea, summon the fish to my aid, and see if any of the mer-people would talk with me. Blake would retreat to Underhill under the guise of summoning an all-Sidhe meeting to discuss deteriorating planetary conditions.

"Mostly, I'm interested in who shows up," he went on. "We haven't had such a council in a long while, perhaps a couple of hundred years."

"Is attendance mandatory?" I asked.

He nodded. "Given we cannot lie, except by omission, I

expect whoever was working with the Merrow won't show up."

"Not so sure about that." Birgit narrowed her pale eyes. "Wouldn't it be akin to proclaiming their guilt."

"It would come down to a hard choice," Blake agreed. "If they're there, they have to face me. But their absence would be noticed as well."

"Are there any acceptable excuses?"

"Aye, being off world and not hearing my summons. Those in the *Dreaming* will hear me loud and clear."

I set my spoon down and took a chance. "What role, exactly, do you play?" Smothering a grimace, I looked right at him. For how intimate we'd been, I should have asked about stuff like that. Would have if we hadn't been so busy fucking.

He cleared his throat. "The others report to me."

"On a regular basis?" Birgit tipped her mug and finished her tea.

"Of course not. Our hierarchy isn't what it once was."

I took another tack. "Are there other Daoine?"

"Of course."

I slapped one hand on the table. "Blake. Don't make me drag information out of you."

To my surprise, he said, "Sorry. You're right. The Sidhe are ruled by a council of twelve Daoine. Unfortunately, half of them have retreated to the *Dreaming*. They may decide to rejoin the council someday, so we cannot replace them, even if more Daoine were available, which they are not."

He set his mouth in a thin line. "I ended up leading our council by default. No one else wanted the responsibility."

"Good to know," I murmured, pleased he'd shared as

much as he had. The Sidhe are notoriously close-lipped—about everything.

"Do you believe the Merrow will tell us anything?" Birgit asked.

"Not if they don't have to," Blake admitted. "It's why I'm hoping to determine who forced them to help construct the Hawthorne markers."

Interesting. "Why forced?" I arched my brows into question marks.

"Because mostly they capture sailors."

"What if they didn't know?" Birgit speculated.

"Didn't know what?" I turned to her.

"Why they were infusing their essence into the wood. What else?" she countered.

"It's possible," Blake said, "but we could spin theories for hours and not get it right." He rose to his feet, and the air around him developed the pearlescent appearance that meant he was about to leave.

I stood too. "Wait. When and where will we meet."

The shimmers in the air settled. "Two days' time back here."

"Nay. Two days' time at my place. 'Tis safer," Birgit suggested.

"Done," Blake said as he vanished.

"A man with a mission," Birgit smirked.

"Something like that." I ferried our plates to the sink. The witch joined me and we cleaned up the mess from supper in silence. Finally, I asked, "Do you have plans?"

"I always have plans." She offered me a smile that had too many teeth and accentuated the hook of her nose.

I dried my hands on a towel and handed it to her. "Care to tell me what they are?"

"I'm coming with you. Running around on your own isn't wise." She hung the towel on a nearby hook.

Hands on my hips, I faced her. "I don't get it. We barely know one another."

She stood still beneath my scrutiny. "You came to me. Your unrest was so palpable, I felt it before you arrived. When I chose to open my door to you, I'd already made up my mind."

Her words touched me. I haven't had many friends. Hell, I haven't had any, not for a very long time, and I'm not sure I could count the mages who tolerated me when I was much younger. That tolerance came to an abrupt halt when my variety of magic manifested.

"Thank you," I murmured.

She tilted her head, so her gaze met mine. "'Tis a lonely life, child. Best accept comfort and aid where it's offered."

Truth suffused me. Covens had come and gone, but she remained. Perhaps my experience wasn't as much of an outlier as I'd always assumed. "Why'd you stay here, knowing you'd be all alone?" I asked. At least I had animals for companionship.

Her thin lips parted in half a smile. "You're not the only one."

I smiled back, remembering Jethro, her cat. Probably, it was more of a familiar, but that was her secret to keep. And then I realized she'd plucked my thoughts about animals and magic right out of my mind. Never one to wallow in anything close to emotion, I asked if she was ready to leave.

"Aye. We can drive the first part. I'll take care of the second."

I frowned. "Sounds as if you know where we'll be going."

"There's a place along the North Sea between Lybster and Wick. The beach is rugged and sealed off from human incursion."

I chewed my lower lip. I'd planned to drive east toward Buckle or Portsoy, but she was routing us back through Inverness. Probably safe enough with the two of us. I didn't realize how badly my confrontation in the alley had rattled me until right now.

Birgit headed for the door as if it were decided. I opened my mouth to protest, but shut it quickly. It didn't truly matter where we entered the sea, and perhaps she knew something about the spot she'd selected. I'd been shooting blind. Not that I haven't spent time with the Selkies and such, but water has never been my first choice since I have to drain my magic to bedrock to breathe.

I snatched up my bag and my keys. Somehow, Birgit's battered leather satchel hung from her right hand. I hadn't seen where she'd dropped it or how she'd picked it up. Maybe it was a magical bag that didn't obey normal rules. We got into the car, and I drove through Nairn, moving west.

When we got to the intersection with the coast highway, I turned right, taking us north. "Why, exactly, did you open the door to me?" I asked.

"Hard to say, dearie. I considered shrouding my energy and pretending I wasn't there."

"You wouldn't have had to try very hard. My magic is weak. I'd have sensed your essence but chalked it up to you having been there recently."

She gave a little shrug. "Fate tossed us together for a reason. I've learned not to question Her hand too deeply. Plus, I haven't had a worthwhile goal for many a long year. Jethro and I, we keep to ourselves. Mortals drop by from time to time with one insipid project after another. Nothing worthy of my talents."

"Why have you stayed?" I pulled to the shoulder, slowing to allow the car that had been tailgating me to pass.

"Why have you?" she countered.

"I knew I wouldn't be here forever, but it's where I've made my current life."

"Pfft. This is where I've made my only life. Nowhere to pull up stakes and move to."

"Not even to be near others like you?" A wistful note had crept into my voice. How I longed for even one other mage like myself. Yeah. May as well wish for the moon to plummet out of the skies. The other animal mages Blake had described didn't sound like BFF material.

Silence stretched between us, lasting so long I was certain she wouldn't answer. When she did, her voice jarred me out of wondering why someone had painted a bullseye on my back.

"Covens have their downsides," she murmured, a rueful note in her voice. "Unlike the Sidhe, magic varies widely from one witch to the next. Some are weaker than you—"

"Hard to believe," I cut in.

Birgit ignored me and went on. "And some want to scorch the earth until nothing is left but ruin."

"Huh? I don't get it. I thought your kind had an affinity for the natural world." I steered toward the shoulder again to accommodate a bus lumbering behind us. Damn it. I was driving the speed limit. Where were the boys in blue, anyway? The ones who handed out tickets for going too fast.

"Only for those whose blood runs pure. Our ability—and our wisdom—has become diluted. There was a time when witch only mated with witch. Not anymore. Our ability can't sustain itself once the percentage of magic drops much below half. And we have plenty of witches exactly like that. They show up at covens demanding entry. No one wants to turn them away because our numbers have been dwindling."

Hmmm. Maybe my solo status wasn't such a bad thing after all. Nothing like perspective. "How far are we going?" I changed the subject since a few minutes had passed, and Birgit didn't seem inclined to add anything to her retrospective on her kinsfolk.

"I already told you."

She had. I dredged through my memory and came up with a spot between Lybster and Wick. A road sign obligingly suggested Lybster was still thirty kilometers. A glance at my fuel gauge was reassuring. We should have plenty of petrol.

"You did," I agreed and asked, "How is it witches have chosen to mate with mortals?" It might be a sore topic, but she was plenty capable of telling me to go screw myself.

Breath hissed from between her teeth. Before I could tell her to forget answering, she said, "I've asked myself that a hundred times. A thousand. And I have yet to come up with an answer.

"Congress with humans isn't forbidden. Probably our first mistake."

I banged a hand on the steering wheel. "Even I have enough skill to ensure I don't get pregnant."

She made a snorting sound. "I assume the logic went

something like: well, one won't hurt. And one wouldn't have, or even two or three."

"Oh my. How many..." I stumbled as I hunted for a word. Tainted witches wasn't right. Neither was fallen. Damaged was even worse.

A bitter laugh filled the car. "You needn't spare my feelings," Birgit said with a touch of asperity. "To answer your question, far too many. Perhaps over half our numbers. It's gotten so bad, and the younger witches so disrespectful, I needed distance before I killed the next one to challenge me."

At least I understood why she hadn't gone in search of a coven. Still, a voluntary separation from her kin was a far cry from me who had none.

Lybster came and went in the blink of an eye.

Birgit straightened in her seat scanning the landscape rushing by. Dawn wasn't far off. The edges of the sky were lightening in shades of pale pink.

"Slow down," she instructed.

I turned on a flasher and moved to a rather inadequate shoulder. It was strewn with rocks. After the line of cars that had formed behind me flitted past, I guided us back onto the highway.

"There." Birgit stabbed a finger at something I couldn't see, but I edged to the left again to accommodate slowing down. The faintest of roads came into view on the ocean-side of the highway.

A declination offered a relatively safe spot to leave my car. "Will this work?" I asked. "Or did you want me to cross over and drive down the dirt track?"

"This is fine. Not much farther. We're better off walking."

"Will I need anything?" I exited the car and glanced at my shoulder bag in the rear seat.

"Why would you?" she countered. "Your phone won't work under water." Done talking with me, she turned and ran nimbly across the road, weaving between cars whose drivers honked in irritation.

Something similar to a shudder tracked down my spine. Usually, I pay attention to signs like that, but a cursory scan didn't yield much of anything beyond vehicles zipping past a few meters away. I hesitated. We'd come this far. She was doing me a favor since this wasn't her war.

Christ, I have to trust someone.

Brave words. Not exactly mollified, I buried my reservations and hoped to hell I didn't regret not listening to my gut that was screaming at me to jump back in the car and drive away.

Chapter Eleven, Blake

I wasn't anxious to return to Underhill, much less announce an all-Sidhe meeting. Everyone would complain, accuse me of being power mad if not a wee bit dotty. Breath wafted from my mouth in little spurts. How soon people forget. Back when the council was led by twelve just like me, no one would have dared voice opposition. And complaints, if there were any, would be whispered rather than thrown in my face.

Get over it, I told myself sourly. Hell, I was as bad as the rest of my kinsmen. When did we grow so squeamish about facing unpleasantness? Probably about the same time so many of us withdrew to the *Dreaming.* No more tasks. No more difficult anythings.

I'd checked the Hawthorne twig twice after my initial impression, certain I had to be mistaken. The Merrow are technically Fae. Loosely related to the Sidhe, they've never tried to capitalize on the relationship. Nope. Mostly, they wanted to be left to themselves. I'd heard through third- and fourth-hand sources they'd turned cartwheels when Poseidon was relieved of his command of the seas.

Which is a polite way of saying everyone was thoroughly sick of his overbearing ways. It was a good reminder to put a positive spin on this gathering I planned to call. Because it was close, I chose the gateway near Rait Castle. As usual, the grounds were deserted. Apparently, the appeal of the ruin had slipped a few notches after the battle I'd fought to rid the gateway of a Cait Sidhe who'd captured one of the changelings I'd left to guard it.

Actually, Abria had done most of the work. I'd watched closely, though, ready to leap to her side if she needed me. I crossed the green and entered the portal. The initial part felt like Earth, but the demarcation where the mortal realm ended and mine began was obvious.

The air thickened, ripe with the scents of flowers and damp earth. Fifty paces later, I crossed the veil and Underhill spread before me. It's always reminded me of a Hobbit village, except we own the original concept. And the rounded doorways all lead into caverns rather than buildings.

Another thing about the Sidhes' home is corridors extend in all directions. They move when they feel like it, so the path to where you want to go usually requires a magical assist. Cuts down on unwelcome visitors. In search of my chambers, I scented the air sucking in deep lungfuls. Nowhere smells quite like Underhill. Everything is enhanced by a factor of at least ten. So roses or honeysuckle or jasmine become addictive.

No one ran to greet me. Seemed odd, but then I wasn't here much. In a hurry to return to Abria and Birgit, I hastened through the central square—the place every corridor began—and scribed a message on gray slate tablets hung on the door to our meeting hall. It had been so long since anyone used this method of communication I didn't have to erase the previous message. It had worn away.

Says a lot because there's no weather in Underhill. No day-night cycles. No wind. No rain. I added a vector to my message that would ensure it was transmitted to everyone within range, range being all of Underhill and Earth and a few of the nearer borderworlds.

I set the time for six hours hence and started for the dwelling I've called home forever. It wasn't where I expected. I shrugged and kindled a spell to lead me there. After wandering this way and that for far too long, I fine-tuned my spell.

The air glistened and shimmered. When it cleared, I stood before my front door. Not trusting my eyes, I ran my hands over the worn wood, located my do-not-disturb enchantment, and disabled it. Despite my ward, had anyone entered?

I took my time and stood beneath the lintel magical antennae extended. Only after I didn't sense anyone's energies other than my own did I walk inside. Throughout everything, I hadn't seen another soul. I left the door cracked, hoping someone would see it and join me.

I needed information. Something had happened here, but I had no idea what. It was almost as if my kinsmen were no more, which was impossible.

Or was it?

The last time I'd been here had been the night of the battle for the Rait Castle gateway. Then I hadn't gone as far as my home. I'd been intent on locating Abria. She'd been injured, and I'd taken her to one of Underhill's many sitting rooms. Time was we were far more sociable than we are now.

After pouring well-aged mead into a tumbler, I sank to a sit on a patterned carpet that dated back so long I was amazed the threads hadn't rotted. I sent out threads of seeking magic to see if I could sense any life. Aye. There. And There. And again.

Sidhe were here, but keeping to themselves.

Perhaps I should have set the meeting for the morrow to offer an opportunity for everyone to get used to the idea of mixing it up. Eh, bad idea. The more time I'd allotted, the more likely mages would have fled.

My door opened a few more centimeters. Kirwan shuffled in. One of the few not employing spells to delay aging, he looked every one of his however-many years. White hair grew in a circle around a large bald spot. Wrinkles sat atop other wrinkles lending him the appearance of a Sharpei.

On my feet, I filled another tumbler with mead and handed it to him.

"Thanks, Elwyn," he croaked and grasped the glass in a palsied hand with liver spots splashed across the back.

I waited until he'd had a chance to drink before growling, "What in Danu's name happened here?"

"You've been gone too long." He drained half the glass.

At this rate, we'd be here until the meeting began, but I'd play along for a while. "What does that mean?"

A sly look added still more creases around his sunken silver eyes, and he made shooing motions with both hands. "Ye may as well go back from whence ye came," he intoned in Gaelic. "Naught here for you. Not anymore."

"But I was just here," I protested. "And not all that long ago."

"Didn't stay long, did you?" A reproachful note tinted his words with censure, as in somehow this—whatever it was— was my fault.

I resisted an urge to throttle him. "What happened?" I repeated and added compulsion to my question. He'd answer me, or I'd beat the truth out of him."

"Do ye truly wish to know?" At my nod, he went on, "Once ye do, there's no going back."

A weight, malicious and foreboding, settled across my shoulders. My next words came hard. "Aye. Tell me, everything. Leave naught out." I matched his Gaelic and upped the ante on compulsion.

Finding Abria's enemies might not be as straightforward as I'd hoped. I didn't want to be sidetracked by internecine squabbles, but I didn't have a choice. Maybe I wouldn't be able to fix anything, but at least I'd be up to speed on whatever had gone south here.

Chapter Twelve, Abria

Still nervous as a long-tailed cat in a room full of rocking chairs, I buried my reservations. Probably, I was still hyper-reactive on account of my near brush with misfortune in Inverness. The tracking bits of Hawthorne wood were gone. Presumably, no one could find me.

Presumably. Big word that really meant a leap of faith on my part.

After locking the car and zipping my keys into a pocket, I ran back across the highway to catch up with Birgit. Along the way, I raised my mind voice, ready to summon an animal escort. Better to alert my honor guard sooner rather than later.

Or not. Remembering my vow not to put any of my friends in harm's way if I could help it, I sheathed my command and hoped nothing had leaked out.

Birgit was waiting for me around a bend in the faint path, concealment spell at the ready.

I stepped into her spell, feeling it wrap me in a heady mix of herbs and damp earth. "Who are we hiding from?"

"Hard to say. Wouldn't you rather be prepared?"

Something cryptic was laced into her answer, but I didn't press her for details. We trod a winding path studded with rocks and small bushes twisted this way and that by the ever-present wind. Meanwhile, the cries of birds overhead suggested they'd discovered my presence and were marshalling resources to stick by me. Rodents chittered from all directions reassuring me they had my back.

"Called in your troops, eh?" Brigit cackled.

"Wouldn't you rather be prepared?" I tossed her words back at her, not bothering to add I hadn't done a thing.

"Don't be impertinent, child."

"I'm probably older than you," I shot back.

"Ha."

Okay. This was going nowhere fast. Last thing we needed was tension between us, so I didn't rise to the bait. Ten more minutes ticked by as we dodged shrubbery that had overgrown the path.

"How'd you find this place?" I asked when it became clear the sea was farther away than I'd thought.

"Hush."

Okay, then. She was done indulging my curiosity. Maybe if I'd dug a wee bit deeper while we were still in the car— My thoughts stuttered to a halt. The salt scent of the North Sea deepened, tickling my nostrils. Overhead a gull cawed a warning. In the next few moments, the North Sea emerged from the overgrown shoreline.

It's always fascinated me with its barely constrained power. The crash of waves on rocks intensified tenfold, and the feel of foreign magic battered Brigit's warding. Rays from the rising sun bounced off the waves as they rolled in, creating quite the lightshow. It was beautiful and somehow terrible. My magic radar screamed a warning. Something lurked beneath the water, something ancient and powerful beyond reckoning. The birds had moved higher, and the noisy rodents fell silent.

I stopped. It wasn't a conscious choice, but my feet were in full rebellion and refused to move closer to whatever lay ahead. My lack of forward momentum must have tugged on Brigit's spell because she turned and gestured with both hands. *Not a good place to be still,* rustled through my head.

"We should go back." I said, not bothering with telepathy. She'd hear me even over the boom of the waves.

I faced the ocean; she faced me, so she didn't see the ocean's surface cleave in two or the rising column of water. I tried to turn and run, but my body wasn't my own to command. Not anymore. In a vain hope my problem was linked to Brigit's spell, I hissed, "Loose me."

Rather than answer, she spun, took a few quick steps forward, and fell to her knees. Her warding, which had turned out to be useless, frittered to streamers borne away by the rising wind.

The tower of seawater stopped twisting this way and that. A tall, bony hag stepped out of it. Clad in tattered black robes sashed in red, she hovered above the water's surface, bare feet skimming the waves. Tangled silvery hair clung to her skull and fell past her knees. Stark cheekbones, colorless eyes, a beak of a nose, and a squared-off chin projected malice.

Warmth surrounded my feet and lower legs. Mice. Rats. Beavers. Badgers. Pine Martens. Their courage smote me, and

I arranged my magic—such as it is—to shield them from harm.

The apparition, except she was real enough, floated nearer. Brigit remained huddled in a crouch with her head bowed. I'd be damned if I'd cower before anyone, least of all the thing spawned by the sea. Damn the witch, anyway. She'd known what we were walking into. She'd picked this spot specifically to raise whoever bore down on us.

The question was why.

I squared my shoulders and waited. I might not be bowing and scraping like Brigit, but I knew enough to keep my mouth shut. A couple of brave badgers crawled to my shoulders.

"Rise," rolled from the hag. Her voice sounded like the sea, gravelly and gruff.

Brigit scrambled upright. With her head still bowed, she said, "Cailleach, goddess of witches, hear my humble request."

I was already as upright as I could get. Shock cascaded through me. I'd thought the gods and goddesses long gone from Earth, yet apparently Cailleach stood—er, floated—a few meters away.

Also known as the Winter Goddess, her power had rivaled the Celts'. I'd thought her more myth that reality, but then I've never hung around with many witches. Careful not to dislodge the badgers, I sank to my knees and bowed my head. Now that I knew who she was, there was no reason to anger her.

And then I remembered her command to rise and scrambled back to my feet.

"You." She pointed a bony, long-nailed index finger in my direction. "I've heard about you."

Several replies crowded my throat. Things like, "All good, I presume?" died upspoken. I can be a smartass, but this wasn't the venue for it. I had a feeling Cailleach lacked a sense of humor. The badgers hugged the sides of my head even closer. I stroked their thick coats, waiting. Badgers can be real sons of bitches, but they're more misunderstood than inherently mean.

The goddess had reached Brigit and stopped. From my vantage point a meter or so away, the scents of snow and storms and winter joined the salt smell of the North Sea. "Why have you come?" she asked.

The question hadn't been addressed to me, but I was interested in the answer. Brigit had brought us to this place expressly to raise the goddess. So much for my plans to hunt for the Merrow. It might still happen. Brigit wasn't who'd been targeted, and we weren't linked at the hip. I could always move my agenda forward.

Maybe. At the moment, I was still locked on the spot of sand where I'd first seen the sea turn into a vortex. Movement in an up and down plane was allowed, but I couldn't step forward, back, or to either side. The animals had me hemmed in along with eldritch magic thickening the air and turning it into a glistening soup of enchantment.

The goddess's attention returned to Birgit. "Why are you here?" she growled.

"To solicit your assistance, my lady," Brigit replied.

"For what?" Cailleach snapped her skeletal fingers.

"My friend has been targeted for death," Brigit explained. "It is possible the Merrow are involved, and—"

"No!" The winter goddess's tone was harsh. "The sea people harm no one."

Not sure where I found my tongue, I blurted, "They may have been pressed into service inadvertently. To protect the real perpetrator."

"How?"

Brigit explained how she'd discovered the Hawthorne tracking twigs and outlined Blake's role in identifying their source.

"Blake Townsend?" Cailleach's busy white brows shot up.

Brigit twisted to shoot me a glance over one shoulder. Of course, she'd have no reason to know his surname. "Aye, the same," I answered.

"Not his true name," Cailleach grated, "yet one he has used for a long while."

At least the information didn't surprise me. Names have power and I hadn't revealed my true one to him, either. So much for trust. Neither of us had much.

Brigit reached into a pocket and withdrew a cloth sack that glittered with spells. "One of the Hawthorne bits lies within," she said and offered the sack to the goddess.

Her thin lips twitched. "You wish me to ask the Merrow who commissioned it?"

"Who better?" Brigit stood tall almost as if she were tossing down a gauntlet.

Cailleach snatched the sack. Once she had it in hand, it vanished from sight. "Remain here," she commanded and left in a flash of blue light. No water this time.

The badgers had wound strands of my hair around their claws. Could I move again? To test that the goddess's presence had been behind my lack of control, I took a couple of experimental strides nearer Brigit and said, "You should have told me."

"Would you have come?" She angled her head to one side.

I shrugged. "Not sure. Maybe."

"I wasn't certain the goddess would show. I've been here many times when she didn't." After a pause, Brigit added, "I believe she was curious about you."

"Me? Why? I'm nobody in the magical realm."

The witch narrowed her pale eyes. "Perhaps in your way of interpreting the world, but others tell a different tale. Your power is...different."

"Pfft. Yeah. Weak as dishwater."

"Your analysis."

Before she could go on, I slashed a hand downward. "I've lived with my power, such as it is, for centuries. I'm the best judge of what I can—and cannot—do."

The birds circled lower adding to the air currents with their beating wings. All the furry bodies crowding around me burst into a cacophony of chitters, squeaks, and squeals. I can't talk with every animal, but most of them respond to mind speech.

"Some of us do not agree," she replied.

Perhaps because her tone was neutral, it took a moment for what she'd said to sink in. "Who might 'some of us' be?" I crossed my arms over my body to fight a sudden chill that had nothing to do with the wind or the sea.

Instead of answering, she pointed toward a declination in the cliffs rising from one side of the beach. The tide was going out, and a number of openings had appeared. "Come on," she invited. "We'll like as not be here for a while, and we may as well be comfortable."

I followed her despite a big part of me wanting to cut and run. Even though my body seemed to be my own again,

Cailleach had instructed us to stay put. Eh, bad idea. Could she enforce such an order in absentia? I wasn't eager to find out. Perhaps the Merrow could shed light on who'd hired them to fashion the wooden bits.

Plus, I was curious about what Birgit might reveal. I'd spent countless years delving for information about myself and never found much of anything.

It sounded as if the witch might know something. Or maybe she'd tossed that tidbit out to ensure I followed her. Yeah. I don't trust much of anyone, and her failure to disclose why we were really coming here was a solid reminder of why.

Lost in thoughts, I wasn't paying attention and would have tripped over a rock if the animals hadn't warned me it was there. I couldn't see my feet through the undulating mass of bodies surrounding me, but I could have used a thread of power to sort my way across the soaked sand. The cavern Brigit led us to was deep and sheltered from wind and elements. All the rodents that had trailed after me crowded inside. A few birds landed and tottered in as well, cawing their support.

Brigit settled on a flat rock and swung an arm wide as if to tell me to take my pick of seats.

"You've been here before," I said.

"Many times. Back in my coven days, we'd often meet on this beach. Cailleach would rise from the waves and join our dances and merrymaking."

Interesting. I'd never known the sea was her home.

"You could have told me," I said again and sat across from her.

"I wasn't certain she'd even be here. My other choice was

coming here alone, but you're in danger and I didn't want to leave your side."

Instead of being gracious, saying thank you, and letting it go, something about her words got my ire up. I slapped the rock I sat on with a palm. "I've managed this far without a caretaker. Hell, I don't even remember my mother. According to Blake, it's because I didn't have one."

"Not trying to be your mother, just your friend. You need them whether you realize it or not."

I winced and looked away. "Drat. I'm sorry."

"No need for that. We have bigger problems than your confused feelings."

I blew out a tight breath, and then another. "I'm still not seeing this as a *we* problem. It's mine, not that I want it, but you can walk away anytime. So can Blake, for that matter." I was on a roll, so I kept on keeping on. "I mean, I understand what's in it for him. He's trying to inveigle his way back into my bed, but you and I have been the faintest of acquaintances."

"Until you showed up on my doorstep."

"Still, my desperation—and I was desperate—didn't turn my misfortune into your problem," I insisted.

"I was waiting for you," she said softly. "Jethro is a seer in one of his other guises. It's one of the reasons he and I have done so well together for so long. He foretold you coming."

"Not a reason for you to drop everything," I mumbled. A pair of rats crawled into my lap. I scratched their short, stubbly fur.

"How could you know? You have no idea what he saw in his vision state."

"Are you going to tell me?"

Birgit shook her head.

"Then why bring it up at all?" I groused. I've never cared for being pushed this way and that by things beyond my control. I may have established détente with the extent of my magic—sort of—but I've never accepted prophecies that included me. They're all flim-flam, smoke and mirrors.

After a few minutes, I understood she wasn't going to answer me. "How long before Cailleach returns?"

A shrug was followed by, "I have no idea."

The sun was moving up the sky. Probably, it would be a couple of hours yet until it passed its zenith. Sitting still has never been my first choice. After placing the rats on the ground, I stood and shook out my arms and legs. Claws dug into my shoulders as the badgers clung tenaciously.

"Knowledge isn't always power." Birgit's voice came out of the blue since she hadn't exactly been in a chatty mood.

"What exactly does that mean?" I asked.

"More often than not, it turns into a millstone and creeps into every decision, even the ones best left alone." After crossing her arms beneath her breasts, she continued. "Not everything foretold in visions comes to pass. We're presented with a variety of possibilities. There are rarely clues which version of the future will end up unfolding."

I considered what she'd shared. "Then why even bother?" I chewed my lower lip.

"'Twasn't me but Jethro," she reminded me. "I rarely understand why he does what he does."

I mimicked her posture and tucked my arms around myself. "If you're not going to offer up details, don't tease me."

"I was attempting to help you understand why the details you crave won't do you much good, and could backfire."

"How?"

"You haven't been listening." She dropped her arms to her sides and rose. "If I relay what Jethro saw, and you pour energy into either supporting or refuting his foreseeing, it could easily be for naught."

"But that should be my decision," I argued. "Not one made for me."

A creeping sensation slithered down my spine, so real I almost reached back to hunt for a snake. Silly of me. The badgers would have made short work of any creature who touched me against my will. They're ferocious warriors and much smarter than everyone gives them credit for.

Besides, snakes are drawn to my magic too.

"I'm going for a walk," I said and strode out into pallid rays of sunlight. Enough clouds whipped along overhead, the sun was bound to lose out to rain. Brigit's gaze bored into my back. I felt it tracking me, following me as I picked my way around rocks and boulders to the place waves crashed against the shore.

Much as I hated to admit it, Fate cut both ways. Birgit may have been privy to a vision that told her I'd show up on her doorstep, but the same energy had guided my steps. Though I knew her, I'd never stopped by her dwelling before.

The animals had left with me. Seals crawled out of the surf and waddled close. Birds cawed and cheeped, circling overhead in droves. When a flat rock rose before me, I clambered high enough to sit on its damp surface and stared out to sea, losing myself in the endless undulation of waves.

Did Blake know whatever Birgit did? Was that really why

he'd shown up? Sensing my distress, the animals surrounded me, warm and furry and fuzzy and feathered. Quieting my mind, I let energy flow outward, wrapping every creature in love and appreciation.

A war was brewing with me at its epicenter, but there wasn't a damned thing I could do about it from this remote beach. Hell, I hadn't been able to do much when I was in the thick of things. The observation comforted me. I've always been an in-your-face-let's-get-the-job-done gal.

I still was, but not much ass-kicking to be accomplished from here. Antsy and far from mollified, I settled in to wait for Cailleach. If it started to rain, I'd move back into the cave. Maybe. Easier to be alone than to deal with the awkward silence that had sprung up between Birgit and me.

If she hadn't wanted to disclose Jethro's prophecy, she shouldn't have brought it up in the first place.

Chapter Thirteen, Abria

An hour marched by. I counted my blessings rain hadn't materialized. Not yet anyway. The gunmetal sky was a dead giveaway. Well into the second hour, the waves parted, and the witch goddess balanced on their surface until her bare feet hit the sand. "Keeping watch?" she inquired.

"What did you find?" I should have waited for her to volunteer information, but my restless need to be gone hadn't abated. If anything, it was stronger than it had been before. I felt Birgit's energy drawing near, but kept my gaze squarely on Cailleach.

No matter what Birgit did, I was out of here as soon as Cailleach was done talking. Sooner, if she was evasive. I wasn't a witch, so she'd be less inclined to include me in anything, including information.

Birgit tugged on one of my feet, indicating I should climb down. Probably a good idea if it would hurry things along.

Even if it didn't, I'd be in a better position to leave. Intuiting my intent, the animals made a path for me. I joined Birgit and a phalanx of seals and sea turtles on the rock-strewn beach.

"Thank you for your efforts on our behalf," Birgit began.

I poked her with an elbow but stopped shy of pointing out we had no idea if Cailleach had done anything. For all I knew, she might have hunted and come up dry. Or maybe she did nothing but kill an appropriate amount of time before returning.

Geez. When did I turn into such a cynic? Or had I always been one?

Despite my agitation, it was barely midday. Plenty of time to return to Birgit's and meet Blake.

It was tough to keep words locked in my throat. I'd already asked about progress pointblank. Prodding wouldn't hurry anything along.

Finally, when I'd almost chewed a hole through my lip in frustration, the witch goddess said, "It was curious. Almost too easy. Most of my time was spent locating the pod, but once I did, they didn't need to look at the Hawthorne sliver."

She drew her gray brows together. "Makes sense. There's little connection between the Merrow and the Sidhe, so when several of them visited, ostensibly under the guise of wanting assistance with imbuing a certain type of magic into carvings, the Merrow were only too pleased to help."

"What do they carve beneath the sea?" Birgit asked.

"Mostly coral, but also stone and kelp."

I uncurled a hand that had fisted, and squeaked, "Several Sidhe?"

"Wondered if one of you would pick up on that," Cailleach chirped like an inveterate gossip who'd delivered a particularly juicy bit of information. "I didn't get their names, but there were six. Four men and two women."

"What kind of Sidhe? Or did they even know?" I asked.

The witch goddess nodded curtly. "In this instance, 'twas simple enough to tell. These were Cait Sidhe."

My rapid intake of breath didn't go unnoticed.

"What?" Cailleach and Birgit asked almost simultaneously.

"The Cait were behind the plot to take over the gateway near Rait Castle, but we killed the leader."

Cailleach aimed a pointed look my way. Her expression was so condescending, it made me wince. "Revenge, eh? They wanted to get back at Blake. What better way than by targeting someone dear to him?"

"But we hadn't seen one another in months," I blurted.

She flapped a hand my way. "Not relevant when you live forever. Were you there when the Cait leader was slain?"

"Yeah, I had an elemental part in it along with a herd of unicorns."

The witch goddess rubbed long bony fingers together. "Och, wish I'd been there."

I wished I hadn't been, but we'd gotten what we came for. I made a grab for my manners. Elusive little bastards, they finally stood me in good stead when I bowed my head and murmured, "Thank you. I'm certain you had a simpler time dredging information from the Merrow than I would have had."

"They want to meet you."

Her words hung between the three of us for a few beats before I managed, "Why?"

"They feel terrible their actions caused you such grief."

"Kind of them," I said, "but we need to get back."

Cailleach's arm snaked out and she closed a hand around my arm. "I promised I would bring you into their midst."

My teeth worried a dent in my tongue. What I wanted was to shout something to the effect she had no right to make promises involving another. In a distant corner of my mind, I feared she'd set a trap for me.

"How about this?" I suggested brightly. "I'll remain here long enough to shake a few fins, but then I really need to leave."

"Here as in on this beach?" Cailleach sought clarification.

At my nod, power sheeted through the air around her. Where it touched me, it tingled and burned. Several seals pushed through it forming a circle around me and nudging me with their snouts. The badgers hissed and snarled.

"No need for that." Cailleach's toe was sharp. "Your mistress is in no danger from me. I am summoning the sea people."

Damn. I wish I'd had a truth spell deployed to test those words—the ones about no danger—but it would have really pissed her off. Some things require a leap of faith. This was one of them.

In far less time than I expected, the waves developed a choppy aspect. One by one, Merrows popped through. Their long hair came in every shade of the rainbow. Their upper bodies look like human females, but with wings. Their lower bodes are scaled and fishlike. A few males joined the group. All shared the unearthly beauty of the faery-folk.

Taking a deep breath to settle myself, I walked into the sea. It wasn't a leap of faith, after all. Sorrow and concern rolled from the Merrow. Even my power, weak as it was, sufficed to know they meant me no harm. Seals trooped into the briny water too, followed by tortoises.

The sea people surrounded us, cooing in a soft language I'd never heard before. Some stroked my shoulders, others my hair. A sense of peace—hypnotic and spellbinding— enveloped me. I could have remained in their midst for a long while, wanted to. The urgency hounding me earlier vanished. Letting my guard down felt right, normal.

They'd quelled my unease with magic. Normally, such a thing would have terrified me. I'd have fought against it, but not here.

As quickly as they'd come, they departed. Good thing because I'd been snared in their enchantment. Freeing myself would have been difficult since I longed for their warmth and gentleness to circle me again.

Still filled with wonder at the encounter, I trudged through the waves. When I reached Cailleach, I bowed my head. "Thank you. They were nothing like that when I ran across them before."

"They are selective whom they reveal their true natures to," she replied, almost but not quite smiling.

Something must have changed for them to decide I was worthy. Maybe guilt was a driving factor, but I had a sense their candor ran deeper than that.

"Time for us to go," Birgit said. "Thank you, my lady."

"Visit more often," the witch goddess urged.

"I promise," Birgit replied.

A wave of warmth started at the top of my head and rolled to my feet. When it cleared, I was dry. "Wish I could do that," I mumbled.

"You could. All it requires is training." Cailleach laid a

hand briefly on my shoulder before shimmering to motes of light.

Training. My lack of a teacher rose up to bite me in the ass. Again.

Birgit and I found the track that had led us to the beach and retraced our steps to the car. The rain that had been threatening since dawn pattered down, big droplets pelting us. I fished in my pocket for my keys and unlocked Birgit's side before circling the car and getting behind the wheel.

"About that drying spell," Birgit said. "Summon air, heat it with fire. Not too much or you'll singe your hair and clothing, but comfortably warm. Let it envelop you. Release it when you're dry."

"Easy for you to say. I'd rather practice where I don't risk turning the upholstery into an inferno."

"Watch," she said. "Learn."

A channel opened showing me how she mixed magics. Air came first, fire second. She hadn't been kidding about not too much. Soon, the puddles beneath me were dry along with my hair and clothes.

"I can do that," I said. My words surprised me, but I'd followed each step. None were beyond my ability.

"Of course, you can." Birgit paused. "You can do many things you've decided are too hard for you."

I tapped the ignition and pulled onto the deserted highway. After a few minutes, I said, "At least we have a direction."

"Indeed, we do. And it's not all the Sidhe who are apparently behind this. The Cait have always been renegades."

"Any idea how many there are?"

Birgit shook her head. "Probably a question for Blake."

I frowned. "Too bad he went to all the trouble of calling his council into session. We got the answer he's looking for."

She shrugged. "Let's wait to see what he comes up with. Just because the Cait approached the Merrow, it doesn't mean the conspiracy doesn't run deeper than them."

Her words were like a slap in my face, or a bucket of cold water dousing me. But she was correct. I'd assumed we had our answer. Because I was the target, I hadn't wanted to look any deeper. Stupid of me.

"We have some time," I said.

"Aye, a whole day, more of less," she agreed, "since we said we'd meet at my cottage in two days' time."

"Are you up for some sleuthing on our own?"

A glance her way showed a smile when she asked, "What do you have in mind?"

"For starters, I want to track down Jerome MacLaren, the one who hired me."

"You won't find him."

"But he has a bank account," I protested. "I cashed his cheque."

"Hmmm. Did that draft have an address?"

I nodded. "It did. Normally, I wouldn't have looked twice, but in light of what happened, I memorized it."

"Where?"

"In Inverness. Wouldn't hurt to drive by there."

"All right. What happens after that?"

"After we interrogate the fucker, I'd like to take a closer look at the Rait Castle gateway. I was there with Blake, but I was so conflicted about his suggestion for us to enter Underhill, I didn't check it out."

"Why conflicted?"

I shook my head in hopes it would clear my jumbled thoughts. Blake had that effect on me. Every. Single. Time. "I hadn't seen him in a long while. He swooped in out of nowhere as my self-appointed protector, and it just rubbed me wrong. I never wanted to be dependent on him. For anything."

"I see. And we're hunting for?" she asked.

"Traces of Cait. Maybe they haven't given up on securing the gateway."

Birgit slapped a palm on the center console. "I should have thought of that the minute Cailleach implicated them. One thing about the Sidhe, it's always been every mage for themselves. Not much solidarity."

I wondered if Blake would agree with her assessment. When we passed through Nairn, I stopped for petrol. Birgit ran into the convenience store and emerged with bottled tea and biscuits. I hadn't realized how hungry I was until I saw the food, and then I considered returning inside to buy more.

"Hang on," I told her.

"Did I forget something?" She settled the biscuits in her lap and twisted the cap on one of the tea bottles.

"No, but I'm starving. They have decent crisps and chicken nuggets."

"Grab some cheese and crackers while you're about it, and we'll have lunch. I'd have gotten more, but I thought you were in a hurry."

"No rush. We have plenty of time."

When I got back to the car, Birgit had moved it away from the pumps. Considerate of her, and something I should have done. Since we were parked in an unobtrusive location, it made sense to eat here.

"Thanks for moving the car," I said around a mouthful of fried potatoes.

"Eh, some jackass was honking at me, and I didn't want to draw attention to us."

Nairn was small. Many of the locals knew my car, but if the honker had been an acquaintance, he'd have gotten out to investigate why Birgit was in my vehicle. Scotts are a nosy lot, and gossip always swirled around the last resident witch in the neighborhood. Although, humans wouldn't label her as such. They saw her as an eccentric old woman with a touch of old blood who could sometimes be of assistance with problems traditional medicine couldn't touch.

"Do you mind?" Birgit's hand hovered over the grease-stained bag of chicken bits.

"Not at all."

We ate in silence. Before we were done, Birgit returned to the store for two more bottles of tea. Not nearly as good as brewed, but beggars couldn't be choosers. While I waited for her to return, I sent threads of seeking power in a full circle. The metal of the car impeded my spell to some extent, but I couldn't sense anything with malevolent intent lurking nearby.

Maybe I shouldn't have cashed the bank draft. It was as good as hanging out a sign I was still alive and well. But then, whoever had tried to nab me in my home knew as much. Blake had defeated them, and they'd fled.

Not gone. I wasn't that stupid. Nope. They were regrouping for their next strike. An involuntary shudder tracked down my spine, followed by another. When Birgit yanked the passenger door open, I gave a muted yelp.

"Erg. Sorry," I mumbled.

"You weren't expecting me to come back?" She handed one of the teas over before closing the door.

"Of course, I was," I replied testily to cover how sheepish I felt for my hypervigilant reaction. After tapping the ignition, I pulled away from the curb, intent on checking out Jerome's address in Inverness.

"You do realize it's probably not his," Birgit said as she gathered up our various food wrappers and plopped everything in the sack she'd carried the tea in.

"Huh? What do you mean? What's probably not whose?" I'd reached the junction and turned the car toward Inverness.

"The address," she explained patiently. "You can have cheques drawn up with anything you want printed on them."

"Sure, but when the bank identified his account and transferred funds, I figured everything else was on the up and up too."

"We'll know soon enough." She cracked her second bottle of tea and drained half of it.

True. Inverness wasn't far. It's a much bigger city than Nairn, but I know it well. A lot of my sleuthing business happens there. Yeah. My sleuthing business. Would I ever return to it? Or was it just as dead as every other business I'd walked away from over the course of my overly long existence? I'd hoped for a few more years before retooling myself. Again.

"Pay attention." Birgit's tone stopped my thoughts cold.

"We're not there yet," I sputtered.

"We're close."

She hadn't asked a question, so I took a look around to get my bearings. "We are," I agreed. "How'd you know?"

She swore in Gaelic. "'Tis a fair wonder you've survived this long. Can't you feel that?"

Not wanting to appear even more incompetent, I executed a couple of turns and pulled into a parking place. Once the car was stopped, I said, "It's only a couple of blocks. Let's walk."

"Can't you feel the wrongness?" she persisted.

I could have lied, but what was the point? "No. Not exactly." Once I exited the car, I resurrected my seeking spell, but nothing out of the ordinary pinged against its weave.

Birgit dragged us between two buildings so old, one had developed an inward cant. Once we were out of sight, her magic caught me up in a ward. At least, she'd quit chiding me.

We covered the distance to the address on the cheque quickly. Birgit seemed to know the way without any assistance from my quarter. I still didn't sense anything, even after we bypassed the lock on the front door of the building. From the looks of things, it contained several flats, four on each of six floors.

A glance at the mailboxes confirmed Jerome was on the top floor in flat 6D. The place felt quiet, almost uninhabited. We started up the stairs. By the time we passed the third story landing, the fine hairs on the back of my neck prickled. Not exactly an early warning system, but my power wasn't totally defunct.

Birgit set a quick pace. I was panting when we reached the top floor. Even a human could have smelled something was amiss. Maybe. The scent of blood scoured my nostrils. Not living blood, either.

I'd quit moving, but Birgit stood in front of the flat labelled D. A flare of power from her fingertips would have defeated the latch if the door had been locked. It wasn't. My momentary paralysis abated, and I glided next to her, hand on the knob which turned easily.

The sounds of feet on the risers pushed me into the flat with Birgit right behind me. She pulled the door tight and spun the deadbolt. We stood in the center of a combination living room-kitchen. The smell of blood battered me as I crossed to a door.

No need to open it, but I did, anyway. I'd have yelped, but Birgit clapped a hand over my mouth in time. I'd expected to find Jerome dead, but not like this. Blood splattered two walls, half the ceiling, and the floor. His body had been ripped in half. The leg end had been thrown into a corner, while the torso and head lay atop the bed.

I nodded; Birgit let go of me. Apparently, my guess that Jerome had been a stooge, a means to an end, was correct. "What in the hell did this to him?" I croaked.

"The same thing that wants you dead," she replied grimly. Warding snapped into place around me. Her teleport spell kindled to life about the same time as the door to the flat crashed against its stops and splintered into kindling.

Too late, I remembered the footsteps I'd heard on the stairs. If something powerful was after me, why do anything as pedestrian as walk? I added magic to Brigit's spell. The bloody walls wavered but didn't vanish.

"Come on," I muttered, willing us out of this miserable hellhole.

The witch laced her fingers with mine. We were almost out of time. Bitter shards jabbed at me, stinging, burning, but most of all cold. Might have been my imagination except my teeth wanted to chatter. Fuck. I'd sort things out later.

I dug deep, tried harder. Jerome was dead because of me. I refused to be an agent of destruction for any more innocents. Anger rolled through me in a quick, hot tide. It did the trick. Voices chanting in a guttural language full of consonants faded as we got the hell out of there.

Chapter Fourteen, Blake

O nce Kirwan began talking, he didn't require any prodding at all. From time to time, his narrative wasn't exactly on point, but I didn't redirect him. Furious at being thwarted, the Cait had launched a Sidhe-to-Sidhe campaign. Their message had been simple, easy to digest.

In true Cait form, their "ambassadors" had been rational, reasonable. Every species of cat is a master at manipulating others to see things their way; the Cait are better than most in that regard.

Their argument went like this: the age where a council manned by Daione Sidhe was needed had run its course. Once they'd thrown down the gauntlet, rather than telling other mages what to believe, they'd asked a series of questions. Things like, when was the last time we'd actually had a meeting? For that fact, when was the last time anyone had laid eyes on me? I winced at that. The truth hurts, particularly when it cast me in an unflattering light. One where I didn't give a flying fuck about anything, much less upholding ancient Sidhe covenants.

My annoyance didn't alter the facts or make them any less damning. My few trips to Underhill had been quick and quiet. I hadn't demonstrated interest in running anything, let alone the Sidhe council. Never mind my boastful words to Abria about picking up the reins because no one else wanted the job.

The last part had been accurate. No one wanted the job, but "no one" included me. I was regent in name only, and I hadn't done jack shit squat in at least 200 years. It took a while, but my slipshod approach to leadership finally came around and bit me in the ass.

While my back was turned, the Cait had become far more numerous. They'd split up the task of delivering their message. If Kirwan was to be believed—and he didn't have an axe to grind one way or the other—agreement had been close to unanimous. Why would any Sidhe retain loyalty to an outdated hierarchy, particularly when the supposed head of it had checked out?

From now on in, it was every mage for him- or herself. Not a quantum leap since most Sidhe viewed themselves as autonomous. On the surface, nothing would look any different. Until we were set upon by those intent on taking over, draining our power, and diverting it for nefarious purposes. The last Sidhe war occurred half a millennium ago. People remembered it, but dimly. Most had convinced themselves such an event could never happen again.

Deep in a spate of self-castigation, I didn't notice Kirwan had slipped out. The mead bottle was empty. Running on autopilot, I stood and headed for the armoire where I stored spirits but stopped with my hand on the latch. Much as I longed for oblivion, it was stupid, and an indulgence.

Somehow, I needed to gather my people back into a cohesive whole.

It had never seemed important before, but that was when I assumed we'd continue as we always had. Why wouldn't I?

Kirwan was of the opinion no one would show up at the meeting I'd posted. He might be right, but I'd find out for myself.

The appointed time was close, so I left my rooms taking care to seal the entry with unbreakable spells. I called on the earth spirits that keep Underhill whole and secret to aid me. At least they responded to my call. Maybe they hadn't gotten the memo the Sidhe didn't require either council or leadership.

Or if they had, they didn't care. It was one advantage of being regent. They only responded to me, none other could summon their assistance. That they still answered gave me hope. The Cait had probably done their best to sabotage my connection to Underhill and failed. The best they'd managed was to turn my subjects against me.

What was done, no matter how cunningly, could be undone, I told myself.

Not could be, will be, an inner voice popped up.

I hurried along curving corridors. Things shift in Underhill, courtesy of the earth spirits. Nothing is ever in the same spot twice. It means using magic to locate destinations, but it also ensured anyone lacking power would be lost in a trice. From time to time, mortals slipped through the veils separating Underhill from Earth. They never lasted more than a few hours. Something about the energy frequency here drove them mad.

Responsibility for my people caught me up. I would not be the one to break millennia of tradition.

Maybe I already had, a sour inner voice droned. Different from the previous internal commentator, this one was harsh, bitter.

If I broke it, I'll fix it, I replied.

Not in the habit of holding internal conversations, I shut this one down before it developed a mind of its own. I'd searched for other Sidhe on my way to my rooms. This time, I kept my energy close. No need to hunt for my kinsmen. They'd either show up. Or they wouldn't.

I had a nagging hunch the Cait had bigger things in store once they'd cut off my lifeline to my people, but speculation was a waste of time. I'd see what I could accomplish by way of damage control, and then I'd meet Abria and Birgit. Once I was certain Abria was safe, I'd return to Underhill and pick up the pieces.

It would mean I'd have to take up residence here—at least for a while. Hard to manage from a distance. Not that I'd tried very hard.

Or at all.

I grimaced. I'd have loved to be easier on myself, but soft-soaping the truth would buy me exactly nothing. The corridor turned from dirt to fancy interlocking stones. Our formal meeting room was close. After a couple more twists and turns, huge double doors embossed with glyphs and runes rose before me. Crafted of Hawthorne, they'd been shaped by one of our master woodworkers long ago.

Sidhe don't have to work, but most of us are drawn to a

particular craft from an early age. We have bards and seamstresses and stone masons and woodworkers. Cooks and scribes and armorers and weavers. Swordsmen and archers. The list is endless. I'd been a historian with sideline interests in swordsmanship and the assassin trade.

I splayed my hands over the smooth wooden surface of the doors. They parted beneath my touch, swinging inward. Breath clotted in my throat. Woodworkers. Why hadn't I made a connection between them and the Hawthorne slivers earlier? There might not be one, but they were my top suspects. Some of the Cait dabbled in woodworking. It was as good a place as any to start looking for who'd decided to get even with me for their leader's death.

The great hall was empty. After propping the right-hand door open, I strode to the front of the room and turned to face the entrance. A large, round table took up half the available floorspace. It could easily seat two dozen with no crowding. Bench seats angled around the table on all sides. Bookshelves overflowing with scrolls lined two walls. We kept a separate library, but the reference materials in this room were handy to have close in a pinch.

As I recalled discussions about which books would remain in the library and which ones would serve us best in the council chamber, sadness washed through me. I pushed it aside with both hands. My careless ways had gotten me in trouble, but I'd rectify things.

I wasn't the only one impacted, or even the primary one. Nay, our strength lay in coordination and numbers. Thanks to the Cait's sly intervention, the Sidhe had lost almost all our advantages. Except no one would figure it out until it was too late.

I ground my teeth in frustration and stared at the open door willing someone—anyone—to walk through. My thoughts turned to Abria and Birgit. At least they had each other. I might not have been able to pry myself away from Abria if she'd been on her own.

I gave myself a brisk shake. That, right there, was why she'd kicked me out of her house. I'd been treating her as if she didn't have any sense, as if without me looming over her, she'd be lost. How could I have been such a dumbfuck? And a paternalistic one at that.

Lesson one. Abria did not need me. She'd been managing fine on her own. Even my intervention the night she'd been attacked had arrived after the fact. She'd escaped on her own, gotten home on her own, and would have been fine without me jumping to the rescue.

Sitting quietly proved beyond me. I was on my feet wearing a circular track in the woven carpet covering the floor.

"Elwyn!"

The sound of my name in a strident female tone brought me up fast. I halted and inclined my head. "Breanne. 'Tis been a while."

"No shit. Nothing like showing up after the ship's sunk... captain." She faced me, hands on her hips. The last time I'd seen her, luxuriant white locks had cascaded to knee level. For some incomprehensible reason, she'd shaved her head. It set off both the stark planes of her face and fog-colored eyes nested under gray brows. Swathed in the robes she favored—this one deep green—she stood tall before me, broad shoulders square. Her battle axe was clipped into a sheath strapped across her back.

"Let's not get ahead of things." I kept my tone as neutral as I could.

"Nay. Let's not since you're already woefully behind."

I bit back hot words, instructions to leave if my decisions were so distasteful. Problem was, she was right. "Is anyone else coming?" I inquired.

She shrugged. "I have no idea. We're all independent now. The Cait said so, or haven't you—?"

I sliced a hand downward. "I've heard." Breath rattled as I exhaled. "Nothing's occurred that can't be undone."

"Keep telling yourself that," Breanne smirked.

I closed the distance between us. "Care to offer your version of what happened here?"

"Depends. What have you heard?"

Cutting to the chase, I used as few words as possible to synopsize Kirwan's version of events. Breanne nodded from time to time. When I was obviously done, she muttered, "'Tis close enough."

"Why'd any of you fall for the Caits' lies?"

"Mayhap because they weren't lies." Breanne extended one calloused hand and lifted her index finger. "One, you haven't been here for a long while." Another finger. "Two, we've gotten along fine absent the Daoine or the council." Another finger. "Three, so long as you hold a title in name only, the earth spirits will never harken to another's bidding."

Something in the depths of her gray eyes flickered ominously.

"That's at the bottom of this?" I spluttered. "The earth spirits?"

"Them and control of the gateways. We heard about a battle—albeit a smallish one—at one of the portals."

"Did you also hear the Cait's leader was killed?"

"We did. And that his death was unjustified. That he'd done naught to explain such Draconian measures."

Fury pounded through me. This was what came of not being here. The Cait had spread lies, except to their way of thinking everything that rolled from their mouths had been the unvarnished truth.

"Elwyn?" She prodded me with a couple of fingers.

"Remember the two changelings we set to guard the gateway next to Rait Castle?"

"Aye. Vaguely."

"The Cait kidnapped Roya."

A sharp intake of breath suggested it was news to Breanne, and probably all the rest of my kin as well.

"Go on." Breanne poked me again.

"The reason for the battle was to get her back. I returned her to Underhill. If you search, you'll find her. She'll corroborate my tale. The Cait are furious with me. They blame me for their leader's death. Ever since, they've conspired to damage me."

"There's more." Breanne narrowed her eyes.

"Isn't there always?" I tried to deflect her interest, but once activated, her instincts were as unrelenting as a bloodhound trailing a scent track.

Kirwan shuffled into the hall and glanced around. "I was almost right," he said.

"About what?" Breanne demanded.

"I told Elwyn no one would come."

"Is there anyone else in residence in Underhill? I felt the presence of other mages when I arrived." If mages had left en masse—to avoid this meeting—it would explain why the meeting hall was so empty.

Two pairs of eyes grazed mine. Two heads nodded.

"If they won't come to me, then I'll go to them." I still had time before I was supposed to meet Abria and Birgit.

"I will gather those I can," Breanne said and paused. "If you fill in the cracks in your story."

I swallowed a snort. Yeah. Like a bloodhound, except even more determined. Hitting the high points, I started with running into Abria's unique magical signature, being drawn to it, and tapping her to help get Roya back. While I mentioned the attraction between us, I definitely downplayed the sexual aspect.

"Between Abria and the animals loyal to her," I continued, "particularly the unicorns, we prevailed at Rait Castle. Ever since, the Cait have made it their personal mission to end her. They're doing it to get back at me, but also because she played an instrumental role in their leader's death."

The air around Breanne turned violet streaked with a soft blue as she raised her mind voice. Soon, mages trooped into the council chamber in droves. Gods, I'd sensed a few, but how could I have missed this many?

"When the Cait couldn't turn the earth spirits to their needs, they altered the weave holding Underhill together in such a way you'd be invisible." Breanne answered my silent question. Either she'd been lucky, or she'd plucked it out of my head.

"Why didn't it impact you or Kirwan?" I asked softly.

"We were absent the day the Cait strutted through here after most of us voted to do away with out council structure."

I didn't get it. Voting against formalized government wasn't the same as voting to be ruled by the Cait Sidhe.

"Ruminate later," Breanne said softly and moved out from between me and the rapidly filling hall.

I didn't need to titrate my words, or pick them with care. Facing the murmuring throng, I said, "I am so sorry. I have failed you and our long, proud history. I'm hoping you'll offer me enough latitude for a second chance."

The crowd pressed toward where I stood.

"The Cait said you didn't care," someone shouted.

"Aye, they told us you'd set yourself up in Galloway and wouldn't ever return," another Sidhe called.

"I did accept an Earldom in Galloway, but in no way did it lessen my commitment to you." I paused for emphasis. "You are my blood, my people. The Cait were mistaken—or perhaps they were mostly angry because I foiled their plans to take over one of our portals."

"Tell us," a woman urged.

"Aye," another chimed in. "Everything."

I was about to invite someone to drape a truth spell around me, but it happened without my invitation. Normally, such a transgression would have infuriated me, but I welcomed it. They'd know beyond a shadow of a doubt that I, their regent, spoke true.

Without hesitation, I dove in.

I was precisely where I needed to be. With the Sidhe. Sneaky dealings were a brutal wakeup call, but I could fix this. Maybe. I hoped. Once the dust settled, though, I had to be here. Not all the time, but enough to be a resource and a presence. It flew in the face of the plans I'd nurtured for Abria and me, but my path was clear.

Duty first. If she couldn't understand or appreciate the near miss I had yet to navigate my way through, then she was right, and we didn't have a future together.

Hell, I was deluding myself, anyway. She'd been serious when she'd shown me the door.

Nothing much about that had changed.

Chapter Fifteen, Abria

❦

"Way too close," Birgit panted as she swiped a hand across her forehead. Her skin was beaded with sweat despite the chilly temperature.

It took me a moment to recognize the entry hall for her dwelling. "Why here?" I asked.

"Do I hear a complaint?"

"No. Not at all."

"This is the safest spot I know." She answered my why question, crooked a finger at me, and headed through the tunnel connecting the entrance to the remainder of her abode. Once we were both standing in her kitchen, she raised both hands. Jets of light flew from her fingertips, and the doorway turned into a solid wall.

I blinked at it. "Neat trick."

"If they get this far—and they might since they could have

penetrated my warding and recognized me—they won't be able to move past the mud room."

My legs were unsteady. I hooked a foot around the bottom of a chair, turned it, and dropped onto its wooden seat. My stomach had twisted into a hard, painful knot making me regret the meal we'd slopped down in my car.

"Did you, erm, recognize them?" I gritted.

She drew her gray brows into a thick bushy line. "Not individually, but their dark power was unmistakable."

I waited, but she didn't seem inclined to add to her description. "Not to me," I mumbled.

She angled a pointed glance right at me. "Demon sprites. I can't believe you haven't run across them before."

"I have."

"Well, then?"

I took in a breath, let it out, and did it once more. Either I kept my mouth shut, or I spoke up. With my puny magic, what did I know about anything? Even though I was looking at the floor, the weight of her gaze battered me. "Not the take I got," I said finally.

"If you think you know better, let's hear it." Birgit settled veined hands on her hips.

Gathering my gumption, I met her scrutiny squarely. "That's just it," I clarified. "I don't know better. Some days, I don't know anything, but the dark sprites who've crossed my path didn't feel anything like the malevolent force blasting through that flat."

I expected her to dismiss my impressions. Instead, she crossed the kitchen, filled a kettle, and set about making tea. The room filled with fragrant herbal scents from rosemary, lemongrass, and mint.

It gave me a moment to compose myself. I was still shaking from the combination of Jerome's grisly remains and our near-miss with having to fight our way out of his flat. I'd expected we'd breeze in there, have a nice little face-to-face while Birgit and I drummed information out of him, and leave. The reality had fallen so far from the mark it was unnerving.

I raised a mental eyebrow. Unnerving was an understatement if ever there was one. Terrifying fell closer to the mark.

"No love lost between Sidhe and demons," Birgit commented. Perhaps she'd been monitoring my mind and waiting for me to latch onto an island of relative calm. Not much point in talking with me until I was ready to listen.

"You could say much the same about the Sidhe and any other magic-wielder," I retorted. "They seem to get along fine with everyone until there's more than one of them, and then the whole rest of the magical world turns into persona non grata."

I considered the added ripple of dark power. Like as not the Sidhe had never gotten cozy with the lord of Hell, his princes, or garden-variety demonspawn.

"I have a theory." Birgit poured tea into two heavy, white ceramic mugs and carried them to the table.

"Thank you." I picked mine up and drank deep. Perhaps she'd spelled the herbs because I felt much more settled, more like myself as the spicy beverage warmed my mouth and throat.

"Magic has been on the wane for a long while now," Birgit said in a thoughtful tone. "Some, like your Blake—"

"He's scarcely mine," I cut in.

She flapped a hand my way. "Regardless. A few like him have chosen to blend in more closely with mortals. These decisions often come full circle. Given enough time, I'm certain he would have returned to the Sidhe. It's in his blood, no matter how much the weight of leadership drags at him."

I started to ask what Blake's decisions had to do with whoever was out for my blood, but opted for silence. Birgit had her own ways of dealing with adversity. No reason for me to urge her to spit out the bad shit any faster. Once I'd heard, it wouldn't be anything I could unhear.

A corner of her mouth twitched downward. Had she been in my mind? Was she dunning me for being a coward?

"The only way out of this for you," she said softly, "is to claim your magic."

I thumped my mug on the table and breathed a sigh of relief it didn't shatter. "But I did that eons ago," I protested.

"Nay. You gathered the parts of your ability that you found easy, comfortable and never looked any farther."

Stretching my memory as far as I could, my beginnings refused to come into clear focus. As usual, they were hazy as if someone had purposely cast an enchantment, so I'd never stumble onto the truth even by accident. The bigger question was why it hadn't ever bothered me enough to try to dismantle the barrier.

Had part of the spell been woven to keep me fat, dumb, and happy? Someone had figured—and rightly—the animal bonds would fulfill me, and I wouldn't cast my net beyond them.

I wrapped my hands around the still-warm mug. "While I can appreciate the advantages in having more potent magic at my command," I murmured, "I'm not seeing how me claiming some latter-day birthright will make any difference in what we're facing."

"One step at a time."

I cast a pained look her way. Talk about cryptic.

"You're not the target here. Blake is. All you've been is a mechanism to lure him into making enough bad decisions others can move in and turn his spot as head of the Sidhe into an anachronism."

"How can you know that?"

The witch shrugged. "Intuition. Instinct. I just do."

I rubbed my forehead. "But who has it in for Blake?" I could sort of see the why. In terms of the magical heap, Sidhe ability sat just below that of the minor gods. Moving in on their territory would be a coup for anyone.

"You said you had a theory," I reminded her.

The witch nodded. "Aye. The Cait feared their numbers wouldn't be sufficient to sabotage the other Sidhe, so they coopted the Merrow and a few demonspawn. They needed Hell's army to do their dirty work with men like Jerome since the Caits' ability to hold onto a believable mortal form has always been sketchy."

Breath hissed from between my teeth. "Blake's that important, huh? Worth all that effort?"

"He is. With him out of the way, others could commandeer important portals. Even Underhill itself."

"This whole mess started when he had me help him secure a gateway," I agreed. "The Sidhe placed two changelings there long ago. One had died, and the other was gravely wounded protecting it from the Cait."

Not much of a relief for my trials to be relegated to collateral damage. I'd be just as dead if they caught me.

"This changeling. Did she survive?"

I nodded. "I believe she's in Underhill. It's the last spot I saw her. Why?"

Brigit looked askance at me, a gesture she'd turned into an art form. "To corroborate Blake's account when he meets with his people."

Breath oozed from my nostrils. I must be more exhausted than I realized to have missed something so elementary. Sleep would have to wait, though.

"I'm going to collect my car," I said as I stood.

"Not wise."

"Probably not, but I'm going to do it, anyway. I'll drive back here, and we can wait for Blake."

She released her mug and got to her feet. "We're already waiting for him. What earthly difference will your car make?"

How to explain I needed time to myself to make sense of everything.

Was that really it? Or was I hoping for a mini-break from the chaos my life had turned into?

Jethro chose that moment to stroll into the kitchen, tail pluming. "Mrrrowwww." He rubbed against my legs.

"You called for reinforcements," I muttered.

"Perhaps." Birgit sounded smug.

"How about this?" I countered. "I'll just take a brisk walk, clear my head so I'll be more help when we plot our next steps."

The witch narrowed her eyes. The cat who wasn't one purred louder. The faux wall vanished as quickly as it had formed. I started to say thank you, but didn't. I shouldn't have to thank anyone for not holding me against my will.

"Be back soon," I said brusquely to cover how vulnerable I felt.

A few steps brought me through the tunnel and into the mudroom. Jethro was still by my side. Understanding dawned as I glanced at the oversized black tomcat. "You're coming, aren't you?"

"Mmrrrowwww."

"There's really no need—"

The friendly meow turned to a not-so-friendly hiss. Apparently, he and Birgit had come up with a compromise. One they hadn't bothered to fill me in on. It annoyed me, but I'd deal with it later.

Much later. I had bigger fish to fry.

I pushed the door open—no reason to use magic to open it—and strode through with the cat by my side. The rain from earlier hadn't abated. If anything, water sluiced from the skies with more enthusiasm than earlier. Tugging my totally inadequate hood into place, I started jogging away from Nairn. The highway was mostly quiet, and I set a quick pace along the shoulder that offered me a head on view of any oncoming traffic. It was raining so hard, I didn't trust most drivers to notice me with my black jacket and a hood covering my bright hair.

Roads in the UK and most of Europe began their lives as horse and donkey tracks. They've been widened and modernized, but they don't compare with the expressways I've seen in other countries. In this case, the highway was two lanes, one in each direction with pullouts every so often along both shoulders. Absent a pullout, the shoulders were only a meter or so wide.

Hunching my shoulders against the chilly wind, I

refocused my attention. I hadn't come out here to resurrect the history of roads in northern Scotland. Nope. I'd come out here to consider what might happen next. Birgit had seemed certain about sensing demon presence in Jerome's flat.

So certain, I hadn't questioned her conclusion. But I'd wanted to since the feel of whatever it was hadn't screamed demons to me. If I got to choose, I'd far rather have the whole of Underhill after me than Hellspawn. The moment my thoughts went there, a graphic vision of what had been left of Jerome assaulted me.

A started meow from Jerome both reminded me of his presence and alerted me he was tracking my thoughts. Good to know. "It was pretty awful," I murmured, figuring he'd know what I referred to.

Unfamiliar magic threaded blues and greens that shimmered in the damp air. It had Jethro's magic stamped all over it, or I'd have been alarmed. I started to ask what he was about, but I'd find out soon enough. Pavement flashed beneath my feet as I picked up my pace.

I couldn't see the cat anymore. Maybe I'd never been able to between his coloration and the bleak weather. Couldn't see him, but I still felt his steady presence. The irritation I'd battled when he'd announced he was coming with me faded. I was grateful for his company. Even though he wasn't exactly a cat, I was used to traveling with an animal escort.

A final trill of power and a man took shape. Insubstantial at first, he grew more corporeal. Black hair covered his head in unruly curls. An old fashioned tartan with fabric winding around torso as well as hips covered a finely woven linen shirt. Of course, it was soaked in moments.

I slowed and then stopped to get a look at him. Taller

than me by perhaps a third of a meter, he had impossibly broad shoulders and a full black beard. Stained deerskin boots laced around his calves.

"Do I meet muster?" Dark bottomless eyes twinkled with mischief.

"Sorry," I mumbled. Too late, I realized I'd been staring. I started jogging again, each foot sloshing in my soaked shoes. I'd known he could take another form, so his transformation shouldn't have surprised me.

But it did.

"Why reveal yourself to me?" I asked.

"Why not?"

Not in the mood for sparring, I ran faster.

"That wasn't fair. You asked a question, and I brushed it off." His deep voice buzzed against my ear. "I read people better when I'm in this body, and 'tis far simpler to communicate."

"Did you find what you expected?"

"Nay, not at all. You're an intriguing woman, Abria MacLeone."

I glanced at him, hoping for more. He didn't disappoint. "Allow Birgit to teach you about your power."

My feet ground to a halt; I spun to face him. "Is that what all this was about? The reason you insisted on coming with me?"

"Partially. Neither of us were comfortable with you being alone."

I gave up and rolled my eyes. He was so much taller than me, perhaps he didn't notice. "I've been alone for hundreds of years. No one's ever protected me—except my animals."

Laugher rolled from him. "Pretend I'm still a cat."

"Won't work, and you know as much."

He cocked his head to one side as if listening to something. "Time to return," he informed me.

"What did Birgit say?"

"Blake isn't there yet, but he's close. So are other less favorable elements. We must protect Birgit."

Today was one for surprises. I'd never have believed Birgit needed protection—from anything. It also cast her relationship with Jethro in a far different light. If there was protecting to be done, I'd have guessed it flowed the other way: from witch to cat.

So much for assumptions.

A spell simmered around Jethro, lending the murky air a golden hue.

"I can walk back," I sputtered.

"Aye, I'm certain of it, but this is quicker." The ambient casting wrapped me in its tentacles. I'd have fought against it, but I didn't want Birgit stuck defending herself from my enemies. A side benefit was Jethro's casting kept the rain at bay. I was so wet, I couldn't get any wetter, but a break from the incessant thumping on my head was welcome.

I examined his power. Full of the scents of wet fur and warm hearthstones, it remained as unfamiliar as before. What was he? Shifter? Changeling? Something I'd never heard of?

It would have been rude to ask, so I didn't. Instead, I let his spell sweep us from where we stood to a small, dark chamber. From the homey smells of herbs and flowers, we had to be somewhere in Birgit's domicile I hadn't yet seen.

Jethro placed a finger across his lips and morphed back into a cat. The transformation was barely complete before he streaked out the door. More cautious, I threaded power outward to see what threat faced us. If the cat was correct, it was already here, except I couldn't sense a thing beyond Birgit's essence.

Done cursing my inadequacies, I followed the cat, albeit far more warily. Surely, I'd hear something to alert me to enemies who'd breached Brigit's wards.

A frantic yowl was followed by stern words from Birgit in Gaelic so old I had trouble interpreting it. My heart beat like a tripwire; my throat went dry.

What if something like the demons who'd ripped Jerome limb from limb were here?

If they were, I'd deal with it. Somehow. I warded myself, taking care not to let anything that might give me away leak through. Once I was shrouded, I marshaled defensive magic, holding it between my cupped palms. It stung, but I ignored the pain. More important to hang onto my element of surprise than to be comfortable.

Adrenaline beat a track along my nerves until I felt frayed, raw. After the yowl and Birgit's words, silence reigned. The back of the kitchen came into view. One more crook in the hallway, and I'd be able to see what we faced.

Or not.

The kitchen was empty, but the opening leading to the mudroom hadn't been resealed. I crept forward wishing for a weapon other than magic. Obligingly, a sword hovered in front of me. Nice, but I couldn't rework my warding to grasp it.

It settled to the ground without a clatter as if to tell me I knew where to find it.

The cat that wasn't one yowled again, harsh and mournful. I rushed forward. The time for stealth was done. Jethro had said Blake was close, but he wasn't here yet. Something snarled low and menacing. The unnatural sound iced my blood.

I kept going.

No matter what was out there, I couldn't let Birgit face it alone.

Chapter Sixteen, Blake

T ime dragged as I answered question after question. What had begun as a comfortable margin eroded quickly until I was beyond late for the agreed upon rendezvous with Abria and Birgit. Still, my lack of presence in Underhill had spawned the current near-disaster. It meant I couldn't check my cell phone for the time and make excuses.

Not that my phone would even work in this magical realm. Something about the faery world was hard on electronics. Hard as in, it killed circuit boards. I'd ended up with enough dead phones and tablets, I'd taken to leaving them behind. It was anyone's guess whether the iPhone carelessly tucked in my jacket pocket would still be functional when this interminable meeting ground to an end.

Finally, no more of my kinsfolk stood and waited for me to recognize them before speaking. I gave it a few more moments before I arched my brows and asked, "Did we cover everything we need to today?"

A lissome blonde with jewel-toned pink wings and acres of hair tossed knee-length braids over her shoulders. "When will you return?"

Of course someone would have to ask since me not being here was at the root of the Cait moving in and sowing misinformation. I opted for honesty. "The Caits' reach has grown long. I'm dealing with a..." My voice faltered before I tried again.

"Dealing with one of their victims on Earth," I plowed on. "They targeted her to get back at me."

"Why is fixing it your job?" someone else asked.

"Aye, is the victim one of us?" the blonde tossed out.

"Will you tell them, or shall I?" Breanne glided to the front of the room near where I stood.

I held a neutral expression. This was what came of confiding in anyone, particularly a blabbermouth Sidhe. "I will manage," I informed Breanne and sketched out the highlights—or lowlights—of Abria's trials at the hands of the Cait.

"In any event," I continued, "I'll ensure she's safe, and then I'll resume residence in my quarters here. All will be as it was a few centuries ago. We'll have regular council meetings and figure out if we can't fit into the modern world better than we have."

"What do you mean?" Kirwan rose to his feet from where he'd been sprawled on a marble bench near the back of the hall.

"Look at our numbers in the *Dreaming*," I countered. "They left Underhill because they felt hopeless, tired, useless, and a whole lot of other things. Some have told me magic has seen its last flicker and they're sick of struggling to resurrect it."

"You're hoping to lure them back?" Breanne waggled fingers my way.

"Some of them. Aye." I scanned the group. "Any more questions? I'll be back within a fortnight. Sooner if I can manage it."

Small groups of Sidhe rose and walked out of the meeting room. When only Breanne and Kirwan were left, she said, "We'll hold things together. Us and the remains of who used to sit on the council."

"Thank you."

I left it at that as I summoned a journey spell. It had been generous of her to offer, and Kirwan hadn't refuted her words, which meant he'd help. Underhill would be in solid hands during my absence. At least the two of them had been worried about Faery's viability.

I planned my egress near Rait Castle. It's naught but ruins and doesn't draw much in the way of tourists. I had no idea what time of day it would be until my spell faded plopping me in the midst of a drenching downpour under darkening gunmetal skies. Afternoon was fading. It would be dark very soon.

Not wanting to waste the time or the magic, I resisted an urge to wind a ward around myself. Instead, I set a quick jump to cover part of the distance to Birgit's home. I'd never been there, so I tied into her distinctive magic and let it lead the way. On the outskirts of Nairn, I felt wrongness.

Poor choice of words. Pressure from the nether realms was so overwhelming, a mortal could have tied into it. Not that they'd have labeled it as Hellspawn energy, but they'd have broken out in a cold sweat despite the rain and figured they were coming down with the flu.

Aye, a Hell-born flu. How had the Cait managed to get Satan's buy-in for anything? What had they offered the King of Hell? Or had they gone through a side door and seduced one of his princes? Female Cait can be seductive as all get out. Perhaps two or three of them had tag teamed a prince and addled his mind. Anything even remotely related to sex, destruction, torture, or pain would have been a winning combination.

I'd been cautious up until now. No more. Enough demons were north of Hell to saturate the Highlands with their poison. I didn't have to reach downward to know the hills and barrows were in full rebellion.

"Soon," I crooned, angling my words into the muddy soil. "Retribution is coming."

After a quick check to make certain I still had a bead on Brigit's energy, I crafted another spell. This one landed me on the coastal highway north of Birgit's dwelling. So far so good. Despite my lack of warding, no one leapt from the shadows to dissuade me.

Should I go back for reinforcements?

It was the prudent course, but there wasn't time. Whatever was unfolding was happing here and now in real time. The air had developed a metallic taste with overtones of sulfur and ozone. It coated my lips and tongue with a sour patina that made me want to rinse my mouth with something to overpower it.

Single malt whiskey would be just the thing.

Breaking into a lope, I did deploy warding. It might buy me a few seconds while I took stock of who stood against us.

The clop of hoofs behind me was accompanied by frantic whinnies. I turned in time to see half a dozen unicorns clatter past.

Had Abria called them? Or had they known she was in trouble through the link she held with all creatures. Regardless, I picked up my pace and ran after them.

"Becca." I kept my mind voice low and hoped she was part of the herd. At least I knew her. Maybe we could craft a quick and dirty plan.

One of the unicorns flashed around so quickly, she had to tilt her head to avoid goring me. "You." Her nostrils flared. "All this is your fault. Show yourself."

Not a time to argue. I released my concealment spell.

The other unicorns had stopped and formed a tight circle around me, horns aimed at my chest. They're about the only creature who can end my immortality. "Aye. 'Tis my fault, indeed." I reverted to Gaelic, hoping their ancient tongue would appease them. "Don't stop on my account. Abria is in trouble."

Becca skinned her lips back from squared off teeth. "You. Will. Fix. This," she hissed.

"Trying my best."

"How, Sidhe?" a black unicorn asked. "You came alone."

"I had no idea I was walking into a shit storm." I was back to English. "By the time I knew, I didn't have time to return to Underhill for help. Come on." I jerked my chin forward. "We can hash this out later. Once Abria and Birgit are safe."

After ducking between bunched withers and sodden manes, I took off on a dead run for the growing maelstrom. Red-tinged flames shot out of the hillside. Distant booming intensified. I pushed myself to run faster and gathered magic into a lethal arc balanced between my hands. Since water was the name of today's game, my casting was heavy on it with an assist from air.

The asphalt beneath my feet rolled, nearly tumbling me to my knees.

Shrieks and squalls filled the air along with rumbling reminiscent of a dirge laced with evil. The unicorns had caught up with me, nostrils quivering as they scented the toxic air. I'd never say this to my kinsmen, but one unicorn is worth ten Sidhe.

A glimmer of hope filled me. Maybe we could kill enough demons to make Satan sorry he'd ever believed a slimy, lying, Cait Sidhe. And if this little shindig had bypassed his knowledge, we'd mete out enough carnage the prince responsible would have no choice but to fess up.

Asphalt cracked, breaking into chunks. It wasn't designed to withstand earthquakes. A dull roar escalated into a cacophony as the earth opened before me. Debris shot skyward, turning into missiles as chunks gave into the pull of gravity.

I resurrected my warding damned fast after a house sized boulder crashed a few feet away. Broken bits of what had once been a front door shocked me into motion. Not that I'd stopped, but I had slowed down. This had to be the entry to Brigit's house. I pushed forward, threading my way around holes and rocks until I passed under the lintel.

Becca beat me to it, but she wasn't moving, and her bulk blocked the hole in the door. "Move," I said, resisting an urge to push on her rump.

She edged over enough to let me through, but angled her neck in front of me. "Let me through," I sputtered.

"Remember," she whinnied. "You asked."

She moved and I plunged forward. The floor vanished beneath my feet, and I fell a ridiculous distance before I gathered enough magic to halt my downward progress. My next move was a mage light.

Breath whooshed from my lungs as I stared into a bottomless pit. At least, it explained the explosion. Unicorn saturated power snared me and dragged me upward. "Thanks. We need to cross over that." I pointed at the hole.

"Wrong again, Sidhe." Becca pawed the crumbling dirt with a hoof. "Abria's gone. So's the witch."

"I can find her," I announced through clenched teeth.

"Then I suggest you do it because I already tried." If the unicorn had been human, she'd have crossed her arms over her chest, or tapped a foot, or slapped me. As it was, she focused both liquid eyes my way.

Redirecting the power I'd pushed into defensive magic, I reached for my link to Abria. She had to be close. Had to be. I expected the warm glow of her energy to bloom in my mind. It didn't.

Why couldn't I locate her?

I shut my eyes, focused all my concentration, and tried again. If Becca had criticisms, she kept them to herself. Even she recognized dunning me wouldn't bring us nearer to Abria. Meanwhile, the other unicorns had crowded in behind us.

In the distance, the blare of sirens suggested the police were on their way to investigate the quake and subsequent explosion. Or perhaps it was the local fire department. Regardless, I did not want to be here when they arrived. They'd detain me as a material witness.

I could obliterate their puny minds with magic, but my

top priority was locating Abria and extricating her from wherever she'd been dragged.

Becca laid her horn on my shoulder boosting my magic. At first, it didn't help, but finally a weak pulse of flowers and summer and birdsong fluttered through.

"She's down there." Becca sounded mournful.

"We cannot follow," another unicorn said. "Hell is barred to us."

News to me, but smart on Satan's part. A dedicated herd of unicorns could wipe out him and his fucked up princes and minions.

The sirens were growing closer. "Don't let them see you," I cautioned.

"Do not return without her," Becca growled just before she and the others vanished, leaving me standing on the edge of the pit by myself.

Wisps of Becca's magic clung to me and carved a path to Abria. Nothing to do but jump.

Chapter Seventeen, Abria

❧

Jethro was back in his man form. Birgit and him stood in the center of a circle of demons. Complete with red scaly hides, horns, and tails—and over three meters tall—they would have been bad enough on their own. Crouched within the circle was something far worse. Creeping evil straight out of my scariest nightmares.

Maybe not. Even within the bounds of sleep, I'd have been pressed to imagine anything this hideous. My heart pounded like a tripwire, banging against my ribs; my mouth went dry.

A cross between a serpent and a dragon, it sported two sets of wings, a mottled black hide, and legs jutting off at odd angles from between the segmented portions of its thick body. The thing was probably over eight meters long. Tough to judge since part of its nether regions was coiled. Alligator jaws, about a million teeth with gnarly bits clinging to them, and a row of beady red eyes across its forehead completed the picture.

It opened its mouth. A grunting snarl started low and rose in volume until I clapped my hands over my ears. It was the same unnatural sound I'd heard from the relative safety of Birgit's kitchen. And it had the same effect. When I tried to swallow, the sides of my throat stuck together. My feet wanted to spin me around and run as fast as they could.

Nope. Not going to happen. Whatever this turned into, I'd ride it out. Shooting pain down one side of my face reminded me to unclench my jaw. The sword beckoned, but I couldn't see where it would help me. Even with a magical assist, I wasn't strong enough to use it to cleave through demon or serpent scales.

Birgit had drawn a pentagram in the dirt encompassing her and Jethro. It glowed golden. So far, it was holding the demonspawn at bay, but for how much longer? Power flowed from the witch at an alarming rate. No way could she keep up that level of exertion without falling on her face.

Jethro wound an arm around her, hopefully sharing power.

She noticed me, narrowed her eyes, and commanded, "Leave."

Her voice was surprisingly strong. Perhaps she wasn't as depleted as I feared.

I didn't waste energy on words. I wasn't going anywhere. How could I live with myself if I left the witch and her familiar—or whatever he was—to face the apocalypse alone?

The monster's tongue snaked out, quivering as if he were scenting the air. His head swiveled on his thick neck until he stared at me. I stared back. That's the thing about being weak magically. I've learned to compensate. Now was not a time to appear feeble or cowed.

Two of the demons sidled toward me, red eyes gleaming unnaturally. *Oops.* The phrase "fake it till you make it," rolled through my mind. I leveled my gaze at them too. They had to know I was bluffing. Even if I could manage to do away with one or two of them—and I couldn't—there were twelve. Maybe thirteen. I hadn't taken the time to count.

What for? There were way too many. Even if Blake showed up now, it wouldn't even the odds by much. Not unless he brought a Sidhe army along. Unlikely, since any of them lifting a wing to aid a non-Sidhe was as remote as goose grass in the Sahara.

"Go. Now. Someone has to let Blake know." Birgit's words pounded home just how desperate our situation was.

He could fit the pieces together without help, but I was too busy glancing from the demons to the serpent to answer. They could come round behind me, trap me. Why hadn't they?

Maybe they're as dumb as they look...

I quashed my inner voice. Even the stupidest hellspawn was a tough adversary—especially for me.

The serpent thing howled again. Or growled, or whatever the fuck it was doing when it opened its mouth. In addition to the horrendous noise, the stench was unbearable. A cross between roadkill roasting in the sun and a charnel pit, it burned my eyes and the back of my throat. My stomach lurched against my diaphragm; my mouth flooded with saliva.

At least the horrible dryness was gone.

A small victory, and short lived. I swallowed, once and

again, tasting bile. In a contest between a dust dry mouth and vomit, I'll take Door Number One any old time. Throwing up in front of the demon mob would blow the cool, nonchalant image I was doing my damnedest to project. Maybe it was even working since no one had gotten too close.

Not yet.

Mice and rats streamed from goddess only knew where, surrounding me with their furry bodies. Spiders and beetles joined the party. Telling them to retreat wouldn't work. I was in danger, and they loved me.

The knowledge both heartened and shamed me. I needed to do something other than hold a pity party. I'm not okay with Satan's minions squashing me like a roach, but I'm way less okay with even a single furry strand or carapace or wing sustaining injury at the hands of my enemies.

The wolf's death in Inverness still stung, but if I didn't drag my head out of my ass and launch a credible counterattack, all the rodents and insects clinging to my lower body would die just like the wolf had.

Protecting me.

"I'm ordering you to leave." My mind voice was aimed at the loyal animals surrounding me.

They ignored me. I'd figured they would, and I'd be lying if I said I didn't crave the warmth of their small bodies pressed close.

If they refused to budge, I had to pull out all the stops to shield them. Everyone was convinced I had a whole hell of a lot more magic than I believed.

If Birgit, Blake, and Cailleach constituted everyone.

The ticket was I had to believe in myself—and do things

differently than I had in the past. No reason to hang out a sign alerting everyone I was about to play fast and loose with my power. Regardless of how big a crapshoot it was, I had to do something. Birgit and Jethro were in this fix because they'd tried to help me. Wringing my hands and perseverating on how badly we were outnumbered was a losers' game.

Never mind the monstrosity bugling his black heart out with his demon honor guard curved around him. Did they have mascots in Hell? More importantly, who was running the show here? I'd assumed it was one of the demons, but maybe they reported to the serpent.

I gave myself a sharp mental shake. Wasting time dredging for answers to questions that had none wouldn't help any of us. Wishing I'd had more practice time—or any at all—I asked the dirt beneath my feet to open a channel deep into the earth.

A shining band of magic flowed into my feet and through my body. I glommed onto it and shaped a transport spell, looping a corner to encompass Birgit and Jethro. The spell's shape was awkward, so I sidled as close to them as I could without alerting anyone what I was up to.

Turned out I could only alter the distance by a couple of meters.

Four of the demons shouted louder and formed a loose line in front of Birgit. It didn't require scrying skills to know they were about to breach her warding. They might not succeed the first time, but eventually her defenses would fail. It was a matter of who ran out of magic first.

It wouldn't be the demons. They'd shore one another up.

My journey spell was almost ready. Where should we go?

My cottage back in Nairn was a non-starter. Underhill would be safe, but none of us had the proper credentials to make it past the veil. Somehow, I was certain being friends with a Sidhe—Daoine of otherwise—would make zero difference.

Maybe one of the northern island clusters, like the Orkneys. I rolled my mental eyes. Like I'd have a fraction of the magic needed to get us that far. The four demons had ditched any pretense of subtlety. Dark jets flew from their paws right at Birgit's warding.

So far, it was holding, but lines carved deep into her high forehead. Veins throbbed in the gnarled fingers extended in front of her. Jethro was breathing hard.

Waiting for the perfect destination to pop into my head wasn't going to work. Not that any such thing even existed, but moving us away from here and into something even worse would be stupid. After a major magical blitz I'd need time— and sleep and food—before I could do this again.

If I could even do it now.

"For fuck's sake, get on with it," I sputtered.

A quick check of my fledgling spell told me it was light on damn near everything. A crack splintered across Birgit's ward. A word from her, harsh and unintelligible, repaired it, but her attention had been diverted.

Two of the demons crashed against the ward. It held, but looked like an automobile windshield with safety glass held together by threads. A couple more blows like the last, and Birgit and Jethro would be history.

Or prisoners, an even less savory option.

Tossing all my reservations aside, I told the animals still clinging to me to hang on for dear life. Next, I propped my magical center open and summoned all four elements. Never mind they're supposed to be mixed in proper proportions. I didn't know any formulas, so I'd have to wing it.

More of everything had to be better. Right?

The air turned thick and heavy, sweet with the scents of oleander and roses. At least it cut the stench from the monster. He'd lifted his head off the front set of legs. Clearly, he'd figured out something was afoot.

Before he figured it out and snapped me up in the morass of teeth in his mouth, I upped my request, shouting, *"Come to me now."*

Demon heads swiveled my way. Too late. Spells have a place where they develop terminal velocity. I'd blown past that a few seconds before. Guiding the disparate weave of the magic was growing harder.

Major understatement. More like impossible as power dug its claws into me. I've always been conservative with my use of magic. What had I unleashed?

The ground heaved, an explosion deafened me and made my bones ache. Fluid drained from my ears. I'd overdone this, but stuffing the genie back into the bottle was hopeless. My entire body vibrated as fire, air, water, and earth pummeled me from all sides.

Not the actual elements, but power sitting behind them.

A second explosion and the dirt beneath my feet collapsed. I clung to the unruly corners of my spell willing Birgit and Jethro to be here somewhere. Too late, I understood the demon horde must have fallen into the swirling vortex along with me. Birgit would be safer where she was.

Air currents spun me end over end. Somehow, I clung to

my casting. No more reason. It wasn't doing anything I wanted it to. Judging from the direction of travel, I'd dropped us straight toward Hell. Convenient for the demons—and the monster. Less so for me.

The hole I'd fallen through was still visible far above. A jolt of familiar magic told me Blake was staring through it. Along with Becca. Where had the unicorn come from? The furry horde holding onto me had been silent.

Crap. I couldn't drag them into Hell. Even if we didn't get that far, being this deep in the earth would be their death knell. I hunted for Birgit and Jethro. Couldn't find them.

Had they escaped my net? I mouthed a prayer to Danu, hoping for their safety. Determined to be more than dead weight who'd fucked up what should have been a simple travel spell, I pushed magic this way and that until I stopped tumbling and could hold my head above my body.

Harsh and unforgiving, breath stuttered through my teeth. There had to be a way to reverse what I'd done—not for the demons or monster, but for me and the animals hanging onto me. Claws had scored my flesh in multiple places. I didn't blame anyone. In their spot, I'd be terrified too.

Bellowing from below suggested the monster had landed and wasn't thrilled about it. I'd be even less happy if I ended up anywhere near him. It decided me, not that there was any true choice to be made. Something scraped my ankle. At first I figured it was one of my passengers until strident cursing identified the missed grab as a demon determined to drag me down.

"No more Mr. Nice Guy," I mumbled and turned my full attention to the elements coursing through me.

My spell was awkward, unwieldy. How to turn it back on

itself? Was it even worth the trouble. I could start over. Do another much shorter travel spell and bounce us out of here.

Before I talked myself out of it, I began untangling my magical essence from the failed casting. Easy to say. Much harder to do. The damned thing stuck like glue, as if it had turned into a part of me.

I stymied another ankle grab with a shot of pale lightning.

Time was running out. I'd stopped falling, but nothing said I couldn't be dragged out of the bubble I'd forged for myself.

I was breathing hard. So hard I felt dizzy and disoriented. And stuck. I couldn't get enough distance from the first spell to craft a second one. If the first spell wouldn't let go of me, I'd have to reshape it.

Daunting, maybe impossible, but I couldn't go there. Nope. I need to be methodical, cool-headed...

"What in Danu's name are you doing? Trying to blow up the world?" Blake's voice shocked me. I dropped a few bits of my casting, but they bounced back and slapped my sides.

"Can you get us out of here?" I demanded, ignoring his question. I'd admit my stupidity later. Maybe.

"I take it to mean you can't."

Defensiveness rolled through me. "Working on it. I figured since you were here, and your magic is fresh—"

Instead of answering, the familiar feel of his power encompassed me, cutting off my flow of words. Full of the scents of damp evergreens and ocean salt, it reminded me how much I'd missed him.

"Did you see Birgit and Jethro?" I demanded before he kindled his spell.

"Nay. They're trapped down here too?"

"'Fraid so. Can we gather them, and—"

His power shot us upward. Once we were through the hole and into the wreck of Birgit's entry area, he untangled his working from me, barked, "Take care of her," to Becca, and dove back into the hole I'd made.

To clean up my mistake.

Fuck. This was what came of trusting others' opinions about my abilities. I'd jumped in with more than two feet, and look what happened.

Becca pushed me with the side of her horn until I stood in the middle of half a dozen unicorns. Nickers, neighs, and horsie cooing soothed the rough spots in my soul.

"It's all right," I told everyone. "Don't waste your magic on me. Birgit and Jethro are down there somewhere." I pointed through the opening.

The rodents and insects dropped away from where they'd been plastered against me. *"We'll be close,"* one of the rats said before all of them raced for safety.

I sucked air into my fried lungs, and then did it again. At least no one had died on my watch today.

"How many demons were here?" a black unicorn asked.

"Aye, and what's that other reek?" a silver one chimed in. "Like demon, but not."

I told them, skirting over my major faux pas.

"You say the serpent landed somewhere down there?" Becca waved her horn toward the chasm.

I nodded. "I think so."

"Not in Hell?" another unicorn sought clarification.

"Not sure. I've never been there."

"Did you pass through gates?" Becca asked.

"I don't think so. I fell for a long while, so I might have missed them."

The black unicorn whinnied. "No missing Hell's gates. Passing through them is…unpleasant."

I peered around unicorn withers and rumps. Still no sign of Birgit and Jethro. The whine of sirens caught my attention, ebbing and flowing as if emergency vehicles were driving in circles.

"Who's with me?" Becca swished her tail.

"What are we doing?" I asked her.

"Going monster hunting, what else? If you're coming, hop aboard."

My mouth stretched into a grim smile as I vaulted to her back.

"I'll remain to shore up the magic that has the gendarmes chasing their tails," the silver unicorn said.

"What gendarmes?" I asked.

"They materialized when you blew up the world," the unicorn smirked.

"I did not blow up the world," I bristled. "Only a teensy corner of it."

Becca tossed her mane and addressed the silver unicorn who'd volunteered to hold down the fort. "A few more circles, and you can withdraw the spell. None of the police will even recall why they were here."

From a great distance, much farther than the police siren, I heard the monster roaring. So did the unicorns. The wreck of Birgit's entry hall took on a golden glow as five unicorns wove magic together just before all of us leapt into the breach.

My magic wasn't needed, so I shaped it into a seeking spell. Becca was intent on sinking her horn into the demonspawn, but finding my friends was far more important. No one had died today because of me.

Not yet, and I aimed to keep it that way.

Chapter Eighteen, Blake

Abria's power lit the world. Beautiful, terrible, untamed. Had she created this chasm? Only explanation I could come up with. Locating her was simple, all I had to do was follow the waves of her unique blend of magics. I nodded sagely. Surely, she'd seen the light and claimed her full birthright.

Except, if it was true, how had she ended up deep inside her own working when she should have been outside its weave, controlling it. She came into view. The lower half of her body looked as if it was encased in living fur. I readied lethal energy. Thank all the gods I didn't loose it.

Once I got close, I made out all the small animals hanging onto her for dear life. Her honor guard. They'd probably been in more or less that same position when the earth opened.

I also figured out damned quick her surfeit of enchantment had jumped the gate, escaped her control.

Censure ate a hole in my throat, but I bit back anything she might construe as critical. Things between us were shaky enough. Instead, I silently offered her points for courage.

She's never trusted her magic. Too bad when she finally decided to go balls-out, it ricocheted back in her face.

Nothing a spot of training wouldn't solve.

She was nattering on with excuses about why she needed me to extricate her when I simply did it. After leaving her in the unicorns' capable hoofs, I reentered the hole with feelers out for Birgit and Jethro. I'd never met him, but I assumed if I located her, he'd be in the same vicinity.

Sulfur fumes singed my nostrils. Ozone made my throat achy and dry. Why hadn't the demon horde beelined it back to Hell?

Good question with only a couple of possible answers. Either whoever was behind this shitshow had ordered them to stay put, or this was one of the spots where it was impossible to access Satan's realm.

Hell has gateways. Lots of them. Orders be damned. Satan's minions have never been especially malleable. If a portal was near, I suspected the contingent scattered through this newly formed cave would have been long gone.

First things first. I poured more juice into my seeking spell, but there was no sign of Birgit. She might not be here after all, or she could be warded. The Sidhe delude themselves about their magic being exceptional. In truth, many mages carry equally powerful enchantment. It looks different, but that doesn't mean it's inferior.

Enough rambling. I moved to the edges of the cave, hunting for tunnels or other potential escape routes. The cavern was constantly reshaping itself, the sound of rockfall loud against my ears. After the third dead end, I stopped to regroup.

Birgit could teleport. If she'd been dragged into the hole, my bet was she'd—

Golden light bursting with the feel of unicorn magic bathed the dank space. I flashed around in time to see five of them galloping downward. Abria sat astride Becca.

If there'd been something to drive my fist into, I'd have done it. I'd rescued her. She'd been safe. Becca had no right to—

"Stop, just stop," I mumbled and shunted my wits into better shape where I was thinking rather than reacting.

Abria was a free agent. Maybe running squarely into danger had been her idea. Perhaps it had belonged to a unicorn, but no one had twisted Abria's arm. She was here because she wanted to be. The unicorns would never have forced her into something she didn't want to do.

My hunt for Birgit and her familiar had turned into a dead end. If a battle was afoot, and there damn near had to be one, my magic would be put to better use aiding the unicorns.

And Abria.

I dropped lower, riding the coattails of unicorn power down.

Abria saw me first, or maybe she was merely the first to acknowledge my presence. "Where's Birgit?" she shouted.

"Warded or not here," I replied.

A tightening around Abria's eyes suggested she was fighting an impulse to order me to try harder.

"*Ssht.*" Becca's mind speech was more like a neigh than a word.

The unicorns had fanned out into a rough circle. Below, sprawled on a wide shelf was the serpent Abria had described. It was even more disgusting in person than she'd let on.

No wonder she'd thrown every kind of magic together, hoping for the best.

Demons stood guard around the monster. Was it injured?

"Is that all of them?" I asked Abria.

"No. At least three are missing."

"Any chance they're dead?"

Abria shook her head. Tangled red hair wound around her tall, spare frame.

Fuck. Not good news. They could be anywhere, but my money was on them hunting for reinforcements. You can get out of Hell almost anywhere. It's just the getting in that requires a gateway.

"Do we have a plan?"

Becca shushed me again.

Fine. This wasn't my circus. I'd help as I could, not that unicorns needed much assistance. Their horns can kill anything. Permanently. Even vampires. No second chances once a unicorn has gored you.

If the herd was talking amongst themselves, I couldn't hear them. As one, they clopped onto the rocky dirt. Demons ranged between them. Not for long. Casually, as if they had all the time in the world, each unicorn drove its horn into a demon's chest. Black fire flew from hands that turned lifeless. It flickered and smoldered when its maker expired.

Impressive. One more round, and we'd be done with the demons.

We? Ha. If I wanted a piece of this action, I needed to hurry. Selecting a flat area behind a trio of demons, I landed with magic at the ready. Almost before my feet touched the ground, I blasted the nearest demon dead center in his back. It wouldn't kill him, but it should knock him out long enough for me to finish him with a sword I conjured from the air.

So much magic jockeyed around the cave, it was simple to borrow from the various strands. The resulting broadsword was just the way I like them. Heavy, requiring a two-handed swing. Sharp. Deadly. Before a unicorn could poach my target, I ran forward and sliced head from body. Stinking black blood geysered upward. I leapt sideways to avoid the worst of it but still got drenched.

Gagging from the smell, I wiped my blade on my pants. They were so filthy, more blood didn't make a whit of difference.

Squeals and grunts filled the air, but not for long. Soon, only the monster was left. Howling and heaving and thrashing its bulk from side to side. Had the fall injured it?

Abria hustled to my side and gripped the hilt of my sword. "Whoa. Nice. Where'd this come from?"

"My imagination with a liberal sprinkling of pixie dust." I grinned. I wanted to crush her against me. It wasn't why we were here.

"I'm worried about Birgit."

I was too. "She's been taking care of herself for a long time," I reminded Abria.

She shook her head. "Sorry. Doesn't fly. I'm why she's in this mess."

I gripped one of her hands. "Don't give yourself too much credit. As I recall, she volunteered."

The unicorns had taken up positions around the serpent,

but out of reach of its jaws and flickering tongue. I caught the scent of poison and understood why. I wanted a chunk of the serpent, but the unicorns appeared to have the situation well in hand.

"What was that?" Abria peered into the gloom, moving her head from side to side.

I hadn't been paying attention to anything except her. A low, rolling rumble vibrated in the pit of my stomach. I felt more than heard it, and it was definitely coming from below us.

"Look sharp," I cried, not bothering with telepathy. Who cared if the serpent heard me.

"Sharp about what?" Abria extended both hands; power turned her fingertips silvery-blue.

"Someone put out a call for help."

"The ones I couldn't account for. Damn it. They're like a cancer."

"Worse." I pushed with magic, selecting spots that looked weak to me, but nothing gave way. The serpent's bellows escalated; my ears ached. Unicorns gored it systematically, working from the head toward its distant tail.

Abria's magic tracked the length of the serpent. She vaulted forward screeching, "Wait!" Doubling back, she grabbed the broadsword from my hand. No one was more surprised than me when it didn't vanish. Usually, props like that only work for the one who conjured them.

Pushing between two unicorns, Abria began sawing at the serpent's scaled hide. She wasn't making much progress, but that type of weapon is better for chopping than fileting.

I hurried to her side. "What are you doing?"

"Birgit and Jethro are in there," she shouted and went back to trying to carve them a path to freedom.

Power augured from me into the serpent, but I didn't sense anything except its fell presence. "How do you know?" I didn't want to undercut her belief, but neither did I want to waste energy on a wild goose chase with Hell's minions bearing ever upward.

"It's the cat. I can feel him."

I'd been searching for the witch, not her familiar. With a flicker and a flash, I crafted a hunting knife sporting a wicked serrated blade. "Use this," I told her.

Becca cantered close, black blood dripping from her horn. "Can't kill it," she wheezed. "It's borrowing power from somewhere. Every time we sever its essence, it bounces back."

Intent on sawing through scales, hide, and gristle, Abria didn't even look up.

"Birgit and Jethro are in there," I told the unicorn.

She pawed the ground in fury. "Ashamed I didn't figure that out. The twisted bastard is stealing magic from them."

How much more could it take before they died?

"Tell the others to back off from this section," I told Becca.

"Stop." Her equine voice bounced off the walls. Rocks cascaded down on us.

I snapped up the broadsword, funneled enchantment into it to make it heavier and longer. Once I had what I wanted, I stepped a couple of meters behind where Abria was working, raised my blade, and brought it down on the monster where two segments fit together.

We had to fix this fast, before a bunch of hellspawn

mowed through our scant numbers. Once I'd figured out they were coming, I could feel them clawing their way through layers separating Hell from where we stood.

My first blow did nothing. Undeterred, I struck again. And again.

Chapter Nineteen, Abria

Christ on a fucking sawhorse. No wonder we hadn't been able to find Birgit. She could have been screaming her head off, or blowing through magic like there was no tomorrow. No matter what she did, the serpent's power would have obfuscated hers.

Sweat poured down my face and sides as I carved away at scales that may as well have been made of granite. Behind me, Blake brought his blade down over and over. Each time, the solid thwack reverberated through my hands and arms.

Neither of us was making much progress. The unicorns trotted up and down the length of the serpent jamming their horns in at intervals, but avoiding the area where Blake and I worked.

Had I been right about this being where Jethro's energy shone brightest? After one brief flash where I'd been positive I felt the cat, nothing else had materialized to reinforce my belief.

Was he dead? Were we too late?

I put the brakes on my worst imaginings and assessed the spot I'd been winnowing the blade between two scales. I'd hoped to pop one loose. Ha. Not going to happen. In the spirit of the grand experiment I'd begun earlier, I held the blade at an angle, stuck the tip between the scales, and called fire. It ran down the blade and between the scales.

My fingertips rebelled in agony. I ignored them and pushed harder. Fire disappeared between the scales. Encouraged, I sent another blast.

Thwack.

Thwack.

Thwack.

Blake had settled into a rhythm as he cursed up a storm in Gaelic. I thought I heard him say, "one more," but the majority of my focus was on the spot between scales where I was funneling fire.

The next part happened fast, so fast I'm still not certain quite whose magic did what. Blake's sword cleaved through the serpent. Fire shot out the hole along with a screeching black cat.

Relief sheeted through me. Somehow, against all odds, I'd guessed right. Or my fragile magic had come through when I needed it most. Blake snatched the cat and covered his fur with clods of dirt to put out the fire.

"Where's Birgit?" I shouted to make myself heard over the din of the unicorns and dying serpent.

"Right here." The witch crawled out of the hole Blake had made, her hands curled into claws. The ends of her hair smoldered; her face was streaked with soot. The moment she was clear, she opened her fingers and tossed fiery balls back into the cavity she'd slithered out of.

Fascinating. The fire hadn't damaged her because she'd fashioned it into weaponry. Neat trick.

"It's finally dead," Becca neighed from a few meters away, punctuating her words with victorious whinnies.

Blake still cradled the cat, but he'd quit hissing and writhing. Birgit held out her arms, and Blake handed Jethro over. The blade he'd used shimmered to motes of light; my knife followed suit.

Blake clapped his hands together sharply. "We have to leave. Now."

The unicorns had been frolicking around the dead serpent, kicking it for good measure. Blake's words cut into their victory dance, and they formed a tight circle around where we stood.

"Aye. Satan's army is on the move. I heard them talking with the serpent." Birgit made a face and spit something black and disgusting out of her mouth.

Unicorn energy threaded around us full of the scents of new mown hay and sun-drenched pastures.

Blake raced to where Becca stood. "Follow my lead. We're going to Underhill. It's safer than anywhere on Earth."

I fully expected the unicorn to gore him, or kick him in the shins with her razor sharp hoofs. Instead, she opened her magical center. Where before there'd been unicorn essence, now it blended with Daoine Sidhe magic.

Birgit stood by my side. "Thank you."

"What? You thought I'd just run off and leave you?" My tone was far sharper than I'd meant it to be, but if anyone should be doing the thanking, it was me.

The witch shrugged. "As you've pointed out, we don't know one another all that well. When Cailleach accepted you, I felt certain I'd made a good choice. I wasn't surprised you did everything you could to rescue Jethro and me, but 'tisn't a reason not to thank you."

Power swept me off my feet; the dirt walls glistened, developing a radiant aspect. About the same time, I heard klaxon horns and the baying of Hell's hounds. Damn, we were cutting this way too close. The stench of Hell raked my nostrils, but the damnable cave—the one I'd carved because I didn't know what the fuck I was doing blending magic and elements—fell away.

Suspended in blackness, I caught my breath. Not an easy proposition since my heart felt too big for my chest cavity.

"I do believe we escaped," Birgit muttered and shook her filthy gray hair. Bits of serpent guts rained from her tangled locks.

Jethro hissed.

"Sorry, love." Birgit rearranged her grip on the cat. "We'll find you a healer in Underhill."

"All I need is clean water and time," the cat growled into our minds.

"If you'd have asked me even fifteen minutes ago," Birgit went on, "I'd have said we were on our way out. Even if Hell's minions had arrived and saved the serpent, we didn't have any way out of him."

"He was sucking us dry." Jethro shuddered. *"It was disgusting, and I was helpless to escape. I tried. Took this form and clawed forward. The moment I hit his mouth, he started chewing me to bits. The other direction grew too narrow."*

"I cursed him," Birgit said. "Every wild oath I could think of. If he'd survived, he would have been miserable."

"I'm sorry," I muttered.

"For what, dearie?"

"Involving you in the mess my life has turned into." I blew out a frustrated breath. "This isn't over, you know. Not even close."

"For now it is." Birgit patted my shoulder with the hand not curved around Jethro.

I opened my mouth to argue, but shut it before words came out. My life was up in the air. I couldn't return to my cottage in Nairn. Not safely. It's the first place my enemies would look for me. Continuing my private detective business was out of the question. At least here. Maybe if I moved to the States or South America or Australia.

"Just get through today," Birgit suggested dryly.

I cast a sidelong glance her way. "Been reading my mind?"

"Um-hum."

The spell that had yanked us from disaster weakened. I felt it shift just as we plopped down in Rait Castle's ruined courtyard. It was nighttime. Around midnight from the looks of the sky. For once, it wasn't raining. Or sleeting. Or snowing.

Becca laid her horn on my shoulder. "Until next time, mage queen."

Mage queen? If I hadn't been so trashed, I'd have furled my brows. "When will that be?"

She brayed what might have been laughter. "Sooner than you think." She shook herself from head to toe. Her mane and tail twirled in the night breeze as she cantered away with the other unicorns surrounding her.

Blake mimed a low, sweeping bow. "Please. Enter my realm as my guests."

We'd been at this juncture before. Last time, I'd run the other way. Still uncertain if I was doing the right thing, I dropped through the gateway with Brigit behind me and waited for Blake to join us.

"We'll find a healer for Jethro," Blake said as he landed next to me.

"I'll be fine," the cat who wasn't one growled.

"Then you'll make it easy on our healers," Blake murmured. After gliding around me, he led us down a channel with a ceiling so low I had to duck.

Jethro was still protesting he didn't need anything. If it hadn't been such a mirror image of what I'd said the last time I was here, I'd have laughed. Maybe. Every bone and muscle in my body ached. I still didn't totally understand what I'd done to be targeted by Satan and his ilk. There had to be more to it than them trying to fuck with Blake via me. Or maybe not. I hadn't been able to figure it out when I was at the top of my game.

Not much hope of doing anything but plopping one foot ahead of the other in my current depleted state.

Light flared, illuminating a declination in the ground. As I watched, it grew into an opening with stairs leading downward. Blake's intense gaze burned into me, but he didn't try to talk me into moving any quicker than I was comfortable..

The Faery realm was intimidating. Power flowed around me, impossible to ignore. Maybe bad things happened to those who breached Underhill's borders. Everyone appeared to be waiting for me. I sent a few threads of magic—all I could muster—forward and tested the path. If anything beyond the circle of light meant me ill, I couldn't sense it.

Because I had no options—like I said, home was a non-starter—I nodded curtly and walked down stone stairs that curved into infinity. As I moved along, the stairway lit ahead of me. Blake's magic? Or something built into the walkway? The last time I'd been here, Blake had carried me because I was unconscious. If there'd been a light show, I'd missed it.

Birgit followed me down with Blake behind her. He spoke a few words, and the breeze tracking through the hole abruptly ceased. I didn't need to look up to know he'd shut the entrance, disguising it to flow seamlessly into Rait Castle's foundations.

Because I was traveling on autopilot, eyes at half-mast, the bottom was a surprise. Blinking blearily, I noted a junction where three corridors came together.

Jethro bleated miserably—a cross between a meow and a groan.

"Is there somewhere I can take him?" Birgit asked. "A quiet spot with warm water and—"

"Of course. Of course," a deep throaty voice floated to us before its owner came into view. Tall and thin with silvery wings folded behind her back and acres of white, curly hair, the Sidhe wore a cream-colored robe sashed in deep blue. Runes traced the length of the fabric, and a leather belt studded with pouches had been slung atop the sash.

Blake inclined his head. "Thank you for coming so quickly, Viona."

The healer bowed back. "Good to be needed. It's a rare enough occurrence. We need more wars." She latched onto

Blake's gaze with onyx eyes. "Any day we strike a blow against evil shines brightly for all Sidhe."

"Indeed, it does," he agreed.

"Come. Come." Viona crooked a long-nailed index finger at Birgit. "Let's assess the damage. Soon, the shifter-seer will be well on the mend."

Shifter-seer, eh? First I'd heard of that particular iteration of mage. I'd wondered what Jethro was. Now I knew. The tap of bootheels said Birgit and Viona were on the move.

"We'll leave soon," I called after them.

Birgit stopped and turned to face me. "Really? And where might we be going? Neither of our homes are safe, and—"

"You are welcome to remain as long as you want," Blake cut in.

It seemed to mollify Birgit because she trotted after Viona.

"My apartment is this way," Blake said and pointed down another of the corridors.

I walked slowly, taking in the occasional painting, wall hanging, or statue. It was comfortably warm, not cave temperature as I'd have expected. Breath swooshed from me. I squared my shoulders, determined not to reveal how the days' events had rattled my faith in any future at all.

To his credit, Blake didn't say a word. Neither did he drape an arm around me or do anything else that might make me even more skittish than I already was. He and I both knew I was only here because there was nowhere else to go.

Sad commentary, particularly when I looked back a few short months to our Bacchanalian romps. Hard to fathom I'd been so carefree. So ignorant of what the future held.

Yeah. Back then, I'd had no inkling what waited around the corner.

We reached a carved set of double doors. They opened of their own accord, or else they recognized their master. Perhaps, unbeknownst to me, Blake encouraged them with a spot of magic. It didn't matter. I walked through feeling a pleasant tingle.

"Warded?" I cocked my head to one side.

"Of course."

"Even this deep in Underhill?"

He shook his head. "Pfft. Up until I set things straight, the Cait had all but overrun this place, but none of that is important. If you go through that door to the right, you'll find a bathroom. Feel free to clean up. I'll find something that will fit you and make us a meal."

I crinkled my nose. Both of us still reeked of demon and serpent. I wasn't the only one who needed a bath, but Blake was a big boy. He didn't need me to suggest his next moves. Part of me almost, almost invited him to share my bath, but wisdom prevailed.

My life was such an ungodly fucked-up mess, the last thing I needed was to compound things by resurrecting our troubled relationship. After nodding thanks, I trudged through the door and into another hall with doors on both sides. The third one I opened yielded a luxurious bathroom.

Gold-veined white marble shone with an inner light. A deep tub was already full of perfectly warmed water. Flower petals added the scents of rose and jasmine to the steamy room. Guess magic was good for some things after all.

Magic that's done properly, I reminded myself and winced at my earlier fall from grace. I'd tried my damnedest, but my almost total lack of formal training had come round to bite me in the ass.

I perched on a chair and unlaced my boots. Once they were on the floor, I stripped off my stockings. My trousers followed, and then my jacket and top. I hadn't bothered with a bra, but I skinned out of my panties and lowered myself into the king sized bathtub.

Soap, shampoo, and scented oils complemented the flower petals. For some reason, the water remained the same temperature. I muffled a snort. Nothing should surprise me in magicland. Once I was soaped and rinsed, I lay in the water, luxuriating and not thinking about anything.

I must have closed my eyes because a tap on the door brought me thudding back to consciousness. "Clothes are outside," Blake called. After a pause, he added, "Jethro is doing fine. He'll make a full recovery."

Footsteps faded as he retreated. Relief surged through me. I hadn't realized how worried I'd been about the shifter seer. Birgit must have been anxious as well. Otherwise, she'd never have carped about my "leaving soon" comment.

I pulled the plug and climbed out of the tub. Thick, warm towels hung over a rack. After wrapping one around myself, I cracked the door and grabbed soft doeskin pants and a fuzzy, woolen tunic marveling at the workmanship. My panties were as filthy as the rest of my garments, so I skipped them and dressed quickly.

A comb and brush sat next to the sink. I went to work on my tangled locks. At least they didn't have bits of serpent clinging to them anymore. A quick glance in the mirror wasn't as alarming as it could have been. Circles scribed under my eyes, but I was clean, my damp hair starting to form ringlets around my face.

Scooping up my discarded clothing, socks, and boots, I padded out of the bathroom and toward the entry hall. The scents of food drew me to a formal dining room with a table that could have seated twelve.

"There you are." Blake rose from where he'd been seated at one end of the expanse of mahogany. Or maybe it was teak or some wood specific to Underhill. His hair was wet too, and he wore a pair of gray slacks and a pale blue sweater.

"Any place I could wash these?" I waggled the bundle of clothing in my arms.

"Sure. Follow me, and then we'll eat. I'm famished. Bet you are too."

Before I'd been so tired I could barely keep my eyes open. The bath had helped, and now I was, indeed, hungry. "Food would be wonderful," I murmured.

He led me to a small laundry room and instructed me how to place my various clothing items on a conveyer belt. "When they come back around," he explained, "they'll be clean."

I started to ask how, but didn't. Regardless of what Birgit did, I wouldn't be staying, so how things worked didn't matter.

Once we were seated at the table, dishes floated in from somewhere, settling silently on the tabletop.

"Hope I remembered what you like," he said as he passed me dish after dish.

"You did, but this is too much," I protested taking a few spoonfuls of several yummy smelling casseroles. Fresh bread and a fruity alcoholic wine reminiscent of mead comprised the rest of our meal.

After we'd eaten in silence for a while, he skewered me with his direct dark eyes. "How are you doing?"

Fine almost popped out, but it had been a serious question and deserved a serious answer. "Not very well. Trying to figure out what to do next." I shook my head and laid my fork next to my plate. "No matter how many ways I dissect things, I keep coming up with the same conclusion."

"Which is?" he prodded.

"I have to leave the Highlands."

"For once, we agree." After a pause, he said, "You truly are welcome to stay here. Not as my lover, but as a free agent."

Sadness rolled through me. "It would never work."

"Why not?"

"I'm not like you. Not Sidhe. Sooner or later, the others would resent my presence. Plus, I'm not used to being dead weight. There's nothing for me to do here."

"I disagree. You could learn about your magic."

His words hung between us, and I flinched. "This isn't the right place for that," I blurted.

His black brows shot up. "Where better? We have an extensive library, and—"

I splayed my hands on the table and stood. "How would that unfold?" I demanded. "I hang out, get room and board gratis while I study magic? I'm not a youth any longer, haven't been one for a long time. No one gets a free ride. Sooner or later—probably sooner—people would resent me, expect me to do something beyond smiling pretty before I bury my nose in a book."

"Sit down." Blake didn't raise his voice, but those two words were laced with compulsion. I fought its pull.

Anger boiled through me. "Stop that," I gritted.

To his credit, the compulsion part subsided. "Please sit. There. Is that better?"

I shook myself from head to toe. Were my clothes ready yet? How long did that conveyer belt thingie take?

"Yes. It's better, but I should go."

Blake was on his feet so fast, I missed the transition. He spun me to face him and gripped my shoulders. "If today didn't scare the holy hell out of you, it should have. You're lucky all you did was drill a sizeable cavern under Birgit's home. If it hadn't been her house, and filled with white magic, you could easily have wiped out veils that hold Earth separate from a myriad of evil realms."

My eyes widened. I tried to shake clear of his grip, but it was hopeless. Before I could protest, tell him his premise was absurd, he continued. "Your magic is strong, so strong it's a potential danger to the rest of us if you don't learn to control it."

Defensiveness joined anger, tightening my muscles into rocks. "The only reason I did what I did was because Birgit and Jethro were in danger."

"Good intentions only travel so far." His tone was chillier than I'd ever heard before. "You can do things for the right reasons and have them turn sour fast."

"So? I'll never do anything like that again." A quick, hard twist broke his grip on me. I backed away a few steps.

"Until next time. And there will be a next time. You'll feel cornered, desperate, and you'll throw the kitchen sink at the problem. Kind of like you did today." His mouth formed a stern line. "Birgit said Cailleach will help, and—"

"Setting aside the fact you're all talking about me behind

my back, I don't care about any of that," I cried. "Why is anyone after me? What did I do to piss off the gods?"

He nodded slowly. "You're not the target. I am. Accessing the full range of your ability will place you in the best position to sort everything out. Once you understand why this is happening, we can compare notes. Together, we'll devise effective countermeasures, so you don't have to spend the next couple of thousand years staying one step ahead of annihilation."

I swallowed hard around a lump that had formed in my throat at his couple of thousand years observation. "If I had the ability to do that, it would have already happened."

"Nay. Not true. You need access to the full spectrum of your power, or the roots of this problem will elude you forever. Plus, this is a problem we must solve together."

"How could you possibly know that?"

"How could you not?" he retorted and closed the distance between us. This time, he cupped the side of my face in his hand and held my gaze. Somewhere along the line, he'd dropped his glamour. Wings wrapped around me, not tightly, but creating a warm cocoon.

An island of safety.

Oh-oh. Watch it.

I straightened, testing for magic, but he wasn't using any to convince me of anything. "No magic," he murmured, having helped himself to my thoughts. "Except what we make together."

When he lowered his mouth to mine, I didn't pull away.

Chapter Twenty, Blake

I'd have given even odds of Abria slapping me or kicking me when I took a chance and kissed her. She did neither. The hot tide of passion that had bound us together for so many months pounded at the door, but I chose a different path. If we slept together again, it had to be because she wanted me—not because she felt backed into a corner.

Her lips softened beneath mine as she kissed me back, but the wild abandon I remembered wasn't there. She was being cautious too. After a few moments, she tilted her head away, grinned crookedly, and murmured, "Easiest thing in the world would for us to tumble back into bed, but my mind is a muddle. I'm tired and confused, and—"

"Hush." I brushed my thumb over her full lower lip. "Everything will come together. You're important to me, and I don't want to make things harder than they already are."

"I never had any problems until you hunted me down to help with your Cait Sidhe and portal issues."

I nodded agreement. "True. It's a starting point to untangle what's happening."

"It is." Her forehead crinkled in thought. "Since I'm not the target, but a way of someone trying to punish you, all I am is collateral damage." A sigh bubbled from her. "There won't be much I can do about that."

I stroked a lock of hair back from her face and tucked it behind an ear. Tenderness welled through me, a fierce need to protect her.

"Why are you so lukewarm about kindling the full extent of your power?"

Her green-eyed gaze skittered away, but she did answer me. "It will change everything. Maybe the animals won't... won't be the same."

I thought about it. They'd been her whole life. Of course, she'd be concerned. "Why wouldn't they be?"

Abria shrugged. "I don't know. Now, we're equally matched, balanced. If I'm suddenly stronger by a factor of ten, they might feel I no longer need them. Animals are quite intuitive. I couldn't change something that elemental about myself without them noticing."

"Your honor guard from earlier didn't shy away from your display of power, and it had to have been far more ragged and undisciplined than it would have been under—different circumstances."

The corners of her mouth twitched. "You're being quite restrained. You mean if I hadn't—what was the phrase you used?—thrown the kitchen sink at it."

"Not restrained so much as practical. We can't go back,

Abria. I want you to remain in Underhill where Faery can protect you." A pause before I plowed on. "If you insist on leaving, I'll help you find as safe a spot as I can."

"Except there aren't any. The magical world has a long reach. I can't escape notice, no matter where I go. Not for long. And I can't believe the other Sidhe would sit back and accept me being here for anything beyond brief visits."

The part about my kinsmen was true, but they might come around. "Is that what you want? Being on the run, always looking over a shoulder? It would effectively cut you off from the animal world too. Your link with them is the simplest way to locate you, so you'd have to be where they aren't."

She trained her gaze on my face. "You're telling me the truth, not trying to manipulate me."

"Aye, not much point. At least, stay long enough to take a stab at controlling your brand of enchantment. Learning everything isn't critical, but enough to avoid a repeat performance of earlier would help."

I ached to hold her against me, soothe the troubled places in her heart and mind. Instead, I turned and walked out of the dining room, through the kitchen to the laundry. Her garments were ready. I'd known they would be, so I folded them and carried them and her discarded boots back to where I'd left her.

Abria had returned to her seat. She sat with her head in her hands rubbing her temples. I bet she had one hell of a headache from blowing through all that magic. I remained in the doorway watching her, taking advantage of a moment when she was unguarded and unaware of my presence.

My heart hurt for her predicament; guilt swamped me. I'd

done this to her by including her in my Cait Sidhe problems. She had every right to hate me for kicking the pins out from under what had been a balanced life.

I set the stack of laundry on a side table and placed her boots on the floor. By now, she'd straightened and was looking at me. "I retrieved your things," I murmured.

"Time for me to go, huh?" She pushed unsteadily to her feet. "I'll just change and—"

All my promises to myself about stepping back, giving her space to dictate her own path flew out the window. I stepped in front of her. "Please. I don't want you to go."

A brisk knock at my outer door startled me. When I sent a jot of magic to see who was there, witchy energy flooded through me.

Birgit.

Hoping for the best—the witch was nothing if not rooted in common sense—I instructed the door to open. Birgit strode briskly into the dining room. "On time for supper, I see."

Jethro, in cat form, leapt on the table, bent his head over a chicken dish, and began eating.

Abria stroked his matted black fur. "I am so relieved you're all right."

He purred and ate faster. Birgit picked up another dish, a savory fish stew, and plucked bits out with her fingers. "I was hoping you had something to eat," she said between bites. "The infirmary only had mead. It was delicious, but liquor only goes so far."

"I can order more food," I told her.

The witch scanned the laden table. "You already have enough here to feed ten."

"It's an open offer." I retreated to the end of the long table where I'd been sitting. Had the witch's entry been serendipitous? I didn't think so. Abria's mind was simple to tap into. I bet Birgit had known she was on the verge of running away.

Abria shifted from foot to foot. "Um, have you decided what you're doing next?" she asked Birgit.

Jethro had eaten the chicken casserole down to the china dish. He'd been cleaning his whiskers with his paws when he suddenly flowed into his human form. Unlike most shifters, he emerged fully dressed in dark brown leather trousers and a tattered flannel shirt.

"We were talking about that," the shifter seer said.

"Aye, we will assist with your training," Birgit chimed in. "We should begin immediately, right after this meal is done."

Abria rolled her shoulders back. "What if I'm good to go the way I am?"

"You're not." Birgit set the dish she'd been eating from back on the table.

"How would you know?" Abria shot back.

"Child, please." Brigit started toward her.

"I am *not* your child," Abria shouted and hurried from the room.

I started to bar the main door to my suite, but didn't. She wasn't a prisoner. I refused to hold her against her will, but I breathed a sigh of relief when she went back towards the bathroom. Several bedrooms lined that hallway, and she ducked into one of them.

"She cannot be by herself until she has control of her power," Jethro said. "I've seen many versions of her future. The ones where she remains untrained don't end well."

Tell me something I don't know.

"She's frightened," Birgit said. "I'll go talk with her."

I watched her hurry out of the room. "Hope she has better luck than I did," I mumbled.

"You love each other," Jethro said. "It complicates things."

"I love her," I corrected him. "She doesn't feel the same."

"Aye, she does. You're too blinded by fear she'll slip away to see it."

I turned toward him. "What have you seen in your glass or pool or however you scry the future?"

He shook his shaggy head. "You know better than to ask. I'm not one of your Sidhe seers to be commanded by a Sidhe prince."

"Fair enough." I picked up a piece of bread, but my appetite had fled. I still didn't understand why Abria had cut me out of her life. Until I figured out the why, I had no hope of rebuilding the joy and tenderness we'd shared.

"This is all my fault." I spoke the words half to myself.

"Nay. Each of us has a life path. Hers is unfolding as was foretold from the moment of her creation. You may have been an instrument, but if not you, then someone else. Times are changing. What emerges may surprise...everyone."

I stared at him. His usual bland expression had turned somber. Damn seers, anyway. They always know more than they let on. Before it never bothered me, but now I was desperate for any scrap of intelligence I could lay my hands on.

"Will teaching her alter outcomes?"

"Probably."

I waited, but he was done talking. When he morphed back into a cat and went back to eating, I assumed he'd shared all he was going to. "I'll be in the library," I told the cat.

"*Mrrrrrow.*"

"Gathering source materials so Abria can begin her lessons."

"*Mrrrrrow. Purr. Purr.*"

If he'd wanted to talk, he'd have used mind speech. At loose ends, I made good on my promise and headed for the library. There's a larger one elsewhere in Underhill, but my personal collection provided a starting point.

What I really wanted was eavesdrop on Birgit and Abria, but it was the wrong thing to do. Disrespectful. If Abria was ever going to trust me, I couldn't use magic to force her to my will. If it would even work, which I doubted.

Books and scrolls clattered from shelves, landing smoothly on a long table in my study. Turning my mind away from whatever was unfolding between the witch and Abria, I grabbed the first scroll, unrolled it, and marked sections with magical highlighting.

Hours passed. I was still working by magelight, having amassed a significant pile of reading material, when the witch and Abria walked into the room.

This was it. Rubber meets road time. Holding a neutral expression, I looked at the two women and waited for one of them to speak.

Chapter Twenty-One, Abria

I almost ran out of the dining room because I'd be damned if I'd break down in front of everyone. Tears stung the corners of my eyes, and sobs were way too close to the surface. I knew exactly what was wrong with me. I wanted to stay in Underhill—with Blake.

Never mind the other Sidhe would never accept me. Hell, they might make my life as miserable as the Cait had. Blake was loyal to his bones, but it wasn't fair to push him into a corner where he spent the next several centuries defending me from his people.

Maybe they'd get used to me, an insidious inner voice suggested. I shushed it. Reality would do me way more good than pipe dreams. Wishing I'd had the foresight to snag my clothes on my way out of the dining room—and my boots—I cast a longing look at the front door to Blake's rooms.

I could leave wearing borrowed garments, but I wouldn't get very far barefoot. I ground to a stop. Three choices. Leave as is and find shoes somewhere. Stomp back, pick up my clothes, and then leave. Door number three was far more complex. It involved staying here until the fury and desolation scouring my bones retreated.

My earlier exhaustion was back in spades. If I walked away from Underhill, I'd probably fall on my face soon after I cleared its protective boundary. The only thing holding me upright was the mix of emotion churning through me, keeping my stomach tight and my throat constricted. If I put some distance between myself and Underhill, at least it wouldn't happen here.

If.

Such a small word with such huge consequences. I couldn't summon the fortitude to leave, and I hated myself for being weak. The specter of being totally alone forever dragged me down. Before, I'd had the animals. Now, they'd be in mortal danger if they spent any time around me, and I refused to put them in that position.

Reluctantly, I trudged toward the marble bathroom. I'd tried doors on both sides of that hallway on my way to the bathroom and discovered what looked like guest bedrooms. I picked the first. Spartan by the rest of Blake's standards, this chamber held a single bed covered with a rose-colored duvet. A writing desk and chair sat in one corner beneath a faux window with a perpetual view of a sun going down somewhere.

Too keyed up to sit, I paced the length of the room and back again. I should have been thinking about the quandary I'd landed dead in the center of. Instead, Blake overshadowed all my thoughts. It was stupid. He and I had no future. We'd never had one. Our magic was too disparate, for one thing.

I stopped pacing so abruptly, I nearly pitched to my knees. The power I currently commanded was subpar, but what if I took Birgit up on her offer to make myself stronger? Then Blake and I might be more evenly matched...

"Stop. Just stop," I mumbled. Staking a claim to bigger magic for the wrong reasons was worse than doing nothing at all. I'd been on the right track with leaving. No reason to think it to death. Was something about Underhill sapping my free will?

My eyes snapped open wider. Of course. That had to be it. This place conned mortals, got them good and lost, and never let them go. Many wandered aimlessly until they died of thirst.

The door flew open, banging against the stops. "You're far from mortal," Birgit commented dryly.

I bounded over and planted myself in front of her. "Stay out of my head."

"Learn to shield your thoughts." The witch tilted her chin at a defiant angle. "If you don't want others to listen in, adopt countermeasures."

A sudden surge of weariness made my knees weak. I tottered to the edge of the bed and sank onto it. "What do you want?"

"Stop feeling sorry for yourself."

Annoyed she'd pulled my covers, I huffed out a breath. "Next piece of pithy advice?"

Birgit crossed to where I sat and crouched in front of me. "This will catch up with you eventually. You can run, but nowhere will be far enough."

"You can't possibly know that. This should settle out

eventually. A new, more interesting target will pop up, and I can return to—"

She gripped one of my hands. "No. That's a fantasy. It will never happen. You can waste time mourning what you've lost, or buck up and face your future."

I opened my mouth and shut it. She'd lost a lot too. Thanks to me, her home was a shambles and a place she couldn't return to. Not easily. Shame joined the rest of the emotions vying for ascendency.

"Come with me." She stood; a spell bubbled around her.

Before I could protest—or even ask where she was taking me—the bedroom dropped away. After a brief stint in darkness, the same beach where we'd met Cailleach formed around us. Dawn was breaking, lending the restless ocean an iridescent hue.

Cailleach, the winter goddess, stood between us and the sea backlit by the rising sun. It turned her silvery hair to more of a hammered bronze shade. Today, she wore a deep blue robe sashed in white. When I raised my gaze and met her eyes, they'd changed. Instead of pupil and iris, a story played out marching forward much like a film reel.

When she opened her arms, I walked into them. She didn't force me, and I have no idea why I allowed her embrace. But I did. There in the light from the newly risen sun, something warm began in my bare feet and traveled upward. It was comforting, uplifting, and stern all at the same time.

Her eyes told the story of my lost history. Of how the Celts had made me, changed their minds, and regrouped. Of how I'd been sequestered to save me from death. I'd known much of that from Blake, but where he'd used words, Cailleach used imagery. It was far more powerful.

Seeing the goddesses circled around me, I felt their caring and concern. A tightly held place deep within me cracked wide open. The tears I'd held back earlier welled and dripped down my cheeks. Once, I'd been loved. It made all the difference. My earliest memories had been of animals rescuing me from darkness. I'd figured whoever put me there, held me prisoner, valued my misery.

I'd figured wrong.

Those first few years of freedom, I'd spent the lion's share of my time looking over one shoulder or the other. When no one ever came after me, my vigilance waned but never completely departed.

Animals took the place of the family I'd never had.

Apparently, by the time I dropped in on the Celts centuries later, Ceridwen, Arianrhod, and the Morrigan had smoothed everything over. I never picked up even the slightest of clues that my origins lay with the gods. Them erasing my memories ensured I'd never find out on my own.

More imagery filled in blank spots in my early life. For the first time ever, I felt whole. Understanding dawned it hadn't been only the difference between our magics that had made me gun-shy of Blake—or any other man.

I'd felt damaged. The only place my fractured beginnings didn't matter was when I was with my tribe—the insects, birds, fish, and animals who were drawn to me and my magic.

Blake.

Everything always circled back to him, but I was coming to terms with it. No longer fighting the deep-seated longing that spilled through me whenever I thought about him, I relaxed in Cailleach's arms. With surprising tenderness, she stroked my hair.

"The Celts are gone." Her low, gravelly voice vibrated in the bit of my stomach. "If they'd remained, they'd have insisted you marshal the full extent of your ability."

"They never cared before," I murmured.

Cailleach let go of me, and I took a step back. "You can't know that," the witch goddess retorted.

"Best not to compare anything the gods do with expectations you might hold," Birgit said softly.

The soft warmth that had rustled through my body still vibrated with promise. My earlier exhaustion fell away. Merrow frolicked in the surf; seabirds soared overhead. Cailleach stepped aside and I walked into the ocean. The briny smell was bracing. Heart and mind still filled with wonder and an odd sense of peace—odd because peace has never been in my wheelhouse—I dove into the surf and stroked toward the line of breakers rolling landward.

Schools of fish joined me. The Merrow formed rings around me, dipping and swaying in time with the surf. The cold I usually associated with the sea didn't bother me. It was there, but my inner heat kept it at bay. A haunting melody teased the edges of my hearing growing louder and more enticing. I'd heard tales of Merrow song, likening it to a Siren's call, but the reality was so much headier it defied description. High, sweet notes blended with deeper ones in a tantalizing harmony. Runes formed in the salt air, melted, and formed again. It had to be a language, but not one I'd ever been taught.

Where before, the Merrow wanted to apologize for any trouble they'd caused by carving the bits of Hawthorne that had served as homing beacons, now they welcomed me into their midst.

If surprised and humbled me. If they could, perhaps the Sidhe might as well. My harsh edges and cynicism were melting away, and I didn't lift a finger to hang onto them.

The sun hovered a few fingers above the horizon when I turned and swam for shore. As I closed on land, my companions brushed past me with fingers, fins, wings, and long, silky hair. Hundreds touched me, sharing their magic and their love. By the time I glided from the waves, my immediate future was clear. I made my way to Cailleach and Birgit and said, "I accept. Teach me what I need to know."

Birgit elbowed the witch goddess. "Told you she'd make the right decision. Jethro saw it clearly in several vision states."

"Walk with us," Cailleach invited.

I fell into step with the witches, and we headed for the cave where Birgit and I had sat a few days before. I experimented with drawing heat from the damp, rocky sand to dry my borrowed garments. They obligingly warmed around me, growing lighter as water evaporated.

"You remembered what we practiced," Birgit observed.

Suddenly self-conscious, I shrugged. "Tried to." I wrung water from the ends of my sleeves. "Clearly, I have a way to go."

We'd reached the declination in the cliff face. Cailleach patted a flat rock, and I sat. "You've lived many lives. Why cling to this one with such tenacity?" she asked me.

I understood what she meant, but I had to dig deep for an answer. "I've been...comfortable in the Highlands. Before I never truly fit anywhere—unless I was with a group of animals. I never had enough magic to be part of the mage world. Neither was I mortal, so I skated between the two poles making certain no one got close enough to ferret out my secrets."

I paused to take a measured breath. "In Nairn, I could use what magic I did have to solve mortals' petty issues. They were grateful, and I didn't expend enough enchantment to alert anyone—like the Sidhe—who might be offended by my presence."

"Have you ever wondered why Blake showed up when he did?" Cailleach's question caught me off guard.

"Wondered, no. He seemed enough like other men who've been attracted to me. I assumed he was looking for an edge to get closer." I frowned, not liking her implication. "Are you suggesting he was complicit in my problems? Other than in the obvious sense where no one knew about me until I battled the Cait Sidhe."

"Not directly complicit," Cailleach said. "Just because he's Daoine Sidhe doesn't exempt him from the pull of fate. He was as much an instrument as you. Except in this instance, he served as a catalyst to ensure you found a path to your power."

"So he didn't know, either?" I persisted, needing clarification.

"The only thing he knew was he felt drawn to you, child," Birgit replied.

"So drawn, he'd have done anything to keep you close," Cailleach added.

"But are his feelings real?" I rolled my shoulders back and leaned on the wall behind my rock.

"Do they feel real to you?" Birgit asked.

I nodded slowly.

"Then they are," the witch replied.

I scrunched my eyes in thought. When I opened them, I said, "My plate got a whole lot fuller if we add Blake tot the mix."

"Not really," Cailleach corrected me. "Magic comes first."

"It always did," Birgit chimed in. "At least now I understand why I remained near Nairn. Jethro knew, but he wouldn't tell me."

I cast a sidelong glance her way. "Huh? I don't understand."

"Aye, you do." Cailleach spun one hand in a get-on-with-it motion.

"But you've been in the same spot for a couple of hundred years." I aimed my words at Birgit. "It's a hell of a long time to wait for someone." My tongue tangled on itself before I added, "For me."

"You're thinking like a mortal. Think like a mage," Cailleach instructed.

Heat rose from my neck to my cheeks. She was right. Time flowed differently when you lived forever, but I still needed to prioritize. "Talk to me about training. How do you envision it unfolding? Where? And for how long?"

Cailleach's thin-lipped mouth curved in a rare smile. "Are you looking forward to the challenge?" At my nod, she said, "Good. For it won't be an easy undertaking. Not at your age. Because you have so many years behind you, you'll question— perhaps resent—my methods."

"Will it be you, then?" I asked. I'd figured Birgit would play a major role. Surely, the sea goddess had better things to do than watch me bungle one spell after the next.

"We will work together," Birgit said smoothly. So smoothly, I knew they'd discussed me in painstaking detail. It made me uncomfortable. I've spent centuries flying beneath the radar. To be the topic of anyone's attention, let alone two witches and Blake, was squirm-worthy.

Intuiting I was having second, third, and fourth thoughts, Cailleach clapped her hands smartly together. "On your feet. First lesson begins now."

Already? Gah. I'd been thinking I could try this out and quit any time the going got rough. I'd also been within an angstrom of bolting back at Underhill. At least I'd made enough progress to be crack the door on my reservations and give this a whirl. Blake's prediction about me raining gloom and doom down on everyone if I remained untrained rattled around the back of my head too.

Apparently, my thoughts were an open book. I scooted off the rock and stood facing the witches. "The first thing I want to learn is how to shield my thoughts."

Cailleach chuckled. "Smart mage. I'd prefer you learned that last."

I shook my head. Now wasn't a time to back down. We were establishing ground rules and a hierarchy. Sure, I was at the bottom, but it didn't mean they could push me around as if I were a youth.

Birgit and Cailleach exchanged a pointed glance. They weren't trying to be subtle. Good. If we started along this road with them hiding things from me, I'd never fully trust either of them.

The sea goddess nodded tightly. "As with all magic, many paths lead to the same end. For you, since you just heard the Merrow sing, their enchantment can aid you."

"Imagine their song, and the runes that accompany it," Birgit suggested. "Keep both alive and in the background. It should effectively cloak your thoughts from others."

Resurrecting the haunting melody, I let it roll through my head. Once I had it firmly in place, I added what I recalled of the runes. Since they hadn't meant much to me, that part was harder. After a few minutes, I dismissed both and blew out a frustrated breath. "When I do that, I can't do anything else."

Cailleach raised her gray brows. "And were ye thinking this would be simple?" she asked in Gaelic.

"No, but not impossible, either."

Birgit hopped down from the boulder she'd been perched on and placed a hand on my arm. "Since when does a handful of minutes of effort turn into impossible?"

I looked away from her shrewd blue gaze. Defensiveness vied with shame. I'd grown used to how I wielded power, sticking with the tasks that came easy to me. The next few weeks, months, years—oh hell, probably centuries—would push me so far beyond my comfort zone I'd probably forget everything about who I was today.

"Not centuries," Cailleach said dryly. "Even I lack that much patience."

A corner of my mouth twitched. If legends were to be believed, patience was far from her long suit. I swallowed the snort that wanted out. To cover, I mumbled, "I'll try again."

And I did. Over and over until I half-assed got it right by letting the Merrow song ride a weave of air currents. If I set them up just right, they ran on autopilot. Almost.

Deep in concentration, I didn't notice when Birgit touched my arm until she grasped my wrist, squeezed, and said, "Abria."

My eyes flew open; I fought disorientation. "What?"

"You tell us," Cailleach countered.

I'd been so focused inward, the outer world had grown fuzzy and vague. Releasing the Merrow song, I returned my attention to the small cave in the cliff face. Most of the day had flew. Shadows crossed the beach, and the sun was well on its way to the western horizon.

Whoa. How many hours had I burned through? Clearly a whole bunch of them. I rocked from side to side on feet that had passed numb long since. Pins and needles pricked, traveling up my legs.

And then I felt the wrongness. Dread ratcheted through me, stealing my breath. Cailleach had challenged me, thrown down a gauntlet. I could do this. Figure out what creeping evil was closing on our position.

"They're here for me, aren't they?" I muttered, followed by, "Don't bother to answer. Of course, they are. The Cait, or Hell's hordes, or whomever, haven't given up."

"Why would they?" Birgit stared me down. "We killed their pet serpent."

"Narrows it down to demons," I gritted, followed by, "Why are we still here?"

"To fight." A strange light flowed from Cailleach, red-gold mixed with deep-blue. "This is my territory. No one marches on my realm without consequences. Prepare yourself."

I barely had time to craft a ward when the witches raced from our cave. They weren't concealed. Power blazed from their hands. Feeling embarrassed, I jettisoned my ward, transitioned its magic into a defensive strike, and ran after them.

Chapter Twenty-Two, Abria

The ocean rose in unnatural waves, pounding onto the beach. Cailleach had altered the pattern of the tides. Had Arianrhod helped from a perch in Caer Sidi, her special land? Or had the virgin huntress left everything Earthbound behind for good.

Demons flooded the beach. A hundred or more. If I hadn't spent so much time fighting them beneath Birgit's house, they'd have been far more intimidating. Tall and scaly with horns and tails, they projected a total bad boy image. Most were red with a few black ones mixed in.

I caught up with the witches. Cailleach chanted in a language I didn't know. Birgit added discordant notes at intervals. Lightning flared from their outstretched hands. When it connected with demon hide, sparks flew.

I could barely hear the demons whooping over the roar of the North Sea, but their mouths were open and the occasional howl broke through. Clearly, they saw this assignment as a cakewalk. I shook a fist their way. We might look like easy pickings, but I vowed to make those twisted fuckers sorry they were ever hatched.

Birgit clasped one of my hands, Cailleach the other. Their power spilled through me, and I added mine to the brew.

Since they flanked me, I drew enchantment with abandon. The witches would save me from myself if things got out of hand. First I tapped the earth, and then both sea and air. Fire —the demons' natural element—wouldn't burn this near the sea, which weakened them.

Waves crashed around us, soaking me as the ocean rolled forward sucking demons into its maw. Faint at first, the Merrows' song danced along my nerve endings. I thought I was imagining it since I'd spend hours harvesting its power to shield the private places in my mind. But then, I saw the seafolk riding wave crests and drowning demons.

Maybe not actually drowning them, but circling them with magical nets until the water did its work. I'd been scared when Birgit called me back from my trance state. And when Cailleach had announced we were fighting, I'd almost asked why. Leaving had seemed prudent—and far simpler.

Fuck me. I needed a serious attitude adjustment. Between the sea and the Merrow and Cailleach's command over the waves, this was no contest at all. Whoops and laughter burst from me as I picked demons to target, driving them into the Merrows' capable hands.

Strident cawing from above drew my gaze skyward. A flock of raptors converged on the demons pecking out eyes and putting holes in everything they could drive their beaks into. The remaining demons checked their forward rush; turning, they bolted for what they presumed would be a safe exit.

Wrong.

Hawks cut off their retreat. The timbre and cadence of Cailleach's chant changed. Soon, the demons ran in confused circles. Had the sea goddess blinded them?

I let go of the witches and ran to where a demon lay shuddering in agony. One leg had been severed; black blood pumped onto the sand polluting it. I chose him because he wore a fur-trimmed jacket and a small gold circlet around his horns. Hoping it meant he carried rank in demon-dom, I kicked his ribs with my boot. The crunch of bones breaking was satisfying, so I did it again.

"You will leave me alone," I commanded and crouched next to him. "Every army that comes after me will meet this fate. Tell those you report to."

He turned his one good eye my way. The other was naught but a ruined socket with white bone showing through. "You must let me live to relay that message to those above me," he growled.

"Use telepathy." I drilled into his mind with my newly found ability and waited. He knew I rode shotgun in his head. Pretending he'd fulfilled my order wouldn't cut it.

A string of demonspeak—no doubt curses—rolled from his lips. Two nighthawks landed on my shoulders. "Say the word, mistress," one cawed.

"Aye." The other one jumped into the fray. "He has one eye left. And both ears."

Meanwhile, the sea was retreating to its usual trajectory

leaving kelp and crabs in its wake. I couldn't hear a single demon. "You're the last," I told my prisoner. "Or damned near it."

Surely, he'd see the light. Do the right thing and pass my message up the ranks. Instead, his head lolled to one side. His remaining eye rolled upward in its socket. One last, long shuddering breath sprayed me with noxious fumes.

Fury scoured me. I grabbed the arm nearest me and shook it. "Bastard. Fucker. You can't die."

"He already did," Birgit snarled from somewhere off to my right.

I pushed upright and faced her. "How?"

"He was following orders. If they're captured, they must kill themselves."

"Pfft. So? He thought himself dead?" It seemed remote as fuck. Maybe Satan passed out cyanide tabs hidden under fake teeth, but that was way too high tech for an ancient god to figure out.

"I don't know how it works," Birgit replied.

The nighthawks descended on the corpse, feasting on choice bits. Cailleach joined us and dropped a hand on my shoulder. "You did well."

"For someone whose first inclination was to run," Birgit cut in.

I considered apologizing, but I was done doing that. "Knowing when to leave has kept me alive," I told the witch.

Cailleach flapped her other hand at both of us. "You do understand why we made a spectacle of their assault?"

"So they'll eventually back off," I answered.

"Exactly," she said.

"But how will the others know what happened? It was why

I was working on him." I jerked my chin at the nearby demon. More hawks had joined the first two until the entire corpse was covered with shiny feathers, beaks, and dark avian eyes intent on a meal.

"They'll figure it out," Birgit said. "Satan may be a dick, but he's not stupid."

The application of modern nomenclature to the king of Hell made me smile. I turned toward the sea wanting to thank the Merrow, but they were gone. "What happens next?" I asked. "Do we remain here?" For all I knew, Cailleach had a castle somewhere beneath the waves.

"You will return to Underhill," Cailleach said firmly. "You have unfinished business there."

Blake.

The welter of confused feelings thoughts of him always engendered swamped me. "I, erm, assumed magic comes first," I stammered. "Isn't that what you said earlier?"

"How do you know Blake won't be part of your new power?" Cailleach's question vibrated with possibilities.

"Maybe, at some point." I was babbling, but I couldn't seem to shut up. "For now, just learning will take all my—"

"Return to Underhill. Now. I will find you when I'm ready." Cailleach cut me off in a tone that said it wasn't up for discussion. Sure enough, she vanished in a burst of blue light.

"Fine, be like that," I shouted after Cailleach, but of course she couldn't hear me. When I made a grab for Birgit's arm intent on dredging what she knew about Blake and me out of her, she sidestepped me.

"I trust you can find your way back," she said before she too shimmered to streamers of light.

I scanned the beach. Night had fallen. A few stars

peppered Scotland's usually cloud-ridden skies. Birgit had said I could find my way back to Underhill, but I wasn't at all certain of that. No roads led to the Faery realm. Better to err on the side of caution. I'd craft a travel spell and tell it to take me to Rait Castle. Once there, I'd pass the gateway and finish my journey on foot.

A sea tortoise had lumbered to my side rubbing its shell against my calf. I stroked its soft head. They live long lives, and the size of this fellow suggested he could be close to a century old. It had sought me out for a reason, so I knelt next to him and waited.

"We will revere you, love you, follow you, no matter what," he said into my mind.

"Thank you." I scratched the sensitive spot where his neck met his shell and he made a happy, grunting sound.

His words addressed one of my fears, the one where my animal honor guard might balk if I were stronger magically. Had he known, or was his statement serendipitous? Eh, coincidences are rare, so it had to be the former. Tortoises are wise and intuitive. I thanked him again, and he waddled toward the incoming tide.

Rising, I kindled my half-crafted travel spell. The beach fell away, replaced by the ruined green behind Rait Castle. The gateway into Underhill beckoned. Would it allow me to pass?

No way like walking through it to find out. And so, I did.

No stairway this trip. Corridors twisted and turned until any memory I might have held about how Underhill was laid out fled. I must have wandered for an hour before I thought to call Blake's name three times.

No one was more surprised than me when he materialized

a meter away. I'd always thought the bit about calling someone's name three times was a fairytale. I grinned. What better place for the old tales to come to life than fairyland?

"What's so funny?" Blake asked.

"Nothing. It's good to see you."

"You really mean that." He walked near and wrapped his arms around me. I hugged him back, surprised my ambivalence had fled.

"I do."

Always one to strike while the iron was hot, Blake covered my mouth with his. No questions about where I'd been, what I'd done—or why I stank of demon—just the length of his body pressed against mine, his hands tangled in my hair, and fervent kisses. I kissed him with abandon, licking, sucking, biting. When he pushed his tongue into my mouth, I welcomed him and sparred with it.

We'd spent months frolicking in my bed. We knew one another well. I tried to remember why I'd held him at arm's length, but none of my reasons made any sense. Not anymore. Before, I'd been concerned about maintaining my private detective business, the life I'd made in Nairn.

They'd been blown sky high. Nothing left to protect.

Blake lifted his chiseled lips from mine. "Only the most important thing in the world," he said.

At first it made no sense, but then I linked it with my thoughts and crinkled my nose his way. "I learned how to cloak my ideas earlier. Better enjoy your dives through my mind. Those days will soon be over."

"Maybe." He placed his hands on my shoulders kneading and rubbing, and then slowly worked his way down my back.

"What is the most important thing in the world?" I leaned

into the heat of his touch. His hands had reached my ass. Gripping it, he pulled me against his harder-than-hard cock.

"Why us, of course." Wings became visible. He cradled me within their folds.

My heart gave a funny little flip-flop deep in my chest. He really did care about me. How could I have been so blind?

A slight touch brushed through my head before he murmured, "I more than care about you, Abria. I love you, adore you. When you showed me the door, it was one of the saddest days of my long life."

More flip-flops joined the first until my ribcage felt crowded, too small to contain my overflowing heart.

"I love you too." The words burst from me. I couldn't have held them back if I'd tried. Hearing them, they rang with truth, a truth I'd circumvented and denied far too long.

The air turned sparkly. Blake's magic, full of the scents of damp forests and the natural world, surrounded us. "Where are we going?" I asked. "I mean, we don't have to go anywhere. Here is just fine..." I stopped while I was ahead. I'd been about to say we could go for it at whatever nexus of corridors spread around us. It wasn't as if the byways in Underhill were crowded. I hadn't passed a single Sidhe since entering the place.

"I want to take us somewhere special, somewhere private where we won't be disturbed." His voice had lowered to a possessive growl that ignited my blood. Where my breasts were crushed against him, the nipples formed hard peaks. Desire pounded through me, alive with promise.

"Trust me?"

I nodded. Today was full of surprises. Loving him, trusting

him, were brand new. Even during the months we'd rarely left my bed, we hadn't talked of anything beyond how to wring a few more orgasms out of our love-soaked bodies.

The corridor gave way to darkness and then to a crystal-lined cavern with a turquoise pool in its center. Koi swam in the water's clear depths. Light flickered and flared off the crystals, but I couldn't determine its source. The grotto was pleasantly warm, waves of temperate air wafting through from somewhere.

Blake let go of me. Once his hands were free, he slid the fuzzy woolen tunic off my shoulders, and then pulled it over my head. It had dried from my time in the sea. Next he unlaced the doeskin trousers I'd borrowed. No panties. No boots. I was naked in no time. He ran fingertips over my skin, and then turned me toward the pool.

"I'll join you," he said, shucking his jacket and shirt before bending to unlace his shoes.

I backed toward the pool, not wanting to take my eyes off him. He had the most amazing body, his skin a cross between bronze and gold. Broad shoulders were slabbed with graceful layers of muscle. Copper-colored nipples held a scattering of dark hair. A flat stomach and slender hips sat atop legs that were works of art. Rising from a tangle of black curls, his penis curved against his belly. Thick, long, and gorgeous, I remembered how he'd felt inside me. All of me. We'd been inventive lovers.

Kneeling, I dropped first one leg and then the other into lusciously warm water. My body thrummed with desire that only grew hotter as Blake closed the distance between us and jumped into the pool. Circling behind me, he closed his hands over my breasts tweaking and twirling the nipples just the way I liked.

I butted my hips against his erection and moved a leg to the side to capture him between my thighs. It was as if we'd never left off. My desire was as urgent as ever, filling me with imagery of all the things we could do to one another. A highpoint of the months where we'd barely left my bed had been endless resourcefulness. We'd never tired of one another. The more I had of him, the more I wanted until my need scared me.

And then, I came up with an excuse so logical, I'd talked myself into believing it.

He bit the side of my neck, sealed the bite with his tongue, and then bit me again. This time on the other side. I squeezed my thighs together; he thrust between them. The water added a whole new dimension in the way it supported us.

The angle of his thrusting altered. My sex grew slick as the head of his cock caressed my nub. Reaching back, I grabbed his hips encouraging a better angle. Breath came fast—his against my neck and mine a rough pant. He dropped a hand to the vee between my legs, stroking and circling, drumming his fingers on the most sensitive part of me.

I'd wanted to hold out until he was inside. Never going to happen. Lust spiraled pushing me higher, and then higher still until it crested and spilled me down the other side in long, lazy waves of passion.

I was still coming when he turned me in his arms, positioned his arms under my thighs, and lifted me onto his cock. I wrapped my legs around his waist and my arms around his shoulders and held on as he pushed inside me, withdrew, and then settled into a rhythm.

I crushed my mouth over his, breathing him in. I'd missed this so much, missed him so much. How could I have been so blind? So misguided? And then I stopped thinking. Feeling him deep within me ignited something fierce, primal. I dug my nails into his back and fell into another climax that left me shaky and gasping for air around the place our mouths were glued together.

He grew harder, more rigid. I urged him on with my body, my mouth, my fingers, my legs scissored around his hips. Tension in his arms, a slight tremor in his legs told me he was close.

So was I. Again.

"With me," I screamed into his mind. *"With me."*

His cock juddered, painting me with jets of semen. I tumbled down a long, delightful slope as another climax snapped me up and wrung me out. Straining against one another, we clung together as if our very existence depended on being as close as we could be.

At some point, I broke our kiss and laid my head on his shoulder. He lifted me off his still-hard penis and carried me to the shallow end where he sat with his back against the wall of the pool and me between his legs.

"What is this place?" I asked.

"Does it matter?" his deep voice vibrated against my hair.

"No. Not really."

"We're in a little used corner of the *Dreaming*."

"How can I be here? I'm not Sidhe."

"It's not only for us," he said softly. "I've always loved the magic in this spot."

I'd been so focused on him, I hadn't paid attention. When I reached out with my nascent power, peace spilled through me. Peace and a sense of rightness that I was exactly where I was supposed to be.

"Does it have the same effect on everyone?" I asked Blake.

He shook his head. "It enhances what lives within you. Nothing evil can bide here. They'd be overcome with darkness."

I traced the line of his cheek with my index finger. "Took quite a chance bringing me, huh?"

"No chance at all." He smiled. It started in his eyes before the corners of his mouth joined in. "I've seen through to the core of you since before I made a point of accidentally running into you."

"Accidentally on purpose." I grinned back.

"Whatever." His expression sobered. "Say you'll be mine, Abria. Maybe not right away, but soon. Once your time with Cailleach and Birgit has run its course."

"I've always been yours. I was just too stubborn and pigheaded to see it."

His arms tightened around me. "Glad you said that and not me."

"Couldn't resist an 'I told you so?'" I snuggled deeper into his embrace.

"Hush, love. Even magic can't change the past. Let's look forward, shall we?"

We rested with the warm water lapping around us. For once, I wasn't worried about the other Sidhe accepting me or all the hurdles that lay ahead. Sticking in the moment was new for me. New, rare, and precious.

Afraid my newfound peace would shatter if I examined it too closely, I floated in Blake's embrace. We'd return to the world—and my animal honor guard—soon enough. Until then, the circle of his arms was all I needed.

Epilogue, Blake

Two Weeks Later

I still can't believe Abria pledged herself to me. Not quite the right words. They would have been a few hundred years ago, but not anymore. No one had been more surprised than me when I heard her calling my name in Underhill. After the way she left, I figured the only time I'd see her again was when she stopped by to collect her clothes and boots—if she even bothered.

I'd felt her and Birgit leaving my realm, and I strongly considered going after them. In the end, I didn't. Abria's distress had been real. While we'd made it past her hissing and spitting in my face, we hadn't made it that far past her overt rejection of my advances. She knew how I felt. I hadn't come out and said I'd leave the lights on and the door open, but surely she was astute enough to figure it out...

Deep in thought, I walked through my dining area to the kitchen and poured a glass of mead enjoying its heady aroma and mild heat as the amber liquid slid down my throat. Abria was gone for a while. Cailleach had paid me a visit and stressed the need for Abria's undivided attention to her lessons. If the sea goddess was to be believed—and I had no reason not to—there'd be a place for me to assist, but not for some time.

Selecting a side hallway, I walked to my study, mead bottle and glass in hand. I'd review the source documents I'd gathered when I assumed I'd be the one teaching Abria. Good to familiarize myself with them, even if I wouldn't need the information right away.

Fortuitous she'd had the foresight to call my name three times once she realized she was lost in Underhill. My realm is famous for trapping the unwary. Birgit and Cailleach should have known better than to send her back by herself. Not that I didn't have faith in my betrothed—another archaic term— but I'd have done more to ensure her safety.

What a fucking understatement. I'd move worlds, burn through armies to protect Abria. In my own way, I was as smitten as the animals who adored her.

Underhill had known she wasn't Sidhe. While it allowed her entry, it would also have sat back until she weakened from thirst and hunger. The Faery world isn't kind to those it considers outsiders. I'd have to have a chat with the land about that.

From now on, Abria would be one of us. As her power grew stronger, the land would accept her just as it had always accepted the Celtic gods. Her magic was closer to theirs than any other. If they hadn't been gone for so long, Underhill might have recognized the underpinnings of her power.

But I'm wandering off track. I do that a fair bit these days.

My mind and soul are still addled by Abria's sudden change of heart. I'd wanted to set a date for our mating ceremony. Birgit and Cailleach convinced me to wait until Abria returned.

After pushing a few dusty scrolls aside, I settled into a worn reading chair and directed a mage light at untidy piles littering the tabletop. I'd just delved deep into an ancient scroll, working to decipher a form of Gaelic that almost predated me, when a faint knock alerted me someone stood at the door to my apartment.

I set another scroll atop the one I was reading to hold my place, but hesitated. Whatever it was could wait. I was otherwise engaged—in something critical, and—

Shaking a stern finger at myself, I rose. I was still leader of my people. Ignoring their needs had almost been my downfall —and theirs as well.

"All things in good time," I murmured and rose to my feet. Kirwan was at the door. I sensed his energy. Hoping he was stopping by to share gossip or a meal—rather than trouble—I hurried to let him in. As I strode through my apartment, an idea took shape. Cailleach and Birgit were well and good, but the best teachers for Abria would be the ones who'd created her.

Where had the Celts gone? Determined to find out, I opened my door and welcomed Kirwan. If there was something to attend to, I'd take care of it, and then I'd launch an attempt to locate Ceridwen and Arianrhod. The Morrigan would be simple to find. All I'd need to do was brave the gates of Hell and ask nicely if she was able to entertain visitors.

The more I thought about it, the more I determined she'd be the best place to begin. She'd know where her kinsmen were. Whether she'd tell me or not was a whole other story, but I can be charming when I need to be.

"Elwyn?" Kirwan stood in the doorway. Apparently, I hadn't invited him inside yet.

"Come in. Please." I gestured. "I was just having a glass of mead. Would you care for one?"

He smiled. "Of course. And then we can work on what to do about..."

Naturally, another problem. Underhill was full of them. What in the hell had the Sidhe done all the years I wasn't here?

Not very well, an inner voice carped.

Rebuke taken, I focused all my attention on Kirwan as he relayed a dispute. Dragons were involved, and we really did need to stay on their good side. I'd shepherded him into the study. After pouring him a glass of mead, I clapped him across the shoulders and said, "Thanks for bringing this to my attention. Best to fix it before it truly gets out of hand."

"My thoughts exactly." He pulled out a chair, dropped into it, and continued adding details about the challenge *du jour*.

You've reached the end of *Jinxed*. *Hunted*, next of the Wayward Mage series, picks up a couple of years from now when Abria returns from her time with Cailleach, Birgit, and a few unexpected characters Blake scared up to help. Please take a moment to leave a review for *Jinxed*. It means so much to authors, and it's an opportunity for you to let others know what you loved about this book. Read on for a sample chapter from *Hunted*, next in the series.

Until next time.

Book Description: Hunted

Learn magic they said. Or at least shore up your paltry skills. Talk is cheap, and that edict has cost me dearly.

I had a comfortable life, once upon a time. A quiet life. One where I'd carved a realistic niche for myself. No more. Power is seductive, and a bitch of a mistress. Once I pulled the cork out of that bottle, a million genies sallied forth.

None of them were nice. No one offered me three wishes, or any wishes at all. I've been working my fanny off for the last two years. Most days, I slog along from dawn to dusk and beyond. Sleep has turned into a distant memory. When I do lie down—or fall on my face, which is what really happens— my mind whirls in circles as I relive the failures *du jour*.

And the very occasional success.

I am stronger. So much stronger it scares me, but my talent sparkles, flowing bright and clean. Soon, I'll leave the well-hidden spot that's allowed me time to claim what's mine.

Whether my crash course in sorcery was wise remains to be seen.

Hunted, Chapter One, Abria

Dip. Weave. Whirl. Fire flickered from the fingertips of my right hand. My left controlled air. This exercise always reminded me of dragons with judicious use of air fanning flames and turning them into a blowtorch.

When I thought I had the air part down, I switched things up and summoned water. As usual, the trickle I requested showed up as a tidal wave drenching me with cold, salty water.

Huffing and blowing, I let my spell go to wipe water out of my eyes.

"Fuck!"

I pounded my fist into a dirt wall. My practice arena was far underground and impeccably warded. I'd love to claim credit for the ward, but Cailleach had shaped and formed it. Because it never faltered, she had to be funneling a constant stream of magic into its weave.

Cailleach, crone goddess of winter, witches, and the sea had taken an interest in me. Like everything in magical realms, having her for a teacher has been a mixed bag. She's wise, knowledgeable, and occasionally tolerant. She's also impatient with a short fuse. I'm not a witch, but she wouldn't have treated one of them any differently.

Actually, she would have since she's never taken the time to guide any witch's magical ability. I'd never have known, except she screamed the information in my face one particularly difficult day when I'd accused her of handling me differently.

The flood of seawater I'd inadvertently drenched my cave with had developed a life of its own. Rather than settling into a quiet pool, it formed small whitecaps ebbing and flowing like a miniature tide.

Grappling for the water end of power, I spun a different enchantment. "Stop that," I commanded.

Nothing happened. A sigh pushed past my pursed lips before I twisted them into a grimace. Once I formed something magical, altering its structure required a whole lot of work. It would be simpler to start over, but I had to get rid of this mess first.

"Never time to do it right, but there's always time to do it over," I mumbled and gathered my skill to try another tack.

Half an hour later, the white caps had moved from mid-calf to my knees. Somehow, I was making the problem worse. Water was far from my strongest suit, but still this was ridiculous. I'd had plans for today—supposedly, one of my last in residence with Cailleach—and so far I hadn't accomplished a thing.

I caught a whiff of witchy energy. Damn it. I'd hoped to

have this predicament behind me before my task-mistress teacher showed up. I was making little shooing motions with both hands before I stopped myself. If none of the dozen spells I'd tried had any impact on the water level, shooing it into submission wouldn't work, either.

Cailleach's wasn't the only magic heading my way. I stopped, narrowed my eyes, and worked to identify what I sensed. The only ones who'd visited during my tenure here were unicorns, Blake—my Daoine Sidhe boyfriend—and Birgit, another witch who'd helped train me. Jethro, her familiar, had dropped by as well. He's a shifter seer and spends most of his time as an enormous black cat.

An idea poked me; I swapped things up. If I was about to have company, I'd much rather they assumed all the water was here at my behest. In a manner of speaking, it was. For now, I'd pretend I'd meant to create the mini inland sea.

Some things have grown easier. Safeguarding my thoughts is one of them. I tucked shielding around my mind to conceal my turmoil. If I couldn't even solve this simple problem, maybe I wasn't ready to leave after all.

I can't stay here forever.

Correct, but two years is nothing in mage time, I argued back.

Cailleach splashed toward me after ducking to clear the low lintel that served as the entry to my workspace. She was half a head taller than me with a spare, bony build. Stark cheekbones, a high forehead, and a squared off chin surrounded her beak of a nose. Tangled silver hair hung to her knees. Dressed in one of her many robes—this one a faded green—she looked like witches portrayed in children's books. All she needed was a pointy hat, a staff, and a cauldron to complete the picture.

Implacable fog-colored eyes settled on me. "What's all this?"

"I was, erm, experimenting." I resisted the urge to rock from foot to foot or squirm or do anything to suggest I was uncomfortable beneath her scrutiny.

"I can see that," she said dryly. "But what was the purpose of this...experiment?"

Standing straighter, I clasped my hands behind my back. "Water is my weakest element. I was testing various ways to enhance my control over it." I added a slight guileless smile. My words incorporated enough truth, she might believe me.

Colors swirled around her as she spun her unique brand of enchantment. Moments later, the water vanished, soaking into the dirt floor. Even if getting rid of it had worked for me, I'd have been left with a mud slick. Not Cailleach. The floor turned sandy, as if the water had never been here.

Her gaze returned to me; I steeled myself for the lecture I was certain sat on the tip of her tongue. It never materialized. Instead, she said, "You have visitors, Abria. Otherwise, I'd have made you clean up your own mess."

Oops. Guess she figured it out. Thank all the gods she wasn't in a mood to belabor my shortcomings. Or to stand over me until I finally got something right—no matter how many days it took.

To divert her attention away from me and my magical flaws, I asked, "Visitors? Who?" Remembering the other magical signature I'd sensed, I searched but couldn't locate it.

"You'll see."

If I'd had hackles, they'd have raised the length of my spine. I didn't like surprises. I started to say I wasn't in the mood, but the words never made it beyond my throat. I've always been a loner—except for the animals, birds, fish, and insects who idolize me. People—magical and otherwise—never held much appeal, but I was lonely. I've never had this long a period of enforced solitude where even a trip to the corner market wasn't on the menu. There was no corner market. Supplies came from somewhere, but I had no say in what showed up or how it got here.

Cailleach has many dwellings. She's told me about some of them. This compound, complete with a castle, moat, drawbridge, and portcullis, occupied a corner of a small borderworld not far from Earth. In addition to my workshop, I also had a bed chamber and access to an expansive library.

Suddenly self-conscious, I glanced down at my patched trousers, ancient T-shirt emblazoned with "Wolves Bite," and scuffed boots. "Should I change?" I didn't have anything nicer, but I could manage cleaner.

Before we'd ended up here, I'd gathered a few items from my home. I couldn't live there any longer; it wasn't safe. But the winter goddess had created a quarter hour window and told me to make good use of it.

Good use equated to racing up the steep stairs to my second-floor living quarters and tossing everything I could lay my hands on into a battered valise. Since I hadn't had time to pick and choose, I'd ended up with schlocky garments like my wolf T-shirt. Functional but far from stylish.

Cailleach's gray brows shot up. Clearly, changing clothes hadn't occurred to her. A small furrow formed between her brows. "Perhaps 'tis a decent idea. You're soaked, and 'twill save explanations."

I started to ask, "To whom." Instead, I nodded and loped for the stairs beyond the cave's entrance. I'd already asked who these mysterious visitors were. She'd declined to answer. A second query would meet with the same fate.

A few minutes later, I was garbed in black slacks, a teal sweater, and a leather vest. Not wanting to take the time to comb out my mass of tangled hair, I scrunched it into an elastic band and headed for the castle's formal drawing room.

It was as good a place as any to start, but it turned out I guessed right. Moving quickly, I bolted into the room and screeched to a halt. It had been hundreds of years since I'd seen Ceridwen and Arianrhod, but I'd know the two goddess anywhere.

"My ladies," I murmured and dropped into a deep curtsy. I've never been very good at them and swayed alarmingly until I regained my balance.

"For the love of Danu, get up," Ceridwen growled. She'd been sitting facing a roaring fire along with Arianrhod and Cailleach, but she stood over me. I hadn't seen her cross the vast room.

I rose, not sure what to say. "Nice to see you," seemed trite. "Been a long time," was banal as hell.

Ceridwen looked much the same. Tall and broad, she wore hunting leathers crafted from soft, pale doeskin with boots laced to knee level. Her eyes were dark, her forehead high. Black hair frosted with silver hung to her waist in multiple braids. The only thing missing was her cauldron, and I felt certain it had to be close. The goddess never went anywhere without it. Serving as the seat of her seer powers, it was an integral part of her energy.

Arianrhod joined her. About the same height, but with a lithe build, she too wore leather garments, but hers were crafted from a darker colored hide. She examined me from multi-hued eyes: one gold, the other silver. Hair like spun gold had been gathered into a bun at the nape of her neck. A bronze torc studded with turquoise circled her neck, and her hunting bow was secured across her back in a battered sheathe.

Questions crowded the back of my mind; I sat on all of them. Had Cailleach sought them out? Seemed likely since so few people knew I was here. The weight of their combined gazes scoured me up one side and down the other. They were taking my measure, but the question was why.

"You've learned to hold your tongue," Ceridwen observed.

"Aye, that she has," Arianrhod agreed. "Particularly given what a chatty little thing she used to be."

That did it. I crossed my arms beneath my breasts and said, "I have never been *chatty*."

"Don't be argumentative." Ceridwen rebuked me.

"Aye, 'twould take very little to change our minds," Arianrhod chimed in.

"About what?" I tried for a neutral tone, but ended up sounding snarky.

"Independent, isn't she?" Arianrhod muttered.

"I am not a *she*. I'm right here. And I'm..." It took a bit for me to do the math before continuing. "I'm over 700 years old. If I hadn't developed some independence in all that time, there truly would have been no hope for me."

Ceridwen's eyes widened. Arianrhod made a, "Tsk, tsk," clicking sound with her tongue against her teeth.

Oh-oh. I'd been rude. Cailleach didn't tolerate backtalk. Why would I expect anything different from the pair staring at me. The winter goddess rose from her seat in front of the fire. No wood here; magic powered these flames. It was one of the ways she'd taught me to control that element.

I expected her to order me out of the room—maybe out of her castle—but she didn't. That part would probably come later. After she'd chastised me for showing so little respect.

The cauldron I'd wondered about clattered down in front of Ceridwen. Just as I'd suspected, it had been sequestered somewhere close by. The liquid within bubbled and splattered on the tile floor. The goddess snatched a glass rod from the air, stirring and muttering.

When she looked up, she announced, "Naught has changed."

My tolerance for ambiguity has never been high. "Would someone please tell me what's going on?" I demanded.

Cailleach hurried to where the three of us stood and draped an arm around my shoulders. The gesture surprised me since she's never been affectionate. More of a business as usual type.

"You've known your time with me was drawing to an end," she said. At my nod, she went on, "Quite a while ago, Blake and I discussed next steps in your training—"

"Without me?" I screeched before clapping a hand over my mouth and mumbling, "Sorry."

"Of course without you." Cailleach's tone was implacable. "What could you have possibly offered that might have been germane?"

I clasped my hands behind me to squelch a desire to punch her. What could I have possibly offered, huh? Oh nothing much since I was the topic of their discussion.

"In any event," Cailleach went on. After all these months, she knew me well. Surely, she was aware of my inner turmoil, but she viewed it as an inconvenience, not anything worthy of being addressed.

"In any event, what?" I growled, tired of masking my irritation.

"The best choice to complete your magical induction is those who created you," she went on.

"But you were gone." I addressed myself to Ceridwen and Arianrhod.

"Not so gone Blake couldn't find us." Ceridwen grimaced.

"We'd forgotten what good trackers the Daoine Sidhe are. He cheated, though," Arianrhod added.

"Aye, his first stop was a little chat with the Morrigan in Hell," Ceridwen said.

"Not much incentive for her to keep her mouth shut." Arianrhod made a sour face.

It was as if they'd forgotten I was here. To fix that, I spoke up. "Blake would have found you anyway. Even without the Morrigan's help," I announced.

"What makes you so sure?" Ceridwen asked.

"He can be quite determined. And he's in love with me, which means he would have tried even harder than usual."

The goddess's mouth formed an oh. She consulted her cauldron and muttered, "Interesting. I'd missed that bit of information."

She may have missed it, but Blake hadn't said a word to me. He could have. He was just here a fortnight ago.

Cailleach and Arianrhod were conversing telepathically. Power swirled around them. Ceridwen bent over her cauldron. I felt like an anachronism. My future had been decided behind my back.

We'd see about that. "No need to take me on as a project if you don't want to," I announced.

Three startled sets of eyes zeroed in on me.

"She does that," Cailleach said.

"Does what?" I was done being deferential. "Since when is speaking up for oneself a crime?" I blew out a breath. "Never mind. Don't answer that. I can leave, return to Blake. He and I will figure this out."

"Testy little thing." Arianrhod settled her hands on her slender hips.

"Reminds me of you when you were young," Ceridwen said.

"Oh really?" Arianrhod hooded her eyes.

Cailleach clapped her hands smartly. A tray bearing a silver teapot, cups, and spoons floated in from somewhere and settled on a nearby table. "Let's have a spot of tea," she suggested brightly.

I snatched a mug and poured hot water over tea leaves. The heady fragrance of rosemary, mint, and lemongrass soothed me. Before my next words took shape, I grasped Cailleach's strategy. She meant to defuse the tension sitting thickly in her drawing room.

It worked.

"Sorry," I said. "I've never cared for surprises, and I've always needed to plan for change."

"Understood." Cailleach squeezed my shoulder and guided me toward a chair. "I know those things about you, and I should have said something."

I latched onto her fog-colored gaze. Some realizations come too late, but this one arrived in time to do something about it. "You've been kind to me," I told her. "You took me in when you had no reason to. I haven't been an easy pupil, but you stuck it out."

A rare smile graced her gaunt face. "You're welcome."

I'd been looking forward to returning to Blake and Underhill, but now I wasn't in any rush to leave. My years with Cailleach were as close as I'd ever come to having a mother.

"Trust the process," she said into my mind. *"Everything will work out."*

Of course, the others heard her, but no one said a word. I knew without being told that once tea was over, I'd be on my way.

"Where will I go next?" I asked.

"We're working on that," Arianrhod said.

"Aye, our kinsmen aren't any more kindly disposed toward you than they were several centuries ago," Ceridwen added.

At least, the where of things wasn't in my wheelhouse. I've always been good at problem ownership, so I moved on to practical elements. "Will I bring my things?"

"What kind of things?" Ceridwen asked.

I shrugged. "Just clothing."

Ceridwen's brows rose in twin question marks. Cailleach explained, "Abria is a natural. She doesn't require props to support her power."

"Told you." Ceridwen jerked her chin at Arianrhod. "She's a lot like you."

"Better than dragging that damnable kettle everywhere," Arianrhod said.

I fought back a smile. This would be like plopping into the middle of two battling sisters. If I was careful and didn't take sides, I might survive the experience.

About the Author

Ann Gimpel is a USA Today bestselling author. A lifelong aficionado of the unusual, she began writing speculative fiction a few years ago. Since then her short fiction has appeared in many webzines and anthologies. Her longer books run the gamut from urban fantasy to paranormal romance. Once upon a time, she nurtured clients. Now she nurtures dark, gritty fantasy stories that push hard against reality. When she's not writing, she's in the backcountry getting down and dirty with her camera. She's published over 100 books to date, with several more planned for 2022 and beyond. A husband, grown children, grandchildren, and wolf hybrids round out her family.

Keep up with her at www.anngimpel.com or http://anngimpel.blogspot.com

If you enjoyed what you read, get in line for special offers and pre-release special reads. Newsletter Signup!

Also by Ann Gimpel

SERIES

Alphas in the Wild

Hello Darkness

Alpine Attraction

A Run for Her Money

Fire Moon

Bitter Harvest

Deceived

Twisted

Abandoned

Betrayed

Redeemed

Cataclysm

Harsh Line

Warped Line

Cracked Line

Broken Line

Circle of Assassins

Shira

Quinn

Rhiana

Kylian

Grigori

Coven Enforcers

Blood and Magic

Blood and Sorcery

Blood and Illusion

Demon Assassins

Witch's Bounty

Witch's Bane

Witches Rule

Dragon Heir

Dragon's Call

Dragon's Blood

Dragon's Heir

Dragon Lore

Highland Secrets

To Love a Highland Dragon

Dragon Maid

Dragon's Dare

Dragon Fury

Earth Reclaimed

Earth's Requiem

Earth's Blood

Earth's Hope

Elemental Witch

Timespell

Time's Curse

Time's Hostage

Gatekeeper

Shadow Reaper

Rebel Reaper

Untamed Reaper

GenTech Rebellion

Winning Glory

Honor Bound

Claiming Charity

Loving Hope

Keeping Faith

Ice Dragon

Feral Ice

Cursed Ice

Primal Ice

Magick and Misfits

Court of Rogues

Midnight Court

Court of the Fallen

Court of Destiny

Rubicon International

Garen

Lars

Unbalanced

STANDALONE BOOKS

Branded, That Old Black Magic Romance (paranormal romance)

Edge of Night (short story collection, paranormal and horror)

Grit is a 4-Letter Word (nonfiction)

Heart's Flame (post-apocalyptic romance)

Icy Passage (science fiction romance)

Marked by Fortune (post-apocalyptic coming of age story)

Melis's Gambit (historical paranormal romance)

Midnight Magic (paranormal romance)

Red Dawn (post-apocalyptic paranormal romance)

Shadow Play (historical paranormal romance)

Shadows in Time (Highland time travel romance)

Since We Fell (contemporary romance)